Payback

Payback

CLARE CURZON

First published in Great Britain in 2007 by
Allison & Busby Limited
13 Charlotte Mews
London W1T 4EJ
www.allisonandbusby.com

A CIP catalogue record for this book is available from
the British Library.

10 9 8 7 6 5 4 3 2 1

ISBN 0 7490 8055 8
978-0-7490-8055-6

Typeset in 11/16 pt Sabon by
Terry Shannon

Printed and bound in Wales by
Creative Print and Design, Ebbw Vale

CLARE CURZON began writing in the 1960s and has published over forty novels under a variety of pseudonyms. She studied French and Psychology at King's College, London, and much of her work is concerned with the dynamics within closely knit communities. A grandmother to seven, in her free time she enjoys travel and painting. Clare lives in Buckinghamshire.

*This one is for my fellow painters –
Daphne, Mariam, Karen, Martin, Barry,
Janet and Hilary; not forgetting the
incomparable Sue Gray.*

CHAPTER ONE

A grey morning. Only 8.10, and already a traffic tailback up the steep, slow S-bend of Myron's Hill. It reached down to the roundabout where Detective Superintendent Yeadings was held up. Not sufficiently bothered to switch to Thames Valley traffic news, he inserted a CD, Vivaldi's Seasons, and edged a couple of yards farther.

It was the start of the tape – *Spring*, all perky lamb-frisking – and he wryly wished it had arrived, with early tulips opening in the borders at home. Still another week or two before the colours revealed themselves. Last year the garden centre had let in some rogues which threw his whole display out of kilter. And he'd planned it for Nan's forty-fifth birthday. Two yellow and three shrieking pink spoiling a swath of Delft Blue hyacinths. Still, the daffs were pushing up well. You couldn't go wrong with them.

An impatient driver a few cars back was leaning on the horn, as if that could move things on. Locals should be used to a brief build-up here. Traffic would clear in a few minutes.

Wednesday was viewing day at the auctioneer's at the top of the S-bend. Access to the trade car park at the rear was too narrow. Some articulated van would be executing a seven-point turn across both lanes to get in.

He knew Nan would drop in there after the morning school run, looking for a new hall table. By 'new', meaning antique. A place to display winter flowers and her sprays of preserved beech leaves.

In the confines of the car, Vivaldi's strings fiddled on in a fine frenzy, ceased, then gave way to languorous *Summer*. This tailback was lasting longer than expected. Perhaps roadworks, restricting to single-lane traffic. Or a collision. There was no movement in Yeadings's own lane, but the counter-flow had started streaming towards him.

He'd be late. It was just as well, he reflected, that the Hoad family deaths were cleared up. Nothing left now but paperwork. And, thankfully, a blank sheet this time for Crown Prosecution.

The traffic flow was normal as Nan Yeadings arrived on foot, having parked in the multi-storey concrete obscenity near the station. Wandering among the ticketed pieces of furniture, pictures, chinaware and knick-knacks on display she felt the usual stirring of excitement tinged with mild guilt which auction rooms always stimulated. She moved in a sort of child-in-toyshop fascination, coveting a long-case clock here, a ship's bell, a tapestry wall-hanging there: things that belonged to others unknown, and not all of them willingly discarded; objects to which she should have no legitimate access. Maybe these were treasures forced into prostitution through debt or their owner's death.

Sentimental value: there must be a corner in everyone's secret heart for something inanimate that had taken on a patina of love.

'Table,' she disciplined herself aloud. She wasn't here to indulge in proxy nostalgia or play Miriam Rothschild buying up the entire collection. Especially since several objects were undeniably naff. She marvelled that there were people who would go for anything, once collecting mania grabbed them.

Having established her feet firmly on the ground and reviewed the major pieces, she decided there were two possible pieces to bid for: one a seventeenth-century rectangular table, of oak darkened by age and slightly scarred, also a fine early Victorian wall-table with fantastic carved legs ending in balled claws and having a scalloped front. It was in good condition, the wood immaculately waxed: burl walnut with intriguing swirls of pattern.

Either could prompt rocketing bids, except that both were large, unsuitable for the average modern house. For their own square hall the first would look imposing, the other enchanting. There must, thought the seldom-churchgoing Nan, be a patron saint for bidders. If so, she would send up a special double-pronged prayer.

She smiled as Shelagh, the auctioneer's blonde assistant, approached to exchange a few neighbourly words. She mentioned her interest, then departed before further temptation should strike. Tomorrow she would firmly restrict herself to bidding for the tables.

In the auction rooms' cramped little office Charles Hennigan looked up from his computer.

'Shelagh, what now?'

'Sandy's not turned up. I've rung his mobile and it's switched off.'

'Try him at home.'

'I've done that, left a message. And both vans are here, so he's not out collecting.'

'Get someone else in. There's stuff to move and the Simpson chinaware still needs ticketing.'

The woman's lips tightened. *Get someone.* Like, snatched out of air? Or was she to give birth on the spot? To a large, horny-handed gorilla who could lift four times his own body weight? 'Easy to say, Charlie.'

He switched on his professional smile, smothering annoyance with treacly charm. 'You know you can do it.'

He turned back to his keyboard, flicked on to Sotheby's list. Sucking her cheeks in, Shelagh made a beeline to her car. Rout the blasted man out, lying abed when needed at work. Batter on the oaf's door until he'd no choice but to answer. And if someone reported to Charlie that she too had gone AWOL, he could deal with that problem himself.

Sandy Craddock, auctioneer's porter and amateur antiques fancier, heard the car draw up and, through ancient net curtains, watched Shelagh's approach with concern. When the doorbell shrilled he was flat on the floor below the window. The damn woman rang three times, finally keeping her finger on the bell for at least half a minute. He lay on for a further five while he pictured her rounding the outer wall, trying windows and kitchen door. When finally the car started up and drove away he stood, dusted his knees off and swore out loud.

It would be no lie to claim he was sick. He felt like shit. Already he'd thrown up his breakfast by the dusty laurel hedge behind the auction rooms. From the van's driving seat he'd seen what happened: the man in the baseball cap starting to cross from the opposite side, threading between traffic, and the biker, appearing from nowhere, simply mowing him down; to vanish in a snarl of acceleration.

Over in a second. Enough to shake anyone. But it wasn't until, hovering behind the gawkers, he'd picked up the distinctive cap and got blood on his hands, that it hit him.

He'd known instinctively. This had been meant for him.

He had cowered among the scanty shrubs behind Charlie's office window to puke his heart out. When the shudders ceased, with hunched shoulders, chin buried in roll-neck sweater, and still in a cold sweat, he rammed his wool cap down to his eyes and trudged off uphill, bent on getting lost. He reached home to find the bloodied baseball cap still clenched in one hand. It took a lifetime of shuddering to fit his key in the lock.

Last night, when that message came up on his screen it had given him cause to wonder. But he hadn't believed it. An empty threat. No one could get to him. Nobody knew who 'Proteus' was. The words, *I know where you live*, were hollow. They couldn't know that. Not even where he worked. Surely?

But there'd been this attempt. Someone out to kill him.

So had he been spied on, followed? And murdered by proxy?

One thing he knew for sure: it was no accident. The biker had headed straight for his victim. Only, because of the distinctive baseball cap, he'd got it wrong. Distance and speed had concealed the difference in age. Warren was slighter, younger, but both had inherited Alicia's height and hawklike features. So now the poor bastard was possibly dead, in place of his half-brother.

Except that, to be strictly factual, Sandy himself was the bastard, fathered by an anonymous redhead, when Alicia had been barely sixteen.

Which accounted for his abandoned childhood, raised by a strait-laced grandmother, from whom eventually he'd inherited this house, an ex-council semi. Alicia had floated off to an easier life, and at twenty-three married a middle-aged academic with investments. Andrew Laing, Ph.D., had died three years back, from a subdural haematoma, leaving Warren Laing as their sole legitimate, pampered offspring.

Sandy Craddock groaned aloud, hardness like an icy stone inside his chest. It would have been himself on the morgue slab, if it hadn't been for that ambiguous baseball cap.

Alicia, never highly imaginative, had sent them one each at Christmas. She'd bought them in Miami, where she'd gone to soak up sun. It was only last week that she'd mentioned, during Sandy's annual phone call, that both brothers had the same. Which was enough for him to bin his own. He'd gone straight out and bought this navy woollen knitted thing to cover his cropped red hair and keep out the morning chill.

He'd only ever worn his cap as a sop to Alicia, and he despised himself for sucking up to her. It had been a hideous thing, electric blue, with a golden eagle on the front crossed by a bolt of scarlet lightning. Over the weeks since Christmas, everyone at work had known him by it. It wouldn't have been hard for the attacker to pick him out, walking up the hill to the auction rooms. But today he'd driven in, having taken

Hennigan's van home last night, for an early morning pick-up.

So, while he'd sat unobserved in the parked van, for some screwy reason it had been Warren Laing walking up the hill, right into it. Wrong person, in the right place at the right time. And certainly right enough for Sandy, surviving and observing the attack, unseen.

It was deliberate. That biker had meant to kill. And, although the paramedics had been doing their best, he could still have pulled it off. The body had flown through the air for ten yards and landed against the auction rooms' wall. Judging by the bloodied cap, his head had caught the brunt of it.

Don't ask him yet to pity the poor idiot landing in it like that. All he could think of was, *they missed me this time, but what'll they do once they know they got the wrong man?*

CHAPTER TWO

Shelagh Ingram's anger with Sandy Craddock turned to apprehension on the drive back. Charlie, notoriously a needle quivering near hysteria on the emotion gauge, could go berserk over her own absence. At the auction rooms, viewers must already be streaming in, demanding catalogues and registering early bids while her desk yawned empty.

God, what a morning it was turning into, starting off with that horrific accident just outside the showrooms, and Sandy inexcusably doing a runner at the very time he was most needed. No phone warning, nothing. And guess who must act as universal shock-absorber.

Her memory jerked back. She'd been wrong about Sandy not turning up. He must have been there early and then skived off; because both vans were in the yard when she arrived. Then, just as she was checking in with Charlie and opening the safe for the lists, there'd been that hubbub outside with someone rushing in to demand she ring 999; which was why she'd missed seeing the outcome.

Duncan Stott, the other duty porter, said a biker had run someone down in the road. A man, he thought, but such a crowd of gawpers gathered that he hadn't glimpsed much between their shoulders. It seemed that paramedics had turned up promptly, fixed a neck brace and taken the unconscious man off to St Luke's.

End of story. Not for the poor devil injured, though. Shelagh hoped it wasn't one of their Wednesday regulars.

Then, instantly, the coincidence struck her. A man knocked down outside. And a staff member, normally reliable, suddenly missing. And in her heart she'd been *cursing* Sandy Craddock as an absentee! Heaven forbid he should be the one run down, poor devil.

One consolation: if she told Charlie that possibility, he wouldn't have breath left to bawl her out for disappearing. She made a beeline for his office and poured out her fears. His earlier forced charm shattered like crystal. 'You *went* there? You're *sure* he wasn't at home?'

She stared him out. 'Charlie, I need to ring St Luke's.'

He waved a trembling hand. 'Well, do that then. What's the number?'

She produced it out of her head. Two months ago Auntie Phil had gone there with a broken hip and Shelagh had rung her ward sister every day.

She made the call. There was some delay because A&E was at panic stations and couldn't field Reception's query. Finally the admission was confirmed: an unnamed male pedestrian traffic casualty, unconscious and without ID. He was already through triage and transferred to Orthopaedics, awaiting surgery. The hospital required someone to come in and identify him.

'You'd better send Duncan.' Charlie was literally wringing his fine, long hands.

Shelagh baulked. 'He's just opened up for viewing, and

obviously I'm needed on the desk.' She waited while Charlie laboured towards the concept that he, as senior partner of the family firm, was at present the least vital performer. He rolled wounded spaniel eyes on her.

She stood her ground. 'Nothing else for it.'

Reluctantly he rose, reached for the wide-brimmed, plush hat from a mahogany coat tree behind his desk and tenderly retrieved his cashmere crombie from the Venetian cupboard. 'You're only guessing Sandy's involved. It's a wild goose chase.'

But it could be *our gander*. Shelagh had tact enough not to retort aloud.

A stagy lingering. 'Do you think it might rain?' He was wearing his defeated face.

'No. But then I'm only guessing at that too.' She made herself scarce before he could turn the wounded-child look on her. Let the wretched man take a risk for once, and if he got drenched, what harm? She was tired of acting mother hen.

Charles Hennigan had a distinct dislike of hospitals. A healthy dislike, as he saw it. A hospital was no place for anyone to risk being ill in. Such pernicious germs; and the smell! Worse than getting home early for lunch when the cleaner had been spraying that synthetic floral stuff.

Finding the right people to interrogate, the right floor, the right ward, and then the right body concealed behind closely drawn curtains took a deal longer than identifying it. Despite the heavily bandaged head, Sandy's unmistakable nose jutted skywards like a prize-winning piece of twentieth-century architecture – perhaps a section of Sydney Opera House – or the gaunt breastbone of a freshly plucked chicken. His limbs appeared mostly swathed in dressings, and there were flat, circular appendages wired to his bare chest. Charlie had seen their sinister like on TV when fearfully zapping past a hospital drama. A nurse confided in hushed tones that they awaited the arrival of a neurosurgeon.

Hennigan regarded the supine form with regret. Aesthetically the man was never one of evolution's finer works, and now it appeared he hadn't improved the original design. He was distracted by the nurse's demand, 'Well, *is* he?'

Was he what? he wondered.

'The man you thought he might be. We need a name for him.'

'Oh, yes, undoubtedly. Sandy Craddock. He works for me. Or did until now.'

'Sandy?' she queried.

'Er, well, Alexander, I suppose.' Reluctantly Hennigan allowed her to extract his business address, since he'd no idea where the man actually lived. No, he couldn't give a National Insurance number. She would need to phone someone in his office for that.

He struggled to insert a question of his own while she wrote the name on a card and affixed it to a board above the bed. 'What do you suppose are his chances?'

'Are you a relative, Mr Hennigan?'

'God, no.' Why did they always insist on being so cagey about information? What the hell difference did privacy make to someone in Sandy's present condition?

'I'm afraid we can't divulge'

'Oh, stuff it,' he said pettishly, turned on his heel and squeaked his way out over the polished vinyl flooring.

* * *

Sandy Craddock crammed a few necessities into an overnight bag. He needn't take much, because there'd be no scarcity where he was going. He dared not stay on at home, where they could easily find him. The words *I know where you live* kept ringing in his head. The biker would check hospitals to find out his victim's condition. Once he saw he'd missed Sandy on the way to work and got the wrong brother, he'd come on here. It was only logic.

It was also logic that if Laing was standing in for him as a near-corpse, however briefly, he could himself take on the other's life. Or at least his luxury flat until such time as alternative lodgings could be found.

He had never been inside Belvoir Court. Relations were too strained for an invitation, but everyone knew that the landscaped block of apartments on the knoll above the river provided the last word in five-star *dolce vita*. It would take a little care avoiding the uniformed porter in the foyer, but once past him he must take the lift to the fifth floor. That much of Laing's address he'd picked up from Alicia, who couldn't resist cataloguing every small detail of her younger son's successes; and this on the rare occasions that her older, less progressive half-brother checked on her.

With this plan in mind, Sandy hastily changed from working sweater and jeans into his only dark suit, substituting for the navy knitted cap a brimmed slouch hat he'd once bought in a fit of madness and worn only once. It had made him look like a private eye from a Thirties Hollywood B-film, but it could serve his purpose as camouflage now. On the way there, he must drop off at a supermarket for a bottle of black dye. Couldn't risk recognition through his flaming No.2

haircut. As an afterthought he slid into his pocket the current disc from his computer.

The street was almost empty as he left the house on foot. It had its busy times, when neighbours, mostly in their thirties and forties, left for work, taking the children to drop off at school. The few women who stayed home weren't back yet from shopping, and the morning was too grey to bring the old grandads out working in the tiny gardens. If, in passing, he was observed from behind net curtains, he felt well enough covered to baffle recognition. He stepped out briskly, already halfway to assuming his new identity: Sandy Craddock, as such, sloughed off like the work clothes he'd slung in the laundry basket.

In Market Square he caught a bus and sat hunched on one of the sideways seats, staring at the floor. He swung off as the bus was leaving a stop two hundred yards short of his destination, by now almost relishing the undercover role. The furtive fedora appeared to have passed on its aura.

Outside the smoked-glass frontage of Belvoir Court he drew a deep breath before committing himself further. Pausing inside the revolving door, he scanned the foyer ahead. The duty porter, immaculate in an olive green uniform, was hovering with a spray-can over a potted tropical plant beside one of the lifts.

Sandy pressed out the Belvoir's number on his mobile phone. As the man returned to his station and leant across to take the call Sandy strode confidently in, passed by with a quick flash of profile and a lordly wave, making for the vacated space. The lift doors opened with a discreet *whoosh* and he was safely inside. He punched number five on the illuminated board. 'Doors closing,' seductively warned an automated, female voice.

As the lift rose it struck him that the same porter could have been on duty when Laing left that morning in the deplorable baseball cap. So what else would he have worn? Casual clothes certainly. Heading perhaps for the gym?

So that was the first mistake, turning up in a dark suit and slouch hat. Would the porter have picked up on the difference and wonder where Laing had gone to effect the change? Was he smart enough to connect the resident's return with the aborted phone call which disrupted his indoor gardening?

On the fifth-floor landing Sandy Craddock's shoulders were sweating under the unaccustomed weight of a jacket. Not from haste or fear, he told himself: just that he wasn't used to this level of indoor heating. In any case he'd need to be pretty nippy breaking into the apartment in case the porter-concierge, alerted, came up to check everything was in order.

But why should he? – he insisted to himself. Most folks had cloth ears and blinkered eyes. Nor did the man's job demand the little grey cells of a Poirot; deadly monotony most of the time. He was probably brain-dead between mealtimes.

Of course some people might extend equal contempt to an auctioneer's porter; but they'd be so wrong. There was a helluva lot more to it than humping stuff about, sticking on labels, identifying lots as called and holding them up on display. In all the years he'd worked at Hennigan's he'd been learning on the job, reading up the subject, keeping abreast of the Fine Arts periodicals, scanning other auction houses' lists, memorising the Lost or Stolen circulars the police provided. In fact, if Charlie were so unrefined as to drop dead suddenly,

Sandy reckoned he could just take over and do it equally well, apart from the lily lad's fancy diction. Though, on second thoughts, he reckoned he could even mimic that if the occasion demanded.

Anyway, he told himself, listening for the lock's tumblers shifting as he pressed one ear against the door panel, it wasn't Charlie's role he had to take on at the moment. Being Warren Laing was something else, uncharted country. And *Here be Dragons*. It could be risky.

Once inside, maybe he should ring in sick, to get off work. And heaven help him if Alicia suddenly turned up here, to visit her cherished legitimate offspring. Suppose she even had a key? There'd be no deceiving her. How long could he expect to make use of this haven?

There was a comforting click. He withdrew the picklocks, depressed the handle and the door opened.

He was in. Head cocked, he listened for sounds of movement. None came, and he started to relax. There was plenty of time now to look around, take stock, acclimatise himself while considering the next step.

But first, investigate food stocks. The morning's unaccustomed excitement had made him hungry. He wondered if Warren Laing went in for real nosh, or was a champagne and caviar poseur. The furnishings implied as much – all flashy. He went through to the kitchen, which was all modern high-tech equipment: stainless steel, black marble and pale maple woodwork, picked out by halogen spotlights which lit as he entered. Schooled by Charlie Hennigan to appreciate artefacts of age and elegance, Sandy scorned these surroundings as severely as he did his own one-stage-above-squalor living conditions. A real kitchen, to his mind, gleamed with copper pans and dark, seasoned wood, its ceiling hung with bunches of dried herbs and maybe, at best, a smoked ham.

But he couldn't fault what he found in fridge and freezer. Among the expected fast-food bachelor items there were hand-labelled and dated packages containing prepared meals requiring only to be reheated. Also, under transparent film, almost a whole carcass of roast chicken and a clearly home-made apple and plum crumble.

Someone, surely not Warren Laing himself, had either made these on-site or brought them in: which implied paid help – unless, of course, there was a live-in woman. Certainly Alicia wouldn't have risked her manicured hands on domestic goddessing. Either way, that could present a risk of being discovered.

He slammed the fridge doors and made straight for the only bedroom. There was no flimsy nightdress under either pillow on the double bed. No male pyjamas, for that matter. And if maybe Laing preferred to sleep in the nude, so then might any inamorata.

Check wardrobes and drawers, he told himself. If a woman's garment turned up, he'd be out of here like a streak of blue lightning.

A wall of four mirrored, sliding doors concealed the wardrobes. The first contained a variety of suits for town wear, shelves of shirts and underwear, with an astonishing number of shoes ranged across the floor; the second, a smaller collection of tweedy numbers, check shirts and sportswear. Below them were ranged several pairs of stylish brogues, a fisherman's waders and the inevitable pair of countryman's green wellies. Warren was clearly a man for all seasons and occasions.

Sandy unwrapped a canvas carrier to reveal rods and tackle. In the far corner was a locked steel cabinet let into the wall. He guessed this must contain sporting guns. This was a level of living he hadn't suspected.

The further two doors must be the female counterpart of the other two. He hesitated before sliding back the next door. What it hid would determine whether he stayed or fled further.

There were several dresses as feared, but no everyday stuff. They were all floor-length, in vivid satins and chiffons. He pulled one out and the scent coming off it showed it had been worn and put back without cleaning. The low-cut bodice had traces of peachy make-up. So – a glamour-puss, but not too particular. She would be tall, he reckoned, and had large feet for a woman. All the shoes were strappy with high heels. But not a well-endowed woman, because the bras (the only underclothing apart from a few pairs of tights and lace knickers) had been made with hard sponge inserts. Sandy didn't envy Laing this woman.

But then he looked in the deep hatbox: three wigs; one blonde, one brunette, one auburn.

He sat back on the bed and grunted. Amusement and disapproval jostled for mastery. Alicia's all-perfect son was a cross-dresser!

The last wardrobe door was not on sliders like the others. It swung open, bringing with it a wooden extension which caught him sharply on the shin. He stepped back and contemplated the mini-office now revealed. Compact, and complete with computer, printer, scanner, modem: in fact the whole works. There were shelves of stationery, and drawers fitted to take CD-ROMs.

This, at last, was something with appeal. Sandy flicked through the labelled discs, some of familiar musicians, others with handwritten names or merely numbers. He picked out an old recording of Sting, switched on the computer, drew up a chair and settled to enjoy. The lack of a password barred him.

Well, at least he and his half-brother had one taste in common. What else? He selected one of the handwritten discs, labelled 150207. A bank clearing number? It could even be a date. He scrutinised a handful of the others and saw his second guess was more likely. He turned the disc between his fingers. The date was recent enough to give some clue to the man's life. So just what had Warren Laing been up to on the fifteenth of February this year? Sandy wondered. Curiosity gnawed at him. He shrugged as he slid it into his pocket.

Beside him the phone rang, startling him so that he'd picked it up before he'd time to think. He grunted hello, praying for a wrong number.

'Darling, it's me.' Alicia's voice, rushing and flirty. The click of her lighter and a pause while she lit up, audibly sucked in smoke, almost choked on a dry cough.

His eyes closed, he saw her flicking bottle-blonde hair from her eyes, cigarette between bony knuckles, ash dropping on her cluttered diamond rings.

She darted at him with little items of trivial news, demanded to know how he was, what he was presently about; all punctuated by sudden bursts of bright, irrelevant laughter.

Clearly she had no idea he was the wrong son.

Although somewhere deep down he envied his brother, he knew why he could never deal with her at close quarters. She alarmed him, would stifle him. Sounding older than he remembered, she was more brittle; overwhelming yet desperately precarious.

The idea crystallised that she did not really love her other son, but stalked him, voracious, like an industrial vacuum cleaner.

Fervently he resolved to avoid picking up further calls. He would leave them to stagnate on the machine; refuse to be hunted down. Not that she would continue once she discovered her mistake. So far, she hadn't. His monosyllables had given nothing away.

'Darling, if you don't visit me soon I shall come and dig you out;' coy threat with tinkling laughter. But a little crack in the silver bell?

Dig him out. She would do that. Maybe had a key to the apartment, or would bully the porter to escort her up. So much for his asylum; he must quickly find another place to lie low.

CHAPTER THREE

'Mr Hennigan, as I live and breathe!' Batty Bateman, local scavenger of small-town gossip, burst from a side corridor as Charlie made his rapid escape from the disinfected environment.

He feigned deafness, but to no avail. In a crouching hobble the noisome little man executed a rapid circle that brought them face to face, and the quoted breath, poured richly on the auctioneer, reeked of stale tobacco and an indistinguishable form of alcohol.

'It is, so it is!' The delight was as fulsome as the stage-Irish accent he chose to adopt on these encounters. It irritated Hennigan, unsure whether it was due to excessive mateyness or condescension to someone with supposedly a dim ancestral connection to the Emerald Isle.

'There now, wasn't I telling meself,' the reporter bustled on joyously, 'that at St Luke's I was bound to run across someone suitably newsworthy. And here's your good self.'

'In haste. Viewing day,' Charlie fired across his bows.

Bateman tagged along. 'I trust your presence here doesn't imply you're stricken with ill health?' He sounded hopeful.

Was there, Hennigan asked himself, any disease so vile he could lay claim to, that would shake the little man off?

'Visiting an employee,' he threw out as disengagement tactics.

It drew Bateman like iron filings to a magnet. He whipped out his notebook. 'And out of the kindness of your heart. Now, isn't that just the sort of charitable human story that the public love to read about?'

Hennigan stopped in his tracks, reminded that he paid for a weekly notice in the *Argus* to keep the auction rooms in local consciousness. Here, it seemed, was free publicity handed him on a plate. He permitted the man's questions, briefly supplied the required details and glowed at the prospect of proving to Shelagh that, however cloud-bedecked his head, his feet were that much in the marketplace.

Bateman snapped his notebook shut, waved dismissal and scuttled off to confirm the data in person. Barred from entering Intensive Therapy, he crouched to view the inert body through the slats of its blinds. He observed with relish the wires, tubes, video display and all the paraphernalia indicative of crisis. Poor bugger, he thought; wouldn't give much for his chances. Auction rooms porter. Wonder if he's worth an obituary?

Released, Charles Hennigan made his dignified way back to the workplace, gravely acknowledging the greetings of passers-by, all potential customers, and stiffly nodding to any who appeared unaware who he was. Installed once more at his desk in the back office, with a cappuccino (cinnamon-topped and served in Crown Derby) alongside, he related his adventures to Duncan Stott, who temporarily seemed the only person not heavily occupied.

'Dreadful little man,' he summed up the newspaperman.

'Reminds me of that feller who was infatuated with Esmeralda and swung on the bells. What was his name?'

'Before my time.' Stott refused to become intellectually involved.

Charlie sighed: Sandy Craddock would have known. Pity he was the one to be mown down. They were going to miss his ready encyclopaedic knowledge. If he finally fluffed it, they'd need an experienced replacement. Maybe the report in the *Argus* would inspire someone to apply for training. No need in that case to waste money or time yet on an advertisement.

At that moment Sandy Craddock was contemplating his new, black-haired reflection in one of the many bathroom mirrors. But for lack of her Medusan crowning glory, it was Alicia staring indignantly back.

The wretched woman might have endowed him with certain physical features, but in mindset and tastes they were widely disparate. She, ever a fashion junkie, had her flashy parties and upmarket booze. He preferred solitude, rare antiques and incunabula.

He rolled the last word on his tongue, watching his mother's cheekbones moving, but relieved that the firm male mouth owed nothing to her.

Incunabula. Not a word she'd ever have used, he guessed; nor even known the meaning of.

For each of them, diverse tastes had brought about their present predicaments. Not that she'd ever admit to being a ruin. Me being judgemental, he acknowledged: legacy of his upbringing. Granny's Methodist severity. Poor old Gran, with her poverty of outlook and of worldly goods. At least, thanks to a scholarship and good schooling, then finally Hennigan's, he'd surfaced from that morass. Hadn't entirely thrown off inherited guilt, though. That's what had hovered darkly all day, refusing to be recognised, ever since the knowledge that someone else had paid for his own follies. And, by an ironic circling of fate, that had to be his half-brother, the despised Warren Laing.

He turned on the local news at noon, fearing to hear of the motorbike incident and Laing named as a fatality. But the injured man was still in coma at St Luke's. He had been identified as Alexander Craddock, porter employed at Hennigan's auctions rooms, and run down outside his workplace.

He sank back on the lavatory seat, head in hands, and submitted to conscience, thought his way back to the start of the day – all that instinctive evasion, the cowardice of it, the callousness. That poor bugger, doubtless wired up to machines in ITU; and himself here, safe in his plushy place. It just wasn't on. And yet what alternative had there been?

Not that this false security could last. Soon someone at the hospital would check and recognise the mistake. Or Warren Laing would come round and protest that they'd booked him in under the wrong name.

His own cover would be blown. The biker, having failed the first time, could still come after his intended victim, still run him down, in both meanings of the phrase.

But that was for tomorrow. There was still enough of today left, and enough sense of survival for him to make the most of the situation he'd plunged into. He'd eat, drink and – if not be merry – at least sleep in material comfort until Nemesis made her presence felt.

He would have played a few games on the computer in the bedroom but access to that was as protected as Laing's personal data. He regretted the absence of readable books. There were property catalogues galore and back numbers of *Playboy*, even a thumbed copy of *Spotlight*.

He spent the afternoon marvelling at the banality of daytime TV. Towards eight in the evening he opened a freezer package of game pie and carefully prepared it according to the printed instructions. He found ready-chilled Bollinger in the fridge, to toast Gran's teetotal health in the hereafter, but after two glasses decided that a claret went better with the pie's rich flavour.

He barely found his way to bed. Cleaning his teeth with Warren Laing's toothbrush, he again stared down Alicia's reflection in the bathroom mirror. Not only the cheekbones, but her startled eyebrows were there too, but fiercer and thicker under their black dye.

Women! he thought, and got no further. At that point a mental block descended, like thunderclouds booming with the wrath of God. All those leftover *thou-shalt-nots* from Gran, making him feel a shit whenever he stepped out of line.

There was one boyhood sin in particular which bathrooms had the power sometimes to bring back: the lonely night-time building of physical frustration followed by blessed, almost instant relief. Then the furtive bathroom visits to rinse out his man-size handkerchiefs.

There'd been little chance of a girlfriend while Gran was

alive. She'd kept him too busy with the house and working her stony allotment. Adolescent memory for him was of a prolonged and futile attempt to raise pea-sized potatoes and coarse-hearted cabbage.

Later there had been Marge, met in a pub at a Saturday quiz night when she'd knocked over his cola. They'd teamed together, he being strong on history and books, she on show-biz and sports celebrities. That first time they'd won a magnum of champagne. (Had to be a big one because most teams consisted of five or six players.)

With Gran out late at a church meeting, he'd taken Marge home to get a corkscrew, ignorant then of how to get the thing open. Crafty little Marge was a couple of steps ahead, untwisted the wire, rotated the bottle and eased the cork off with her thumb. Eventually got him into bed. Both were horribly sick, and somewhere along the way he lost his virginity.

So there'd been Marge on and off for ages, he one in a queue, because she was good at it. Until, still at school, she started a kid herself, and, like a flock of others, he'd taken horrified flight. By then he'd joined Hennigan's, found a new enthusiasm that really led somewhere: antiques.

How would he get by without them? For the first time it struck him that there could be no going back. And no way ahead. Gone to earth like a pursued fox, he might as well not exist.

He breathed on the glass to obliterate the fearsome image of Alicia, nodded to himself. 'Goo'night, you rotten old rogue. You had it coming to you, mate.'

*   *   *

Morning brought Nemesis, as feared. Her other name was Fiona, or so he learnt later. And he found her beside him in bed when he awoke. She seemed in worse form, fortunately, than himself, neither requiring nor offering explanations.

A keyring beside her handbag on the bedside table suggested she had let herself into the flat, wobbled towards familiar sleeping quarters and fallen in bed, half-undressed. She was shapely, young and, despite her condition, quite lovely.

Beauty was unfair, Craddock considered groggily. Even on his best days nobody would have called him handsome. Craggy, perhaps. And on his worse days, shaggy – like a pond-dripping sheepdog.

Fiona struggled to sit up. 'Hair of the dog,' she ordered blearily.

Craddock, his mind still on the sheepdog, failed at first to grasp her needs. Then he promptly wandered in search of Worcestershire sauce to make her a prairie-oyster: yet another skill mastered through the needs of Charlie Hennigan.

While he groped for daytime normality Fiona regarded Craddock closely. 'You know, dahlin', you've been puttin' on weight lately. Getting quite podgy. That's what happens when I leave you unsupervised for months.'

(Ah, that explained the suitcases dumped in the hall. He'd stumbled over them, making his way to the kitchen.) She nudged him in the ribs. 'Have to watch the calories; up the jogging. Anyway, why're you still here? If you're taking the day off, tell you what. We'll share the run. Twice round the park, then breakfast at Bernie's.'

She swung her feet to the floor. 'Come on. Last in the shower's a fruitbat!'

Craddock shuddered. Her instant recovery had him baffled. Not only was beauty unfair. So was youth.

He let himself be led.

It was in Bernie's breakfast bar, still sweaty and puffing alongside the glowing girl, that he sought refuge from talk in a freebie copy of that morning's *Argus*, immersing himself gratefully in small-town news. On page 3 he encountered the recent Hennigan's staff photograph with his own hawkish features circled.

'Vicious Hit and Run' the headline screamed. Then 'Popular Auction Rooms Personality in Intensive Care'.

It shook him. Not just the mistaken identity, but the sudden popularity earned by supposed near-death status. For a brief second he saw himself propped against pillows, mouth gagged with gadgets; wires and plumbing from every orifice of his body; a machine doing the living bit for him. In a hushed, white room crammed with funereal, hothouse flowers.

Only, of course, it wasn't him because he was here, stertorous and heart pounding and thoroughly bemused.

First it had been the biker who'd been fooled by Warren Laing's appearance. With his head covered, yes, there was a resemblance, and the outrageous baseball cap had added to the confusion, with Laing almost on the doorstep of the Craddock workplace. But that the mistake should be repeated and built on at the hospital, then passed uncorrected to the press, was incredible.

Sandy read on, to discover that not only had his employer visited to enquire into the patient's progress, but also the *Argus*'s own reporter had stood regretfully at his bedside. The news sheet oozed sympathy and outrage above Basil

Bateman's byline. The fatuous blind fool! (Unless Laing's face was so damaged as to make recognition impossible. But then the dark hair? Possibly bandaged or shaved close for surgery.) However it was, the whole business was appalling.

'Dahlin',' Fiona prompted, 'aren't you going to order? I want poached eggs and Yorkshire ham. I suppose you want smelly old kippers?'

In a timeless daze, Craddock lets the charade go on. They return to Belvoir Court, he in Laing's tracksuit, lifted pristine from the walk-in wardrobe and now soiled with alien sweat. She still bobs beside him, almost jogging on the spot, intently athletic.

What next?

They pass the janitor-porter-whatever, with Craddock's face averted, take the lift, regain the apartment. It closes around, trapping him with a further onion-ring of confusion.

He takes refuge in the bathroom, locks the door, lets the shower pound him with sharp pin-pricks of steaming rain. Stunned, he wonders just when all this began, this labyrinth, like knitting wool winding itself round his brain, restricting all volition.

He remembers the last sane moment: Wednesday, sitting in the van, waiting for the routine day to unfold, his elbows on the steering wheel, staring up at the giant crane looming over the new building project in Queen's Street. The distant, miniaturised silhouette of its driver echoes his own slumped figure. But the other man is gazing down. He has been there over days, interrupting his programmed immobility with occasional bursts of action: lifting, directing, lowering bundles of girders and building blocks in apparently pointless but concentrated moves.

Ever a loner, Craddock has identified with him, a man selectively apart, an observer going through prescribed actions for others, but emotionally uninvolved.

About the streets there is someone else, equally a stranger, with whom he shares the same empathy: a small, isolated man in peaked cap, clean-washed overalls and clumpy boots. He wears a council-supplied weatherproof jacket with yellow day-glo patches, as he scavenges pavements and gutters for litter with a spiked and hinged stick. Never looking up, he single-mindedly pursues the job that must be the centre of his life. There should be medals struck for such as him: an MBE at least. So Craddock has made a point of saying good day to him, making him look up and respond, thin, birdlike face bright with surprised pleasure.

But at that moment before it all began, it was the crane driver who had occupied his mind, until the roar of the biker streaking into his consciousness, the thwack of the impact and the body flailing in slow motion through the air to strike the wall. Then the bike, still accelerating, had disappeared. Just a few minutes more of normality left – not more than two, surely – before he picked up the baseball cap, identical to his own, and the nightmare began.

Fiona is banging on the door. 'Why the hell have you locked it? Warren, lemme in.'

Wet-footed, he almost slips on the floor reaching her. She joins him under the downpour, clinging close, moulding herself to him, head level with his heart. He lets it all happen, feels himself drowning in her.

There is a tide in the affairs of man, he thinks idiotically, even while holding her, thrusting desperately.

But this is hardly an *affair*. More a random happening traversing the inevitable takeover of his life.

Thank God, then, for such accidents. There's nothing like sex for overriding self-pity.

CHAPTER FOUR

It was mid-morning before Superintendent Yeadings looked up from his revision of Serious Crimes statistics to find Johnny Barling from Traffic lounging in the doorway. Johnny's preference was for latte. Yeadings nodded him across to the coffeemaker. 'Help yourself.'

'Got one for you, I think,' the inspector predicted, selecting a mug. 'Local, yesterday morning. Hit-and-run on Myron's Hill, by the auction rooms. Near fatality. Could be deliberate. No rubber marks on the road, so no attempt to brake. Not that that's conclusive, but three witnesses say the biker accelerated, sort of wheelied on to the pavement, made the hit and was off. Unidentifiable, of course. Black skid-lid and dark leathers.'

'I happened along for the aftermath,' Yeadings grunted. 'There was quite a tailback by then. Who's the victim?'

'One of the auctioneer's staff. An Alexander Craddock, glorified gofer. In coma with head and multiple internal injuries.' He sniffed. 'You've a new coffee brand.'

'Ugandan Fair-trade. It's a pack Z brought in to try. We like it.' Yeadings rose and joined Barling by the window. 'This hit-and-run is something she could chase up. What did you get from the hill's speed camera?'

'No film in it. That's one all the motorists have learnt about the hard way, so it got chopped in the last economy drive.'

'Not before Nan picked up her SP30, at 7.52 on a Sunday morning,' Yeadings dryly complained.

'Happens to the most irreligious of us. Anyway, I'll let your Acting-DCI have the paperwork. Walter Salmon, isn't it?'

'You're behind the times. He's back to DI again. At long last Angus is home from Kosovo and he's taken promotion.'

'I'd heard he'd returned. Thought he'd be back as uniformed CI. Whose braided arm did you twist to keep him?'

Yeadings grinned. 'For once the cookie crumbled the right way.'

It hadn't been as simple as that. He'd made a deal with 'them upstairs'. Serious Crimes could have Angus Mott as detective chief inspector if Yeadings agreed to retain Walter Salmon on the team. Difficult, because that blocked the promotion ladder for the two younger sergeants. But again, Yeadings hadn't been quite ready to choose between them, and Mott having overall control should relieve the rivalry; also keep Salmon within almost reasonable bounds.

This outcome was due to Paula, Angus Mott's barrister bride, hastening his return by quitting her London chambers and turning up here with a notable swelling below the belt. So Angus, decidedly grimmer after his Bosnian experiences, was now back in harness, with the added responsibility of looming fatherhood. A good result all round, Yeadings considered.

Mott was at present organising a stake-out along with DS Beaumont. Overnight activity at a row of lockup garages beside a warehouse scheduled for demolition had coincided with a snout's report of a large drugs delivery due in from an air drop in Essex. Since midnight DS Zyczynski and DC Silver had been manning a camera trained on the garages from a second-floor office almost opposite.

Until she could be relieved Yeadings decided to look at the hit-and-run case himself: any excuse to quit his desk and minimise the shine on his workday trousers. Today, being Thursday, was when Nan intended returning to bid at the auction rooms. That seemed a suitable place to begin inquiries, and a visit could kill the proverbial two birds.

Before reaching for his overcoat he put through a call to St Luke's hospital and pulled strings to learn that Alexander Craddock's condition was unchanged: still in coma, still critical.

At Hennigan's he sighted Nan seated comfortably on a chintzy three-seater sofa alongside a couple he didn't recognise. She turned, feeling his eyes on her and raised a hand. 'Is that a bid from the corner?' Hennigan demanded tetchily, knowing full well she hadn't made eye contact.

Not the way to please potential buyers, Yeadings thought, threading his way between knees, feet and bulging handbags to join her. He was careful not to look in the auctioneer's face until safely roosting on the sofa's arm at Nan's side. She rolled her eyes at him, reacting childishly to the rebuke

He grinned back, then surveyed the room. Prospective buyers (and mere spectators) filled the main body of the large showroom or hitched their backsides on furniture of suitable height. Others leant against the walls, uneasily jostling heavy Victorian oil paintings. There appeared to be a massive collection of chinaware arrayed on shelves behind the rostrum.

He had yet to see Hennigan professionally in action. It was an impressive, if narcissistic, performance: silver-tongued, mobile-featured, his eyes darting, speech rapid as he accepted the next bid, pointed, repeated the price, invited a further advance and flirted for a response. Yeadings was put in mind of a Proms conductor. He was slick and vigorous, as much hustling his orchestra as persuading. For any but veterans in the gathering it would be easy to lose restraint, swept into a bidding frenzy.

Surely not Nan, though. She could be relied on to keep her cool. She was waiting, at first sight calm, but he watched her finger nervously run down the sheet to where she'd marked one item, then a gap and on to another item heavily underlined. These were the two tables, one of which she hoped would be within her self-imposed limit.

A Japanese officer's sword had just gone for £490. Her finger tapped the paper, five items above the first one she was interested in. Becoming tense, then.

There was a slight pause as one of the porters failed to locate the next item for sale. Hennigan's lips tightened into an uncompromising line at the hold-up. The woman clerk, at a table beside his dais, scuttled to sort the matter out and returned, flushed, to her seat.

'They've got a stand-in for the injured assistant,' Nan murmured. 'You heard what happened?'

Yeadings guessed it was a safe moment to risk nodding. The bidding resumed, for a Clarice Cliff Art Deco bowl. Nan drew a deep breath: four items short of the desired Victorian table. It seemed there were half a dozen porcelain and pottery enthusiasts on the floor and the bidding was briskly competitive. The bowl went for more than Yeadings expected.

'Dealers,' Nan whispered. 'That stuff's very collectible at the moment.'

He hoped there weren't any furniture specialists present, or Nan could be leaving disappointed. Bidding moved on to a long-case clock which reached £1750: not a terribly distinguished face, but with a handsome mahogany exterior. Yeadings began to feel doubts for his wife's aspirations.

There seemed little point in his hanging on. There'd be no let-up in the sales to allow him an interview with anyone, and he doubted Nan needed his support. In fact it might be his presence that was making her uneasy. He half rose. 'Unless you'd like me to stay, I guess...'

She fluttered her brochure at him impatiently, intent on following the present sale. He took it as dismissal and left.

Back at the station he borrowed a uniformed constable to change into plain clothes and relieve Zyczynski at the stake-out. Then he settled again to his paperwork, determined to make up for his bumbling and fruitless attempt at active policing: paperwork, which the advent of computers had been intended to eliminate, but in fact seemed only to spawn more.

When DS Rosemary Zyczynski knocked at his door some half-hour later his directions were crisp and terse: to locate and inform next of kin of the injured man in St Luke's. Basic details to be obtained from Inspector Barling of Traffic.

'Sir,' she said compliantly, sparing a sideways glance at the coffeemaker on the window sill. Without raising his head, Yeadings grunted. 'Well, go on then. Find a mug and take it with you. I'm busy.'

She was handed little enough info to work on: just the mother's name, Alicia Laing, née Craddock, and the vague address of 'believed living abroad'. With all the world to seek her in, Z opted for telephone directories for the entire Thames Valley. Neither Craddock nor Laing was all that common a surname, but there'd be a deal of dialling before she could be sure that locally there were no living relatives of the injured man to contact.

'I should go home.' Fiona is seated on the edge of the kitchen table while he sorts packages from the freezer. Her slender legs are wound about each other with fantastic bindweed suppleness. They intrude on his concentration.

'Home.' He repeats the word, not as a question, but he is wondering. Home to what? Some safe carapace long familiar, where her parents raised her and she reached puberty, grew into a beautiful woman; where the narrow bed is still cluttered with teddy bears, fluffy dogs and childish glitz? Or return to a shared mortgage, routine duties? – because certainly in the background there'd be a husband figure. She was too vital and attractive to have missed out on that.

'Or maybe not.' She is watching him, assessing his reaction.

Then his heart leaps as he realises she's turned down her own suggestion. Wherever this 'home' is, she's been away from it long enough to cohabit with Warren Laing. He needs to know more. But go carefully.

'Those months away,' he reminds her. 'How was it?'

'As if you care.' It sounds contemptuous, but her face is wary. She's testing him.

'I want to know.'

She stares back. 'You don't need to.' Defiant now, resisting any hint of authority.

Would Laing have persisted, demanded she tell?

She rises from beside him, stalks across to the draining board, comes back with the copy of the local paper filched from Bernie's bar, spreads it open at the page showing Hennigan's staff photo. She would have discovered it while he was making their coffee.

She taps the ringed face. His face. 'You know him, don't you?'

Difficult question. 'We're sort of related.' Then as she waits he has to fill the silence, admitting, 'My half-brother. We don't keep up. Alicia had Sandy when she was only sixteen: he's the abandoned bastard.' He hears bitterness in his own voice.

'*Sandy?* This report calls him Alexander. So, just a contraction, or?'

He watches her, feeling precarious, his seaside sandcastle crumbling. Somehow she suspects him.

'Time to come clean,' she suggests slowly, spacing the words for emphasis. 'Did you really think I'd not *feel* the difference? All along, your reactions have been wrong.'

She placed a hand flat on his chest. 'It's not flab with you, but muscle. Laing couldn't develop that much in four months. Not with his lifestyle. And then in the shower – such a deceitfully dyed head of black hair. But not black elsewhere. You're Sandy. This photo is of you.'

He stares at her in horror. The charade is over. Now he remembers her plucking at the curling hair on his chest. He'd been too involved elsewhere to have given thought to it at the time. Even then she had known. But they'd gone back to bed since; made love again. Did that mean she wasn't all that bothered by the deceit?

'Look, I can explain.'

'You'd better, mate. I'm waiting.'

So he spills it all: the shock of recognising the baseball cap as identical to his own; the knowledge that Laing had been mistaken for himself; knowing the hit had been deliberate; the panic; the flight; arriving here and intending to lie low while he thought things out.

'So did you?'

'Did I what?'

'Think it all out?'

'I didn't get the chance. You happened along.'

'So now *I'm* to blame?' She sounds offended but her eyes are merry.

'How well do you know my half-brother?'

She pauses, admits to herself that she too should come clean. 'Not at all. We've never met face to face. I saw him once, in Cyprus, at an inquest. There were reasons I needed to follow that up. I had him watched.'

Everything is happening too fast. Sandy works desperately back to his own first sight of her. 'You were in bed with me,' he accuses. 'Sozzled.'

'In bed with Warren, as I thought. And you – he – wasn't – weren't in any state to argue or remember how I'd been picked up along the way. Actually it was a shock finding anyone there. He was supposed to be away. I'd used a lockpick to get in, and the flat was in total darkness.'

'You got into bed with him. All right, actually me. But you *thought…*'

'I reckoned on him – you – being incapable of anything I wasn't easily able to cope with. I gargled with some brandy to appear in the same state, *et voilà*.'

Yes; he recalls how rapidly she'd recovered from her apparent hangover. And he'd been still so pissed that he'd not had the sense to suspect her.

'At that point I decided to take a more hands-on approach to investigating Laing.' Her smile is mischievous. 'There were risks, but I thought I could deal with them.'

'And then you discovered I was a fake. Because I'd left my chest hair sandy.'

'I was mystified; until I picked up that local paper in Bernie's diner. Then I realised somebody other than me was out to get him. But it still didn't explain why you would choose to walk into his shoes.'

'Because I thought the biker had been targeting me.'

'So isn't it now your turn to do some explaining? What had you done to deserve an attempt on your life?'

'It's a long story.' He glances at her sideways, shame-faced.

She leans over and takes his chin in her hands, pulls him close and kisses him squarely on the mouth. 'So it can wait. There are more important things to concern us. You know, you're a really nice man. I rather care for the exchange.'

Nobody has ever called him a nice man before. A nice man: he isn't so sure about that.

'So, Sandy, while I don't understand your thinking that anyone should try to kill *you*, rather than your stinking ferret of a half-brother, I'm pleased this hasn't turned out to be a further scam of his, to get you to cover for him.'

He shakes his head hopelessly.

'Sandy, you really have to do something.'

'Like sort myself out? Trouble is, that's not what I do.'

He knows that socially he's pretty inept. Vaguely distracted, he wanders into situations. Coming here as his own half-brother is the nearest thing to looking ahead he's done for some time. Now dealing with Fiona is getting too much for him, unaccustomed to grasshopper feminine logic. His mind is still caught up on her previous statement.

'What *I* don't understand,' he complains, 'is why *you* should ever choose to sleep with a stinking ferret.'

Confronted by pages of 'Langs' in the telephone directories, DS Zyczynski was relieved that Traffic Division insisted there was an *i* in the name. She came up with only eleven Laings and twenty-seven Craddocks.

Barling said the spelling had been vouched for by the clerk at the auction rooms who was also responsible for keeping up personnel files, insurance and taxation details. Alexander – she'd referred to him as 'Sandy' – had not given a recent address for his mother as next of kin, beyond that she now lived abroad and he saw no reason to keep a tab on her anyway.

Unsatisfactory, Z thought, and it hinted at bad blood between them. Her best hope was to visit his home and search for an address book. With this in mind she called at the hospital to pick up his keys, signed for a ring with no less than five keys on it and declined a separate electronic one with a BMW tag. It struck her as a classy car for someone loosely described as a gofer.

The house was a modest semi on an ex-council development, but like several of his neighbours Craddock now owned it and had made some external improvements: anything, apparently, to break the earlier uniformity of the densely packed estate.

In the next-door garden an elderly man, in his shirtsleeves despite the chill, was tying up a red-leafed vine that had blown loose from the wall. 'You calling on Sandy?' he demanded in a gravelly voice. ''E's not there, love. Got knocked down and gorn to orspital. You don't stand a chance with them 'Ells Angels these days.'

'I know. I've got his keys,' she assured him. 'I don't suppose you know any of his family?'

'There was only 'is old gran. She bin dead these twelve, fifteen, years. Nah, bit of a loner if you asks me. Not that 'e ain't a decent sort of bloke. 'Elped out when I 'ad a bitta bother with the plumbing. You police then?'

Was it the look of me or the questions? she wondered. There were two locks on the front door, a mortice and a Yale. None of the keys fitted.

''E always went round the back,' the neighbour offered. So she did the same and, out of sight, tried to get in that way. The kitchen door was equally secure, double locked, of solid wood, and equally refused all the keys. Which, though unlikely, probably meant the ITU sister had labelled and handed over the wrong set.

A tour of all sides of the house offered no alternative access. The replacement double-glazed windows were in steel frames and self-locking. The man had been admirably security-conscious, which implied a high local crime level.

She wasn't making much progress this morning. Now traipse back to St Luke's, Z supposed, yawning her head off after night shift on obbo. By the time she'd got hold of this info for the Boss it would be midday and she needed her bed right now.

CHAPTER FIVE

From the passenger seat Sandy Craddock scowled across at the girl. She must take him for a spineless imbecile. Since his initial panic he'd functioned by inertia. Now, in more ways than one, she'd slid into the driving seat. In charge, or so she believed.

But her expression wasn't triumphant; rather pensive. Either driving required of her some special concentration or she was planning the next move. Several moves, more likely.

'I'm not sure about this,' he quibbled.

'Keep your head up for the camera,' she snapped. She had braked at the exit for the Belvoir's underground car park.

'When a car reaches this point a buzzer sounds at the janitor's desk and he's supposed to watch the screens. We want him to remember we've left.'

The striped barrier rose and, starting up the incline, she saluted ironically. They zoomed into the midday traffic. 'You're lucky there was a vacancy,' she comforted him. 'I warned Gordon you were a beginner and he accepts you as a challenge. Most of the class are pretty competent, been attending for years. You'll not like Gordon; he's a Geordie.'

Sandy sat in truculent silence. Why should he particularly

dislike somebody from Newcastle? Did she think he couldn't drink brown ale? And, anyway, in art he wasn't such a beginner: at Hennigan's he'd shown some skill in sketching valuables before they were photographed for the brochures. He could hold his own if he stuck to still life.

The Castle's Adult Education courses had quite a reputation. As well as covering an eclectic range of hobby pursuits they coached for some City and Guilds exams. Set in Berkshire meadowland, the main building was a miniature Victorian mock-up of Windsor Castle, complete with crenellated battlements and a squat tower. The present survivor of the eccentric family owning it had registered it as a charitable educational foundation, adding a laboratory block and studios.

Sandy had often driven past when picking up items in Hennigan's van, but never been through the impressive gates. Now, apparently, it was to offer him asylum.

Convinced that the true identity of the comatose Warren Laing would soon be discovered and a police visit to Belvoir Court follow, Fiona had ordained that they make themselves scarce. And since she was booked in for an art course at the Castle she had taken him on as so much extra baggage. His own luggage – that was to say Warren Laing's black Samsonite case crammed with 'borrowed' contents from the same gentleman's wardrobe – was crammed alongside Fiona's matching scarlet leather set in her Jaguar's boot.

Dead man's shoes, Sandy thought miserably. This was going several items beyond that; and by now, for all he knew, Warren Laing might indeed be dead in his, Sandy's, place.

So far, he had managed to circumvent Fiona's demand to know why he saw himself as the intended victim. He'd need to think up some plausible reason: anything but the truth. Also, he should give some thought to which of several persons on offer might be wishing him dead. Meanwhile he had the opportunity to lie low and decide when, if ever, he should recover his own identity.

Two items he'd brought from home which tied him to the past. One was his Visa credit card; the second, the disc containing financial details of the scam that had gone sour on him. Not that either would be of much use. He couldn't be sure of access to a computer where he was going; and drawing cash on the card would spark suspicion when he was supposedly comatose in hospital. There was the other disc too, the dated one which he'd filched from Laing's mini-office.

He turned on Fiona who was singing along with a Beach Boys number on the car's CD player. 'Why on earth did you register me as Warren Laing?'

She smirked back. 'Don't want anyone to imagine I'm flighty.'

Surely this was a further complication? 'Do the people here know him then?'

'Don't panic, hon. They only know *of* him, through me.'

'How much?'

'The same lie that I told you: that we're an item and that I think he's a shit of the first order.'

Craddock grunted: that would be quite something to live down to. And she still hadn't explained why she'd let people believe she'd sleep with the man when she'd such a low opinion of him. He muttered under his breath and Fiona caught the tail end of it.

She laughed. 'You don't appreciate the female half of humanity.'

His head sunk tortoise-like into his borrowed sweater. 'Actually, I'm not much into women.'

Her eyebrows shot up. 'You could have phrased that better.'

'I guess. It's not that I go for men either.'

'God, you're a sad lot.'

He grinned. 'I've plenty of other interests.'

'Not, by any chance, waiting for the right girl to come along? That fuddy-duddy old thing?'

'Maybe something like that. I do get around to dating now and then: the occasional one-night stand. But it never leads anywhere.'

'Then either you lack practice or you're a very dull dog indeed.'

'One of those,' he agreed, grinning again. 'Maybe both.'

DS Rosemary Zyczynski parked near the entrance steps to Belvoir Court, easing into the space between a crimson Merc and a white Alfa Romeo. Only last week she had replaced her old Ford Escort with the new silver Toyota Yaris and was still glowing with pride at it. Between the other two cars it stood impudently confident. Small, but – as one says – perfectly formed. The janitor in the foyer caught the tail end of her smile and, impressed by her pretty face and pale grey sheepskin coat, assumed she was an attachment to one of his better class residents.

Her request for Warren Laing's apartment reversed his

opinion. When she produced her ID he made a further revision, hoping that justice was about to be served. He regretted, more sincerely than she could guess, that she had missed Mr Laing by a couple of minutes.

'I'm sorry, madam. He has just left with Ms Morgan. Coming in, you probably passed them. A maroon Jaguar.'

Yes, it had been streaking on to the southbound carriageway as she joined the roundabout.

'Perhaps if I leave my card you would see that he gets it?' Hastily she wrote on the reverse side requesting he should ring her at CID office.

'My pleasure.'

It sounded more heartfelt than the usual formality. Laing perhaps not his favourite person? Z wondered. That rather echoed Shelagh Ingram's implied criticism of Sandy Craddock's distant relative: close, being a half-brother, but distant by choice. She'd only heard Sandy mention him once, disparagingly, and never had sight of the man.

In which case Craddock's endangered life might be of little interest to him. But somebody had to be informed. Laing could choose whether to visit or not, but a slim chance was he'd know of some reason why Sandy should merit being deliberately run down.

If Laing failed to get in touch with her by nightfall she'd try ringing again. The janitor was turning her card between his fingers, his mouth pursed. 'I was wondering, miss—' (being police, not quite worthy of 'madam' by now) – 'whether I should inform you of his return.'

'That would be helpful, thank you.' She hesitated. 'It's a question of breaking bad news, I'm afraid.'

'Ah.' Almost emotionless, but not quite. There seemed a shade of disappointment now in his tone. As if deprived of *Schadenfreude*.

Job done, Z told herself. A nil result, but she'd acted as required. Now there was nothing ahead but to get home and drop into bed.

Sandy Craddock dumped his case in the doorway and surveyed the room. It was a double, almost identical with Fiona's next-door. Same well-equipped but minute bathroom, same upright chair, armchair and table, same fabric on bed and at window, same lighting – this last item better than at most three-star hotels. Just a difference in the prints on the wall. His pair showed a conservatory crammed with geraniums, and a lush landscape with grazing cattle. Hers had been a sandy cove with paddling infants, and a still life with citrus fruit, pineapple and peppers. All had been signed, and from habit he had priced them, ranking them as limited editions. If they were a sample of the Castle's artistic output, then the standard of work was quite high. For the first time he considered it might not be time ill spent here.

Fiona was standing in the door frame. 'Food,' she reminded him. 'I'll show you where the dining room is.'

It comprised a pair of large rooms linked by an archway, but only one long table beyond their own was occupied. 'Staff,' Fiona explained. 'The students aren't due until check-in at three.'

He'd already learnt they would be of all ages. 'Sixteen to eighty,' she had breezily promised. 'So don't be afraid you'll stick out. Join in or be standoffish, makes no difference. Just daub away and enjoy the moment.'

Why not? he asked himself. The present was all he'd got. Might as well live it.

The buffet meal was adequate, better than he was used to at midday. After eating, Fiona offered to show him round the main building's public rooms, dropping him off to work through the notice boards in the spacious entry hall while she was commandeered by the principal, an elderly man with thick-lens spectacles from which dangled a conspicuous gold chain. As the pair disappeared down a long corridor Sandy wandered out into winter sunshine for a tour of the grounds, famous – so one of the notices had informed him – for its comprehensive collection of European conifers.

Beyond an ancient larch whose lower branches dragged the ground, he found an unlocked Japanese pavilion containing a clutter of sports equipment and a pair of exercise bicycles. A full-size croquet set challenged him to put a price on it. Rather distinctive, but not everyone's collectible. Like so much Edwardiana, that would depend on who was drawn to a particular auction and how specialised their interests. A bit beyond his own experience, but Charlie Hennigan would have known at once what it should fetch on a good day. Sandy's fingers itched to get at a computer and discover what eBay had to offer on the subject.

Farther on he came to water meadows and a lake, recognisable as the scene which had inspired the original of his bedroom print. The cattle were there too, but distant today, beyond the stretch of water.

In other circumstances, Sandy reflected, this could have

provided a pleasant break. Except that holidays had to be paid for. He doubted the Castle would accept his credit card without question.

He asked Fiona's opinion on this when she caught up with him in the arboretum.

'No need,' she assured him. 'I've covered it.'

'I can't let you...'

'Rest easy. Not my own money. It's Warren's. I found an old cheque book at the flat with one page left in it. The signature's guesswork, but they're not to know.'

He stared at her in dismay. He was in a hole already and the girl was intent on digging deeper.

'It's only logic,' she explained, as if to a backward infant. 'You're here as Warren Laing. You've paid as Warren Laing. No one will ever question that.'

Only Laing's bank, and later his executors, once it became clear which of them was actually dead. And that was another problem. 'I wish we knew how he is,' he burst out.

She threaded her arm through his and squeezed sympathetically. 'It really bugs you, doesn't it? Tell you what, I'll ring the hospital, say I'm Sandy Craddock's sister, calling from India and can't get across to visit.'

'I haven't got a sister.'

'As if that matters. They'll have to divulge. People pretend they're related to patients all the time. Of course, if you'd rather I didn't...'

So he let her. More inertia: it was depressing.

She did her thing with a mobile phone which she whipped from her jeans pocket; waited, explained, waited some more and then grunted softly, nodding as the report came through.

Then profuse thanks, her face screwed into almost genuine concern.

'Well?' he demanded.

'Stable, but still comatose. No doubts expressed about his identity. As yet.'

Which at best offered a breathing space. Perhaps, given time, and if Fiona kept out of his hair, he'd get round to contriving some way out of this mess.

Their stroll brought them round to the Castle's forecourt where a number of cars were already being unloaded of travel bags and equipment. A fleshy, middle-aged woman stood by, a frilled pillow clasped protectively to her belly, while her husband struggled with their bags. She beamed on them. 'I always bring my own,' she excused herself. 'I'd never get a *wi-i-i-ink* of sleep otherwise.'

'Students' assembly,' Fiona announced, 'is in the Great Hall. I'll just go fix my face. Meet you there in ten minutes.'

She never materialised.

A collection of strangers filtered in, many of them boisterously greeting each other. A new boy, he kept his head down. Following a group welcome from the principal, they all dispersed to various lecture rooms and studios. He made his way to the one Fiona had previously indicated. There he was immediately conscripted to help adjust the heavy wooden easels being passed out of a capacious cupboard. Like giraffes, they had a strange way with their legs when collapsed. It kept him busy until he found refuge with his own, plus drawing board, in a corner below a window.

They were arranged in two concentric circles round a low table draped with turquoise silk, on which he assumed the still life would be set out. Still no Fiona, but at least nobody had questioned his presence.

Then she pranced in, barefoot, threw off her robe and mounted the pedestal.

Dear God, it was a life class!

Sandy, embarrassed, regarded the curves he had already possessed – or at best been loaned – and hoped to sink through the floor.

'You know the drill,' a slight, bearded man chirruped. 'Cartridge paper first, in monochrome. Choice of soft pencil or charcoal. Go for it. I'll come round with the register when you've all settled in.'

To reach the door again Sandy would need to weave between the two ranks of easels and mounds of gear piled on the floor. There was no hope: he was penned in. He reached for the box of charcoal sticks Fiona had provided, and scowled at the model.

She posed, bent right arm raised with the hand caressing the nape of her neck, left hand on hip, weight on one leg, the other knee bent.

In a way these fluid lines suggested an amphora. No, she was more like a slender coffee pot.

Think coffee pot, he told himself. You can do that.

A uniformed sergeant stuck his head into the CID office. 'Where's Z?' he demanded.

'DS Zyczynski is at home, sleeping off the night watches,' DC Silver obliged. 'Will I do?'

'Well, I thought mebbe a woman's touch. Fact is we've had a mum come in saying she's mislaid her daughter. Kid of three.

Lost her in the shopping precinct, coupla hours back. A lot can happen to a kid in that time.'

'That's uniform's job.'

'Yeah, well, we're already out looking. But there's something odd about this woman. I took her to the canteen, and now she sort of contradicts herself. I can't make head or tail. Would you have a word, see what you make of her?'

'We're not touting for work.'

'I know, but I don't feel happy about it. I just hoped Z would—'

'Is this mum still in the canteen?'

'Unless she's scarpered.'

'Well, I guess I could do with a cuppa. It's your shout.' Silver shut down the computer and rose. Sidling past the open door to Salmon's office he noted with relief that it was empty. The old aquatic number hadn't given him room to breathe since Angus returned. Itchy scales, like as not: frustrated, so he resorted to kicking the dogfish.

Faced with a tearful young woman across a canteen table, Silver too tried to get the story straight. First she'd said they were in the shopping precinct and the child had hung back to look at a display of toys.

'That would be near the Early Learning Centre then?'

She wasn't sure. No, they'd been farther up towards the Superdrug store. Maybe there'd been a hawker with a tray of kids' things. Yes, that must have been it.

Unlikely, Silver considered. Security, always on duty at mid-morning, would have cleared any hawkers off. And the woman was acting confused.

'So how long before you noticed she' – it was a little girl – 'wasn't with you?'

'Not more than a minute or two. I went back and looked in all the shops.'

'Did you question the hawker?'

The distraught face went redder. 'I – no, he must have cleared off by then.'

If he was ever there in the first place. 'Which was the last shop you'd been in, before Jilly went missing?'

'Marks and Spencer. I tried there. Nobody remembered seeing her.'

'And which was the next shop you'd been heading for?'

'Superdrug. I had a prescription from the doctor. For my nerves.'

Silver's eyes slid to the bulging shopping bag down by her feet. He stirred its contents gently with an exploratory finger and recognised a Superdrug paper bag. The woman obviously hadn't allowed a missing daughter to put her off continuing to shop. 'Are you sure she didn't follow you in there?'

'No, she couldn't.' The woman stopped short, put a hand over her mouth and started sobbing afresh.

He waited a moment. 'Hadn't you better tell me *why* she couldn't follow you in?'

This wasn't a mere crying jag now; it was a dam-burst. Silver patted her shoulder, feeling inadequate.

'She – she – I'd strapped her in. She was in her buggy. Oh God, my husband'll kill me. He made me promise I wouldn't.'

'Wouldn't what, Maisie?'

'Leave it outside. Only she was asleep. I – I'd only just got her off and she'd been grizzling all morning till then. It's hard enough dragging her round and finding the right money and all that. So I thought just for a coupla minutes, no harm done. Only, someone's took her, and I'm nearly out of me head.'

So it wasn't just a wandering three-year-old. It was abduction. And the stupid woman had wasted vital time covering herself when the shout should have gone out to all cars and mobiles.

'Wait here. I'll be back,' and Silver made it at the double to Control to put out the alarm.

CHAPTER SIX

A portly woman had dragged a low table between her easel and Craddock's. 'Hello again,' she greeted him. He recalled seeing her in the courtyard, clasping a frilled pillow to her belly: she wouldn't sleep a *wi-i-ink* without it. The chatty kind. He feared further personal disclosures.

'Actually,' she confided, 'I'm left-handed. Would you much mind swapping easels? It's easier to share then.' A flutter of mascara and she nodded at the table.

He supposed she had a point. 'No problem,' he granted and passed behind her. Satisfied, she started emptying a beach-bag of equipment on to the space in between. There was no sign of the luggage-porter husband.

'George is on another course,' she said brightly, picking up his darting glance around. 'Taxidermy. Disgusting, isn't it?'

Less embarrassing than nudes, Craddock thought ruefully. Maybe there was a chance he could transfer to it. Might even prove useful too. Occasionally a stuffed owl or fox – even once a mummified cayman – would turn up for auction and Charlie Hennigan could hardly bear to look at them, let alone conjure up an estimate.

Then he remembered that all that was in the past, and depression settled in deeper.

'Rosa, Rosa Burford,' the woman told him archly.

'Sa-san, er, Warren Laing,' he managed to get out.

She looked at him sympathetically. A stutterer: nervous. Never mind; she'd soon jolly him round.

He kept his head down, feeling blood burning his ear lobes. He reached again in his pocket for the cardboard tube of charcoals provided by Fiona, and placed it in the small space left for him on the table.

'Settle down, everybody,' bleated the tutor. 'You've all got paper and boards by now. I'm giving you just ten minutes to stare at the model, and then draw it from memory.'

It, Craddock noted, bridling on Fiona's behalf. He stared resentfully round at the circle of would-be artists and observed their businesslike detachment, some measuring her proportions against a pencil held upright at arm's length.

No drooling voyeurs then. He supposed he must try and emulate them. Not easy, though.

Gordon was moving among the easels, checking views of the model. Sandy, conscious of his presence behind him, felt uncomfortable, alien sparrow in a flock of exotic birds. Maybe the way everyone was left unsorted and unexplained was meant to avoid extraneous chatter and cut to the chase, but to his mind it made things awkward.

'I thought you would have introduced us all,' he suggested as Gordon's shadow fell over his paper.

The tutor treated this to a smile, his moist lips red and fruity in their surrounds of facial hair. 'I prefer my students *au naturel* as well.'

'Oh.'

Fiona had said he wouldn't like the man. Sandy thought she

was probably right. He was conscious of a slight tightening of his scalp. Very much a chin man, he found goatee beards off-putting. 'Do you mean introductions are artificial?'

'Totally.' His smile was thin this time, but triumphal. 'Would you have made this approach if we'd been so formal?'

So, Sandy admitted silently, I've declared myself. But the other man had too. He'd shown himself a manipulator. Weak-chinned, with thinning hair, he was pushing what authority he had.

'Point taken,' he grunted, managing a half-smile. No point in antagonising the man. Ten days could be a long time. And anyway he didn't need to know who all these people were. They would never mean anything to him.

By first break that afternoon, over coffee, the men were covertly eyeing each other up, calculating the opposition. The women had already passed into the upstaging routine: first subject, postal locality; next, offspring (including grandchildren); thence to private schooling; finally to foreign holidays. Europe, it seemed, was old hat, although Istanbul still scored a point; Egypt, Tunisia, Morocco a shade more upmarket. Israel, Kyoto, Indonesia (especially with personal recall of the tsunami) really scored. But Fiji was the clear winner, though none of the others envied that traveller's teak skin texture. She was calmly conscious of her conspicuous superiority, dilating her nostrils only slightly as she blew out Turkish cigarette smoke, shrugging bonily when reminded it was a non-smoking area.

The men, emboldened, had started asking each other about cars. These ranged from a current year's Ford Fiesta to a treasured sixteen-year-old Daimler, superannuated, so its owner claimed, from the royal household.

As the wild woman from Fiji stubbed out her cigarette the sexes were mingling and they'd reached discussion of their backgrounds. The wannabe actress was philosophical about her non-successes. The most recent had been a brief appearance in TV's *Casualty*.

'A speaking part?' someone asked, counting on a denial.

'Not even a walk-on. Simply a carry-off. Nice red blanket, though. But I'd splurged a lot on a new outfit for the audition. Then the make-up! Lordy, it took over two hours. I was an RTC casualty, drove under an articulated lorry.'

The others sympathised. She was being modest about it anyway.

Their coffee beakers were cleared and work resumed on the model.

Sandy wasn't having much success with the charcoal outline. Actually, if he closed his eyes, he could see every detail of her desirable body – as she stepped into the shower, arms reaching for him. Trouble was, not the right pose for now. He struggled to suppress a repeat reaction, quite inappropriate in present company.

At the next break for the model, avoiding the others now huddling to trade comments on the afternoon's work, Sandy Craddock looked round for Fiona. But she slid her arms into her crimson silk robe, waved a hand and disappeared from the studio.

He queued for more coffee from the vending machine, took his steaming polystyrene beaker out into the darkness of the garden and scowled at the early ghosts of frost creeping over the lawns. When they resumed sketching – a half-hour pose this time – Gordon went straight into his tutor act, moving among them, assessing and advising.

'M'm,' he pondered over Sandy's effort. 'Post-mortem study. Bring it alive, man. Look at those breasts, those delicious buttocks. Go with those curves. Enjoy them!' He made extravagant arcs in the air with his right thumb. 'See the reflected light below the crescent shadows. Light strikes the flesh of the ribcage, glances upwards, giving roundness. *Round*, lad. Breasts are globes, not flat circles. *Feel* them!'

Trouble is, Sandy rebelled silently, that I feel them all the time, can't get them out of my mind. My fingers still tingle.

He had imagined after lunch that Fiona might join him for a social siesta, but when he'd gone looking for her the door next to his own had been locked. No answer to his gentle rapping on the panels. It seemed she was only available when the fancy took her. Time to remind her he too had his needs. The man thing; not mouse.

After an early dinner, which he shared morosely with the other students – Fiona distant at High Table with staff members, like a college refectory – he found the class moving on from monochrome to pastels.

The expansive lady, Rosa Burford, insisted he share hers, their hands occasionally clashing as they reached for the same colour. Her fingers were covered with rings: outsize stones, intricate settings. Well, for her they would be, wouldn't they?

Without peering too closely, Sandy found himself double-pricing them, as good fake or the real McCoy. Now, give him *them* to reproduce on paper and he'd make a good show of it.

After the final half-hour session Fiona dressed and sought him out. In the bar he brought across a bottle of single malt, two glasses and a jug of water. It was what she'd been drinking in Warren's flat, so he felt on sure ground. They settled in club chairs opposite each other.

This time it was her turn to stare long at him. After a considerable silence she stirred in her seat, cocked her head at an angle. He squirmed, apprehensive.

'It's ironic,' she said. 'You and Warren Laing, only half-brothers, are almost identical, colouring apart. Marty and I were twins but in no way alike. She got the blonde curls, was cuddly plump and found life a giggle. My hair's dark and straight; I'm obstinate and prickly. But I loved my silly little sister like nobody's business. And when she – died, half of me went too.'

Fiona's voice had deepened with emotion. Her gaze went distant. Craddock felt for her, but knew words wouldn't help. She reached into her shoulder bag and produced a photograph. 'This was taken here last year.' She handed it across.

Sandy agreed silently: the sisters looked in no way alike. 'Who's this with her?'

'Don't you recognise Gordon Beasley? It's true he looks quite different now with the face hair and goatee beard. It's put ten years on him.'

She sank back in her chair, seemed to be reflecting aloud. 'The coroner decided it was accidental. The police appeared satisfied, but it didn't feel right. There were too many anomalies. Marty was quick-witted, would have reached forward for the handbrake. Being ambidextrous – even with her right wrist injured – she could have got herself out. The car went down on the driver's side, the back nearside door

above water for a matter of minutes. It wasn't found jammed.
She was conscious. A man on the dockside saw her face
against the rear glass, gasping, pleading as the thing finally
sank. She wasn't afraid of water, swam like a seal. It shouldn't
have happened like that.'

'Coroner,' she'd said. And earlier she'd told him that the
only time she'd seen his half-brother was at an inquest: could
that be the same one? How would Warren Laing have been
involved? Sandy leant forward, enthralled. 'So what do you
think?'

'She was restrained somehow. But they never discovered
anything when the car was pulled out. Nothing wrong
with the seatbelts. The assumption was that she panicked,
froze, and then it was too late. The finding was
Misadventure.'

There was a lot she'd left unexplained, not starting the story
at its beginning. Why was the girl in the back seat? What had
happened to the driver? And whose car was it anyway?'

'Where did this happen?' he asked. 'How long ago?'

She stared at him as though he was a halfwit, then
remembered it was news to him. 'On holiday in Cyprus. The
car went off the quayside at Limassol. It happened five
months ago. Since then I've been out there trying to discover
what really happened.'

And it had strengthened her suspicion, Craddock knew
from the harsh anger in her voice.

'What did you find?'

'That she'd been going around with a tall, dark Englishman
who had money to burn.' She was staring at him again, her
mouth twisted sourly. Almost vindictive.

Sandy felt his flesh creep. He was instantly two steps ahead. She meant Laing; Warren Laing, whom he himself resembled.

And by now Laing could be dead too, run down by a biker.

Could Warren really have been involved in the Cyprus death? – was he this Marty's treacherous lover, who'd ditched her while escaping from the sinking car himself? – a coward responsible for a death and escaping justice through lack of evidence? In which case, back in England, could he have been the biker's intended victim after all, and not hit in mistake for Sandy?

His imagination leapt ahead. And then – why assume that the biker had been a man? Could it even have been an embittered girl set on revenge for a much loved sister?

He shuddered, scared for the impetuous Fiona. Then, fast on the urge to protect, came curiosity, uncertainty, further suspicion. She'd quickly picked up that he wasn't his half-brother. So why, hating Laing, would she pretend to help his own attempt to lie low? Done more, taken over its organisation. If Laing had actually been the intended victim, Sandy Craddock needn't have fled for any good reason.

As he watched, her mood changed. She moved her glass across for a refill, abruptly breaking into his thoughts. 'How did you get on with the life class?'

He tried to explain.

She laughed. 'I *embarrassed* you? You're quite the prude, aren't you?'

She read something in his face and put a hand on his arm. 'No, I like that, truly. I've had my fill of the other sort, believe me.' Sounding world-weary and tough. Only, he knew she wasn't. For a few minutes, while she spoke of her sister, someone vulnerable had shown through.

So what was she doing here posing in the nude? He'd already gathered it didn't pay well. She had brains and personality enough to find some better occupation. Had she an ulterior motive? Some reason to be in this particular place at this very time, and dragging him blindly in tow?

Her Castle arrangement had been set up before he came on the scene. So, even with Warren Laing apparently dealt with, could she still be on the trail of the 'tall, dark Englishman who had money to burn'? An alternative suspect to Laing? Or was she seeking *why* he should have betrayed her sister? Even be looking for proof that could put him away – if he survived his injuries.

Is that why she needed to bring him, Sandy, along? – in order to milk him of information on his half-brother? There must be a reason for her sweeping him up.

Rosemary Zyczynski had caught up on some of her lost sleep. She'd been awake for ten minutes and was brewing tea when DC Silver's call came. A lost child: possibly a snatch. Of course she'd respond. See him at the precinct in twenty minutes.

She arrived to find the town centre swarming with uniformed police. A sergeant directed her to Superdrug where she found Silver ensconced at the manager's desk and manning the telephone.

'Z,' he said, 'we're looking for an unknown pushing a navy blue buggy with a clear plastic rain hood; or else carrying a three-year-old girl, with or without a blue and cream checked blanket. Would you believe? – not a soul admits to seeing them.'

Par for the course, Z thought. There were none so blind to others as customers with their eyes fixed on window displays or their shopping lists. So she went in search of teenagers. Trust them, if anyone, to be observant, keeping an eye open for talent of the opposite sex; and just maybe they'd recall some of the visual context.

There was a group of lads with backpacks, loose shirt-tails flaunted under uniform blazers. Just out of school, they had gathered round one of the red perforated metal benches. Their leader, a redhead with loving-cup ears, struck an attitude as she advanced on them. He rested a toe-cap heroically on the bench and fiddled suggestively in a trouser pocket.

'Thames Valley CID,' she told them, flashing her ID. 'Been here long, guys?'

'Nuh.' The boy removed his foot ground-wards. 'About ten minutes.'

'Long enough to drop your litter, I see. Whose ice-lolly wrappings are those?'

A boy at the rear shuffled his feet, and then bent to retrieve the paper.

'Has anyone told you what we're looking for?'

'Trouble usually,' muttered one boy, sliding behind a taller one.

Z explained. The boys looked at each other, shrugged or shook their heads. One hesitated. His hair stood on end, without the aid of gel. There was a tear in the shoulder seam of his jacket and a smear of something like raw egg all down his shirtfront.

'What then?' Z demanded.

'Not the kid,' he said. 'But I guess I saw the buggy thing.' He was too embarrassed to go on.

'Dumped somewhere?'

One or two of the others sniggered. 'Go on. Tell her,' the redhead prompted contemptuously.

More hesitation, then the boy gave in. 'It's on top of a wheelie bin at the back of Sainsbury's.'

Z nodded. 'I can see you've been inside it yourself. I won't ask why. Come and show me. If it's the buggy we're looking for you might even get a mention in the local *Argus*. OK, the rest of you. You can all push off.'

She watched them dismiss, nodded to the boy and followed where he led. She guessed there'd been a bit of horseplay and they'd thrown the boy in. The sort of thing that just happened to the smallest. She'd had some of it herself way back in schooldays. Best quickly forgotten, if you've guts enough to accept it.

They stood looking up at the unlovely rubbish that topped the bin, its lid still thrown back. 'I'll need a leg up,' Z told him.

He linked his fingers and bent to take her foot, then heaved upwards. He might be small but he was strong. She nearly sailed over the top. The stench of decomposition up there was foul.

'Left back corner,' the boy directed. And there it was, tightly folded, partly hidden under a sheet of green plastic.

Z climbed down. 'Top marks for observation. Will you stay here until I can get a police guard?'

'Aren't you going to fingerprint it now?' He sounded disappointed.

'That's an expert's job. I have to call Scene of Crime officers,' she told him, and watched him swell with pride at the confidence. For at least one undersized boy a bad day was turning round.

But what he'd discovered might not be such good news for an anxious mother.

CHAPTER SEVEN

DCI Angus Mott was running through the witnesses' statements for the hit-and-run.

'They're all agreed it looked deliberate,' Beaumont pointed out, 'but there's nothing to identify the attacker. A biker's gear is perfect cover-up.'

'So we go for the bike. "Did a sort of wheelie on to the pavement," this one says. I've done it a hundred times in my wild youth. Another one mentions hefty springs front and back. He'd be a bike enthusiast to have noticed that much. Let's have him in. A Franco Fellini, chef at the Pizza Palazzo.'

'I know the guy. He twirls the dough on an index finger to pull the crowds in. A bit of a showman, he could be bluffing about the bike.'

'Well, bring him in right now, coming up to the evening rush. That should make him talk sharpish.'

Beaumont ambled off to do his bidding. The old, pre-Kosovo Angus would have shown some consideration for business needs, sidled in and had a quiet word with Fellini over a pizza and a diet Coke. His Balkan experiences had hardened him. Or maybe the cares of impending fatherhood overrode thought for others. He looked different too, no longer the handsome, water-polo champ with floppy blond hair who could pass anywhere for a student. His razored trim was warning of serious business. Blame the married state, Beaumont decided: it wears us all down in the end.

Mott made Fellini wait ten minutes on the public bench. As expected, the man had resisted being brought in. Only Beaumont's mention of attempted murder startled his boss enough to let him leave. When the DCI joined them in the interview room, a box file under one arm, the witness was only too willing to cooperate and get back to work.

'So, this biker,' Mott pursued. 'Did you notice anything special about his leathers?'

'Solid black. Skid-lid with a red logo. Seen a lot like that. They're common as...' He waved a hand inclusively.

'Muck,' Beaumont helped out.

The chef glared at him, then accepted it. 'As muck, yes. But not cheap.'

'The bike,' Mott offered.

'Fast. Good acceleration. Not all that heavy, though.'

'A trial bike?'

Fellini closed his eyes for recall. 'Not so stripped down. Bigger tank. A trail bike, I think: or halfway between trail and roadhugger. Black and silver.'

'Do you mean chrome, stainless steel?'

'I think not. Perhaps parts are resprayed. Else I say – Yamaha?' He sounded anything but confident. 'It all happens so fast. How be sure?' A shrug of the narrow shoulders. 'I have a Yam once. It reminds me.'

'If it was a respray job, think classics. Mostly the owners keep them for years, cosset them. Showpieces.'

Mott opened the file and removed a magazine which he

pushed across the table between them. '*Classic Bikes*. Take a look through. See if you recognise the model.'

Fellini ran the pages quickly through his fingers. 'No, I tell you it all happens so fast.' He shook his head. 'I still think a Yamaha. I go now, please?'

They had to let him leave. Beaumont gave him a lift back to the pizzeria. Making conversation, he asked, 'You still a biker?'

Fellini looked away. 'I buy a car now. Got kids.'

Not such a happy man, Beaumont decided. He arrived back to find Mott grumbling about Salmon's absence. 'Where was he going after the auction rooms?'

'He didn't say. Sir.'

Mott noticed the 'sir' and took warning, straightened. 'Am I riding you too hard?'

'We're not all bastards, Angus.'

'No.' He ran a hand through his hair stubble. 'I guess I have to adjust to that. Give me time.' It sounded like half an apology. Beaumont nodded, took out his mobile and keyed in Salmon's number.

'It's ringing,' he said, 'but he's not answering; must have left his phone in the car. I'll give Hennigan's a buzz.'

He retrieved the number and got through to Shelagh at the front desk.

'He's long gone,' she told him. 'I think he meant to take a look at Sandy's house.'

'I need him here, to carry on with this,' Mott told the DS. 'I've enough on my plate, writing up the drugs arrests and now the missing child.'

'I'll go sniff around some bike repair shops,' Beaumont

offered. 'DC Silver's our computer buff. He can list local owners and interview them. If DI Salmon's gone AWOL, he'll have his teeth into something, you can be sure. Bit of a bulldog.'

He grinned ruefully. 'Actually, *shark*'s more apposite.'

Yeadings was organising the missing-child case as top priority. In the shopping precinct uniforms were abroad, asking questions. Mott had visited the home, met both parents and acquired a recent snapshot of the little girl. This, passed to DC Silver, was now being reproduced on posters and handbills. Bateman of the local *Argus* had seized upon a subject worthy of tear-jerking prose. There was to be an appeal on the national TV evening news.

'I want a wider search,' Yeadings ordered, as Z delivered her initial report. 'The AC has drafted in twenty more uniforms to cover parks, woods, boathouses, building sites, derelict property; and divers are on standby.

'Dumpster?' Yeadings's eyebrows shot up to his hairline. 'What's this, Z?' He waved her report at her. 'Are we officially into American-speak now?'

'It sounded more adult that wheelie bin, sir.'

He tilted his head. 'You may have a point there, but correct it. Try "skip".' He continued reading. 'You say the pushchair was damaged. Exactly how?'

'The rear axle was bent at an angle and the left wheel detached, also the left arm support pushed inwards. It was old and not the sturdiest model, but in the bin we found nothing heavy enough to have caused the crushing. I considered the damage happened before it was – er, dumped.'

'The forensics report on it isn't in yet. Did it look like the result of a traffic collision?'

'If a car had struck it I'd have expected more damage, even paint or blood traces. I saw it as due to heavy wear and tear, with perhaps a larger child habitually riding on the rear axle bar.'

'Where's the mother now? Mrs Maisie Bell, isn't it?'

'WPC June Coleman's driven her home, sir, in case anyone phones in.'

'Right. We'll leave it to Coleman to follow up on previous damage to the pushchair. Ring her to that effect. For the present I'm taking you off the biker incident. A witness has claimed the machine was an old Yamaha trail bike. Mott has tasked Silver with listing local models, all the usual.'

'Yessir.' She hadn't been getting anywhere on that case anyway. The missing child was far more up her street. All the same, she'd have another go at locating Laing and Ms Morgan when she had a spare minute.

He leant back in his chair. 'You'll be glad to know that Angus has mopped up the entire drugs reception committee. And the Met has collared the London end. I'm preparing the paperwork for CPS. Good teamwork all round on that. But every effort now has to go into finding Jilly Bell.'

Following Z's failure to get into Craddock's house and Yeadings's lack of result at the auction rooms, it had fallen to DI Salmon, still smarting at reduction from his temporary promotion of Acting-DCI, to tackle Hennigan and his staff at the close of business. It irritated him intensely to have been kept waiting and his approach was accordingly abrasive.

Charles Hennigan, finding the man unpalatable, reacted with increased finickiness. Shelagh Ingram tried her best with a tray of tea and sweet reason, but the simple fact was that nobody could offer any suggestion why Craddock should have been targeted by a killer, nor why the set of keys, confirmed by the hospital to have come from his pocket, were not those of his only known home.

Salmon's narrowed eyes signalled that, to his mind, the road traffic victim was proving a more tortuous character than these single-track people had imagined. A second, secret home implied a double life, which could account for the man's acquiring a lethal enemy. A career criminal invariably attracts trouble on the streets.

This biker business looked professional, an alternative to the ever-expanding outbreak of gun crime between rival gangs. Craddock would have been dealing drugs or fencing valuables for sure, Salmon decided, remembering the car key with the BMW tag. If, of course, it wasn't due to that old chestnut Another Woman, with a vengeful husband or boyfriend. There was a good range of offensive behaviour on offer, but nobody at Craddock's workplace would allow a word to be said against the fellow.

Duncan Stott, busy with packing auctioned items for delivery, and bugged by an inept stand-in for the missing Craddock, barely consented to raise his head when questioned. 'Look, I don't know anything about his private life. He was a bit of a loner, and neither of us is really a drinking man so we hadn't any occasion to talk. I never heard anything about a second home. It was always the same house we delivered to.'

'Delivered what?' Salmon demanded, bristling with suspicion.

'Stuff he bought.'

'When the bids start to dry up, Sandy will sometimes give a nod for something he fancies,' Shelagh put in hastily to let Duncan get back to work. 'We all do. It stands to reason.'

'Still, if you need to get into the house,' Stott offered, 'I could let you borrow my key for his shed. I sometimes used to deliver when Sandy was off on a long run.'

'What use would the shed be to me?' Salmon snapped.

'He keeps a spare key there for the back door, on the top shelf, behind a can of green gloss paint.'

'Right. Let's be having it then.' At least this was some kind of progress. They wouldn't need to batter the front door in or break a window. And from what Stott had said, there might be an Aladdin's cave to explore once they opened up.

Salmon returned to his car to put in a call for DC Silver to meet him on Craddock's doorstep. Silver, he was told, was unobtainable, and his mobile switched off. Salmon ground his teeth and set off to do the survey on his own.

Arrived at Sandy Craddock's house, he abstracted the house key from its concealment in the shed and let himself into the kitchen. A blue Delft clock on a shelf above the work surface showed three-fifteen. Upturned on the draining-board were a single plate, a cereal bowl, mug, teaspoon, dessert spoon and knife. A smell of washing-up liquid still hung on the air. The crockery implied that the last meal had been breakfast, which fitted with the time of the biker's attack. The kitchen appeared tidy and clean. Otherwise there was nothing of note.

A dim passage led to the front door. The room off it

doubled as dining and sitting room. The furniture was utilitarian; no feminine frills or flowers. A worn leather armchair was pulled up to the gas fire which was switched off. Background warmth came from a long radiator under the window. A massive mahogany bookcase reaching to the ceiling was crammed with a mixture of leather-bound tomes and classic paperbacks, some of them yellowed with age; all of them showing signs of use. Bachelor who reads a lot, Salmon reflected.

The narrow staircase led to a half-landing with a square bathroom extending over the kitchen, then a further six steps offered a choice of three closed doors. One was an airing cupboard with folded clothing and household linen stacked on slatted shelves above the boiler. Inside it, against one inner wall leant a steel rod with a rubber ferrule at one end and a hook at the other. To open a loft trapdoor, he assumed.

A single bedroom over the hall contained only a chest of drawers and a divan covered with a plump brown duvet and two feather pillows. The third door, which expectedly led to the main bedroom, actually opened on to a minor version of Hennigan's saleroom. There was nothing big, but a heck of a lot of knick-knacks, mainly china and silver, closely arranged according to size, on white wooden shelves against each of the walls. One section was devoted to scruffy old teddy bears and Victorian dolls.

We've got a weird one here, Salmon told himself. He couldn't see anyone wanting to run down the man for his collection of almost threadbare soft toys. But if the china was of any value, there might be some sense in it. He picked up a bronze statuette, a naked youth with winged feet and a sort of

WW1 tommy's helmet. It still had a sticker on its base with a number. No price, though. That certainly would have been whatever the last bidder was willing to stretch to.

So had that been Craddock, or was this something he'd knocked off in a long campaign of swindling his boss?

Salmon replaced the wing-sandalled youth. It reminded him of the one in the centre of Piccadilly Circus. People called it Eros, but he thought he'd heard mention of another name. One of those old Greek or Roman gods.

Anyway, nothing of note had struck him on either floor of this two-up, two-down ex-council house. That left the loft to explore. Which was where DC Silver would have come in handy. Salmon stared up at the small, square trapdoor, convinced it would be an awkward fit, even if a ladder came to light.

There was no knob or outer bolt. He fetched the steel rod from the laundry cupboard and poked with the ferrule end. The panel swung down, on a pressure switch, and an electrically operated telescopic ladder was activated. He watched as silently it extended itself to floor level. A tentative step assured him it was sturdily enough constructed. He was left no choice but to trust himself to it.

As feared, it was a tight fit and he was obliged to peel off his leather car coat and drop it behind on the floor. He wriggled through. As his weight hit the loft's boarded flooring a light came on. He stood up under the roof beams and found himself in a well-equipped office.

A modern beech-wood desk had matching filing cabinets to either side. There was a full-size computer screen and printer. A tall cabinet contained compact discs.

Salmon seated himself on the swing chair and attempted to boot up. Instantly the lights went out. A sliding sound behind him warned that the ladder was retracting. He yelled at it and it continued to tidy itself away, while a soft thud announced the trapdoor closing.

In total darkness Salmon suddenly stood up and his head struck an overhead beam, making lights flash before his eyes. Swaying on his feet, he put up a hand in his hair and it came away stickily warm.

Only ingrained strict Methodism prevented him loosing off a string of invective.

Silver was never going to hear the end of this: keeping his mobile switched off while on call.

Not that it could have helped now in any case. Salmon's own phone had dropped to the lower floor in a pocket of his car coat.

CHAPTER EIGHT

The child's pushchair recovered from the rubbish skip at the shopping precinct had been plastic-wrapped and sent on for examination by forensic experts. DS Zyczynski, eager to continue on the case, was still nagged by loose ends to tie up elsewhere, notably concerning the biker incident.

A second and a third phone call to Warren Laing at Belvoir Court had not been picked up. Unsure that Laing was, in any case, related to the unconscious victim of the biker incident, she drove across to question the porter on duty. He was unable to help, having been on a fortnight's winter break in Malaga and had returned only the previous day. Asked about a Ms Morgan with whom the other porter had seen Laing last leaving, the man looked blank.

'A maroon Jaguar,' Z prompted him.

'Ah, you know the car. In that case, maybe I can help. If it's been parked in the underground garage, we'll have it on CCTV film. Then you can trace the lady from the licence plate.' He appeared a deal more cooperative than the previous snooty fellow. Marvellous what a little winter sunshine abroad can do for one, Z reflected.

There had been eleven or twelve cars leaving the building daily, and the current monochrome film, retrieved from the camera and viewed in the porter's back office, showed two cars of that make mounting the ramp that led to street level. Both had left yesterday and were timed, one at 9.30 a.m. and the other at midday. The first Jaguar held an elderly man with no passenger alongside. The other was driven by an attractive young woman with long, dark hair. She had treated the camera to a broad smile and a semi-military salute. Less clearly an equally dark-haired man was seated beside her.

'That could well be Mr Laing,' the porter said, viewing the screen. 'I've not seen the young lady before. Nor the car, for that matter.'

Z copied down the licence number and phoned it in for identification. The address came back as Jasmine Lodge, Winchelsea, East Sussex, but the registered owner was a Major Trevor Barnes. So it appeared that Ms Morgan was driving someone else's car.

Major Trevor Barnes's telephone proved to be ex-directory. A male operator at his local exchange could not make the connection because there was no answer at that number.

Zyczynski weighed in her mind whether to contact Sussex police to trace Ms Morgan through the major, but too many intermediaries were needed when it wasn't at all certain that this Laing was related to the biker's victim. Since the local paper had published details of the Craddock incident, any interested party in the area should have picked up on it already. Dissatisfied nonetheless, Zyczynski left it there, aware that the case ranked lower than child abduction. She returned to base and reported for further tasking.

A Major Incident room had now been set up in an adjoining pair of empty offices at the shopping precinct.

Diverted there, DS Zyczynski found them already equipped
with computer monitors and keyboards. All phones were in
use as the augmented CID team pursued inquiries. Outside she
had passed several closed white vans. Officers from the
Territorial Support Group, including two dog handlers, had
been grouped round DCI Mott. All wore uniform blue
coveralls and rubber boots. She guessed their vans would be
loaded with digging tools and thermal sensors, as the search
would be extended to local parks and woodland. So already
the assumption was that the child could be dead and the body
concealed.

She murmured as much over Silver's shoulder as he sat at
his computer. 'Angus is covering all possibilities,' he said
tersely. It seemed the newly returned broom was sweeping
clean.

'Z,' Mott called, catching sight of her. 'Neighbours have
been questioned, door-to-door, by uniform, but I want you
tackling them in depth, as well as family. But first have a word
with the health and social services. We need a full picture of
the family's home life.'

'Right, guv.'

He picked up on her hesitation. 'What then?'

'Isn't this one for the Child Protection Officer?'

'Ultimately perhaps, but she's on sick leave. So cover for
her. Get addresses from DC Silver.

She watched Silver flick at his keyboard, click his mouse,
and the required sheets slid from the nearby printer. On one a
local map was displayed with the relevant house numbers and
a list of residents. The other contained information on a
medical practice and the welfare contact.

Market Lane Health Centre was a modern, low, brick building with a crowded car park and three cars queuing to get in. Z drove through and slid into a space marked Doctors Only. Inside the windscreen she Blu-tacked a card with Police Inquiry printed on it, and her mobile phone number. Chances were that nobody would insist on her moving on.

A middle-aged receptionist answered her queries in a discreetly lowered voice: yes, the Bell family were registered here, Maisie and the toddler with Dr Roberta Milford, Roger Bell with Dr Chatterjee. Both were working here today, but both had full lists of patients and should not be disturbed.

'Fit me in as soon as either finishes with the present patient,' Z instructed firmly. 'I'm sure you want as little fuss made as possible.'

Huffish, the woman refused to meet her eyes. 'I can't promise, but I'll see what I can manage.'

'Thank you.' It seemed that one at least of the medicos was a dragon. Z took a seat in what resembled a small hotel lounge, with potted semi-tropical plants and a stack of well-thumbed magazines.

The first doctor to come free was a small ethnic Indian whose face was wrinkled like a walnut shell. His overheated room was cluttered with personal belongings. He hadn't heard of the child's disappearance and needed Z to bring him up to date. 'Oh, most distressing,' he murmured, 'but how can I possibly be of help?'

'I understand Mr Roger Bell is on your list.'

'Indeed, yes, but I cannot divulge anything about him, miss – er, Sergeant. That would be quite unprofessional.'

'I don't need medical information, Dr Chatterjee. Simply to

know the sort of person he is: just how he struck you personally. This is a very delicate matter I need to approach him on. The last thing I want is to distress him further.'

The doctor regarded her with sorrowful, brown eyes. 'Oh, quite.' He considered his next words.

'I do not think you will find he is someone – er, easily distressed.'

That appeared to be as far as he would go. Z reminded him that this was a police matter and if necessary she could return with a court order allowing access to the man's medical record. She then thanked the doctor and returned to the waiting room.

'Dr Milford is taking a short break, Sergeant,' the receptionist told her. 'She will see you now.'

The second consulting room was free of plants or clutter, and despite the sharp weather, the window was open a full eight inches. Roberta Milford, a heavily built woman stirring a mug of what smelt to be herbal tea, regarded Z with a pugnacious frown. Her voice, however, was warmly sympathetic. 'You're here about little Jilly Bell? Is there any news at all?'

'It's early yet. Every effort is being made.'

'Yes, I'm sure. How can I help?'

'Understandably you can't give me any medical information, except that if the child needs vital medication...'

'You would certainly be informed. That's not the case.'

'Both the mother and Jilly are on your personal list, but not the father. I wondered why.'

'H'm.' Dr Milford swivelled her chair and crossed a pair of surprisingly elegant legs at the knee. 'Actually ours is a practice where any patient can ask to see whichever partner they please. But for statistical reasons we keep to the earlier system of personalised lists.'

She paused. 'Of course, there are still patients who prefer always to see a doctor of the same sex.'

Z considered this, aware of the cautious tone. So which of the parents had a gender preference?

'Who,' she ventured, 'was the first to register with the practice; the father or the mother?'

Dr Milford's weathered cheeks crinkled. The policewoman's guile wasn't lost on her. 'Mrs Bell,' she said promptly. 'By a good four months. As soon as they moved to this area.'

'From?'

The doctor glanced down at the opened file on her desk. 'Previously they lived in Colchester. Their GP then was a Dr Paul Godwin. A single-doctor practice.'

'Thank you.'

'I'm afraid that's all I can tell you, at least for the present. I certainly hope you'll soon have good news for the family. Until then we shall all feel very concerned.' Again she paused, significantly. 'But I have no special anxiety over the child's general well-being. Given normal care, of course.'

'Given her customary level of care?' Z insisted.

The doctor stared back noncommittally; then her hands straightened the papers lying on the open file.

'As far as I have any reason to believe,' she said, looking away. Her tone was dismissive. Z rose, thanked her again and left, determined not to build on the impressions just received until she had met the family for herself.

Her next stop was at the offices of social services. Although she was ten minutes early for the appointment made earlier, Mrs Parfitt was ready to receive her. A tired-looking woman with greying hair escaping from an untidy bun, she clearly had the child's welfare at heart. After expressing her shock at what seemed to have happened, her first words were warning enough.

'The family was referred to us by the health visitor who had monitored Jilly's progress over the eight months she's been in our area. The Colchester midwife had reported she was undersized at birth, although full-term, and she put on weight slowly. I didn't consider she was dangerously undernourished, but her diet could be better balanced. Apparently, when the mother became unable to breastfeed, Jilly was switched almost immediately to solids. Junk food, in fact.' She sighed.

'The sad truth is that it provides bulk without the benefit of vital minerals, as I'm sure you know. The choice, unfortunately, is most often due to cost. Rubbish comes cheaper than fresh fruit and vegetables, fish and white meats. Nor have I seen anything to make me believe Mrs Bell is an adequate cook. Do you have children yourself, Sergeant?'

'Er, no.' Perhaps that was as well, Z thought. She wouldn't care to be so formidably checked up on, although she'd admit that in some cases it was essential. She rushed in, to escape the personal. 'And otherwise than physically, is she a happy child?'

'She was uncommunicative on most occasions I saw her, and inclined to whine when her mother's attention was drawn away. She's not used to being with other children.'

'A demanding child?'

'All children are, at that age, but I'd say more dependent than most. Uncertain, lacking assurance.'

'Clinging to her mother? Needing protection?'

At that almost-official term Mrs Parfitt sat straighter. 'There was never any question of referring her to the At Risk register. There were no signs of bruising or broken bones.'

'That you know of,' Z offered.

'At no time were there injuries requiring medical attention, Sergeant. No hospital emergencies.'

'But you had your doubts, just the same.'

'It's as well to keep an open mind. We have to be careful. There are risks either way.'

'Like the police,' Z suggested. 'Damned if you dare and damned if you don't.' She thought the woman had finished, but apparently not. There was a pause while she made up her mind how much to reveal.

'There had been an earlier child, Sandra.'

'Who died?'

'Of pneumonia, in Colchester General Hospital. No details on her were passed to us. She was four years old.'

There seemed little else to be got from the woman. Z thanked her, handed over her card with mobile and station numbers, and said goodbye. A glance at her wristwatch showed that she'd barely time to ring social services at Colchester before their office closed, and she had no worker's name to refer her inquiries to.

The idea came instead to contact Colchester police and enquire if the family had ever been brought to their notice. The result wasn't long in coming back. Roger Bell had a record for GBH and affray. He had served a two-year sentence for breaking and entering. One of the items broken and entered had allegedly been a local prostitute, but she had later reconsidered and withdrawn the charge.

Nevertheless it had remained on record, which Z approved. Since the alarms raised over the Soham child-murderer's early investigation notes having been expunged, unsubstantiated at the time, more attention was being paid to preserving negative information.

By now, DS Zyczynski decided, a visit to the Bells was overdue.

Warren Laing drifted through bathroom procedures, then, finding himself unaccountably downstairs, scowled at the other *estranjeros*. He had a strict rule: no small talk before breakfast. They were heavily into it, out-screeching and out-squawking the gaudy macaws swarming in tropical heat outside. All in rapid-fire Spanish.

'Piss off,' he ordered them. Flatly, in English.

This foreign cacophony confused him, already uneasy about the drawbacks in having legged it. What had suited Ronnie Biggs for decades, might not go so well for himself. He felt strangely unwell, distanced from his own sensations. Must have picked up some vicious bug on the way out.

He was aware of unaccountable blanks throughout the final planning. He couldn't remember the journey. It was as though he'd slept through immigration as well as the flight: been beamed down here like they did in *Star Trek*. But his molecules hadn't properly reassembled. This was jetlag in spades.

At that point the scene started breaking up, like a bloody satellite message interrupted by static. Visually objects started floating apart, dissolved into mist, almost re-formed, but quite changed, flowing into a white mirage. He reached out trying to sort them, but they slid through his fingers.

The effort of unscrambling was too much. He let go, plummeting to blessed oblivion. If only the damn parrots would give up their screeching.

'I've twice asked Donald to oil this trolley,' Nurse Halliday complained. 'It squeaks fit to wake the dead.'

Not the most tactful phrase to use in ITU, the young medic reflected. For a brief instant he'd thought his patient was showing signs of coming round, but now it seemed not. The drug trolley's reveille had fallen far short of Halliday's expectations. He scanned the board above the patient's head: *Alexander Craddock*, followed by *Sandy* in brackets.

'Have there been any visitors for this one?'

'Just his boss, a man called Hennigan. And that reporter from the *Argus* has been hanging around. He doesn't appear to have family.'

The doctor nodded. A pity. Sometimes it helped to hear well-known voices or have favourite music played. The subconscious could still be stimulated when the cognitive brain was out of reach. 'Ah well. I'll drop by later.'

'Do that.' The rather frosty face gave way to a smile. 'There'll be a latte if you're lucky.'

CHAPTER NINE

For Sandy the evening had begun to improve. Fiona, more convivial, seemed content to settle with him in the bar, and he had hopes they wouldn't break up at bedtime. The whisky was helping and he was intent on getting her to divulge more about her knowledge of his half-brother.

Unfortunately the Castle's entertainment programme intervened, offering a late evening lecture, illustrated with DVDs and piano, on Russian classical music. And Fiona decided to attend. There was no alternative for Sandy but to drift in her wake, his inner rage rising with Rachmaninoff and reaching fever pitch with Moussorgsky. And at the finale, didn't Fiona slip away with a murmured excuse, and then fail to return.

He searched the public areas as inconspicuously as possible, declining well-intentioned invitations from what he supposed must be his classmates. This time her room was unlocked and empty. He went in, checked in the wardrobe and was relieved to find her clothes and cases still there.

In high dudgeon he returned to his room, pulled on a thick sweater and Laing's sheepskin coat. Frost had given way to sleet and now a snarling wind met him in the courtyard, matching his mood. For a full ninety minutes he slogged against it, revelling in being alone. Or almost convincing himself so. Stomping through the nearby village he passed few lighted windows. The pub had closed. Someone clearing up inside was shifting tables and whistling off-key that he'd done it his way. 'Good on yuh, mate,' Craddock congratulated him in passing.

That's what he'd do too, and Fiona could come begging. Thus determined, he turned to start on the journey back, and found he was hopelessly lost. Worse, the sleet became heavier, charged with cutting little particles of ice. It would probably ruin the coat's suede finish. Sheep at least had enough sense to wear a fleece the business side out. By now he was working up a sweat under it. His cheeks seared by the slicing wind, he felt like a reverse baked Alaska.

It was 2.18 a.m. when eventually the Castle's dark bulk showed up ahead, lit sporadically by curtained windows. A dozy night porter let him in with an offer of hot soup, which he scorned: the remains of the malt waited in his room.

After a prolonged hot shower and spurning the use of Laing's pyjamas, he poured himself a treble in a tooth-mug from the bathroom. He sprawled on the bed and solemnly cursed womankind, borrowed clothes and sleety winds. Then, as the whisky benignly began to course through him, he relented, reversed their order and eventually, with regret, cancelled women from inclusion.

He had fallen heavily asleep when the knocking began at his door. He struggled to surface as the tattoo became more frantic. A drumming of fingernails turned to scratching. Her voice, at first low and insistent, rose to a whispered peak of entreaty.

He fought to free his sweaty limbs from the tangled sheets, moving towards a vision of Fiona waiting outside, as wonderfully naked and impatient as himself: womankind come eventually to heel.

He groped to unlock the door, swung it wide, and recoiled in horror.

Lurching as the woman collapsed on him, he fell backwards to the floor.

As he struggled under the sprawling mass, he reached out for her, fingers slithering, wet and sticky, over fleshy shoulders. Under the recognised perfume there was a different scent, almost metallic. *Organic.*

He pushed her off his belly, scrambled upright and reached for the light switch.

She went on making noises, less voiced: more of a gurgling, like the last of the bathwater going down the plughole. There was a single convulsive jerk, and then he knew.

This was no longer farce. It was real. This was death.

'Put your head between your knees,' Fiona commanded.

Too late. He didn't faint, but made up for it with vomit. She pushed him back on the bed and returned to the body on the floor. The distorted face looked like a Sweeney Todd job, she thought grimly. The length of paper towelling she had swathed round the woman's neck was stained a vivid red, but the bleeding appeared to have stopped. It had poured from her ears, where both lobes were savagely torn, but that wasn't what killed her. Turned on her side, she was seen to have four inches of black knife handle protruding from her back, driven upwards under the left shoulder blade. A single straight blow, and the blade's bulk had sealed the wound, but for a dribble of blood at the edges.

'P-police,' Sandy pleaded, struggling to sit up against the pillows.

'Later. We have to move her. She can't be found here. This isn't our business, and I won't take the rap for it.'

'We can't do that.'

'Sandy, get a grip. Find some shirts, underwear, anything to clean up the blood.' She removed the artificial flowers from a bowl on the window sill and went to fill it with cold water.

Sandy slopped Warren Laing's pyjama top into the water and started to wring it out. Fiona had disappeared to her bedroom but came back almost instantly with an ankle-length plastic raincoat. She spread it alongside. Together they rolled the body on to it.

It was turning into a TV hospital drama, Sandy thought. This was where one of the paramedics says, 'On my count. One, two, three.'

Fiona regarded the soaked carpet. There were two patches now, where Sandy had worked on the bloodstains and on his own contribution.

'You'll have to stay in your room until it's dried out. Put the "Don't Disturb" notice on the door. Pretend you're sick. Something you ate at dinner.'

He became suddenly aware of his own nakedness and dived for sweater and trousers. As he was lacing up Laing's shoes Fiona was at the window, struggling to raise the sash. 'Dammit, it's screwed shut.'

Of course: to economise on central heating. But anyway

this wasn't the ground floor. Surely she didn't intend to drop the body a matter of some twelve feet?

'Nail file,' Fiona muttered, and again shot off to her own room. When she returned she had exchanged her bathrobe for a black sweater, jeans and trainers. At this point Sandy took over. Locks and sealed windows were things he'd some experience with. Then, with the sash gingerly raised, he at last stood his ground.

'There'll be marks on the body if we drop it. And we've nothing to lower it by.'

Fiona considered this, leaning far out to survey the ground below. 'Shrubs,' she told him. 'I think they're ceanothus. It's fairly springy stuff; no actual thorns. Drop your duvet first, then both the pillows. She'll be all right then.'

As all right as she'd ever be again, he regretted. A few hours back he'd thought her a deadly bore. Now just a dead one.

It was still black farce, but with added desperation as they struggled to manoeuvre the heavy body out without disturbing sleepers in the neighbouring rooms. A second after they let go there was a distinct sound of broken twigs.

'Now what?' Sandy asked, gazing down at the pale, shrouded form below.

The answer was obvious. They had to follow. An adventitious down-pipe saved them from landing on the body, and they escaped with only minor scratches and soiling.

Mercifully the sleet had stopped, but the shrubbery they dragged the body from showered them with collected water. Sandy remembered the Burfords' car. The luggage-lumbered husband had turned to flick his electronic key, and lights flashed up from a blue Mercedes parked behind him in the courtyard. Unless he was one of the few accorded garage space, and provided he hadn't gone for a drive since then, it should still be where he'd left it.

It was. The same lamp over the Castle's front porch, which earlier had guided Sandy in after his solitary night walk, threw light far enough to allow identification.

'I do not intend breaking in,' Sandy said stoutly. 'Too risky without gloves.'

'So let's just leave her here, by the passenger door.'

Fiona let the woman's ankles drop, and Sandy followed suit with the bulkier torso. They had to roll the body again to remove the plastic raincoat, which Fiona folded into a tight bundle and tucked under her arm. They stood looking down at the results of their handiwork. Rosa Burford lay spattered with mud in what appeared a drunken sprawl. Sandy unwound the length of paper towel stiffened with congealed blood and offered it to Fiona. She grunted impatiently, undid the raincoat, bundled it inside and refolded it.

'Just as well she'd kept her clothes on,' Sandy remarked. 'I wonder why, at this time of night.'

She still wore the floaty bit of evening wear she'd put on for dinner. It was a décolleté, multi-pleated chiffon number, all crimson, orange and yellow blotches, suspended from narrow straps. By daylight any bloodstains on it would be hardly remarkable at first sight.

He remembered the entrance she'd made earlier, standing in the doorway, heavily made-up, raising her fleshy arms in that ridiculous celebrity pose: *Look at me!*

Her earrings had been miniature chandeliers, flashing

diamonds. They were what had made her bleed so, torn from the pierced lobes. He winced. Poor cow, she wasn't the stuff for such ravaging.

But she needn't have brought her troubles to his door. He'd enough of his own without them.

'You must manage tonight without your bedclothes,' Fiona told him, callous to the last. 'We'll chuck them in the Jag. I have the key with me.'

Such a planner, Sandy thought sourly. But there was no point in protesting. No way could anything so bulky be smuggled in without the night porter noticing. Even in daylight they would need to choose their moment, when everyone was in class.

'Is that it, then?' They had disposed of duvet and pillows as she decreed.

Fiona nodded. 'Yup. Now ring the doorbell. Act normally. Chat up the porter. Say you let yourself out again when you discovered I hadn't returned; found me wandering the grounds, unable to sleep. We'll order a pot of tea off him and charm him round. With any luck he'll enjoy our company. It must be a hell of a boring job, all night alone. Let's hope by tomorrow he'll have forgotten anything unusual.'

A slow smile spread across Sandy's hawkish features. 'Tomorrow. That leaves *you* to get the stuff back in. I'm sick, remember. Can't leave my room.'

He was unaffected by her answering scowl.

'And my bed had better be made up sharpish, for when the management comes round enquiring after my health – to defend their kitchen on the hygiene front.'

Fiona gave him a pitying stare. 'Don't you think they'll have more to worry about, once the body's discovered?'

But apparently it wasn't.

At life class next morning Rosa Burford's place was empty. This caused no more comment than a raised eyebrow or a casual shrug. Fiona struck a more provocative pose on her dais. Gordon delivered dicta. The morning wore on.

By eleven Sandy Craddock had tired of acting the invalid and elected to join the second session. Whether it was due to the pose or to his own heightened tension, he found himself physically responding. With the pastels too, which lay available. He abandoned himself to vivid flesh tones.

'M'm,' commented Gordon, appearing by his free elbow. 'Lit by the fires of hell, eh? I like the new vigour.'

But such a sudden access of inspiration took it out of him. A quarter-hour before lunch break, once he'd removed the chalky deposit from under his fingernails, Sandy wandered off, espied the male Burford through the bar's glass doors and on a whim decided to join him. 'You skiving too?' he enquired jauntily.

Burford slowly became aware of him. 'Nuh,' he grunted, chin on chest. 'Opted out's more like it. For this first part anyway. There are better things to do.' He indicated the tawny contents of his cut-glass tumbler. Then, feeling further explanation was required, 'Waste of time listing tools and being lectured on the finer points of hunting when we have the bodies ready set up to work on.'

Bodies, plural? Sandy caught his breath at the man's open admission, before recalling that the class Burford attended was taxidermy.

'W-what are you working on? The animal, I mean.'

'Polecats. I've three of them to make into a Victorian muff for the wife. Just skinned the one so far. Keeping the others chilled. What course are you on?'

'Life class.'

'Uh. The wife's on that.'

Present tense, Sandy noted. How could the man not have missed her? Didn't they share a bedroom?

Anyone who watched television knew that in murder cases the prime suspect was most often the victim's nearest if not dearest. So was this indifference part of a cover-up?

He downed the lager he'd brought across for himself and offered, 'A refill?'

'Seems a good idea.' Burford swilled the remains of the whisky and proffered his glass. He appeared to have exhausted his conversational output, sitting gloomily staring into the drink when it came, and omitted to stand a round in his turn.

'Well, better move on,' Sandy muttered as other students began to fill the bar. He drifted off. Not back to his easel, however. He left by the Castle's imposing front entrance, lingered a moment ostentatiously sniffing the morning air and wandered across the courtyard, to pass close to where last night he and Fiona had disencumbered themselves of their problem guest. There was no sign of Rosa Burford. The place looked perfectly normal

So, when contriving to get his duvet and pillows returned, Fiona must have moved the body on, to stave off discovery. He hoped she'd taken proper precautions. Though, on consideration, any such precautions had certainly to be *im*proper.

During lunch there was no sighting of her. About to re-enter the life class studio, he was aware of a tall blonde in a peach satin wrap mounting the model's throne. 'Where's F – the other one?' he demanded.

'We alternate with models,' Gordon said shortly. 'You should have stayed on if you'd wanted to finish your masterpiece. Settle down, everyone. This will be an hour's pose with two short breaks. Time enough to change over to watercolour, if you feel you're ready.'

Sandy sighed. By now he was imprisoned in a thicket of easels, and God alone knew what mischief the absent, unsupervised Fiona was getting herself into.

Superintendent Yeadings had been summoned to Kidlington to consult with the ACC (Crime). He had done his bit by bringing his chief up to date on current cases, received grudging congratulations on the outcome of the drugs stake-out and silently endured disapproval of the negative score on other major inquiries. Now he was being treated to a recital of platitudes on the policeman's unhappy lot, as viewed from the padded chair and carpeted office of the public spokesman most hunted by local and national press.

'It is essential – our first priority,' Childers insisted in his tub-thumping voice, 'to get across the message of every possible effort being directed towards this missing child: positive publicity; uniforms on the street; fingertip searches; dog-handlers; house-to-house inquiries.' He paused. 'A visible presence. And yes, dogs. They always look good on the front page. The public likes dogs.'

He spoke, Yeadings thought, as one who didn't.

'Young Mott.' The ACC had pounced on a fresh subject. 'How's he shaping? Making good use of experience gained abroad?'

'He knows his stuff,' Yeadings assured him. Useless to point out that dealing with the aftermath of Balkan sectarian bloodlust had little in common with moulding a first-class investigative team on home ground.

'We have a good man in the right job there,' he went on in words the other would appreciate. 'Solid family man, with a baby on the way.'

'Oh, splendid! Wife was a barrister, I believe.'

Yeadings nodded. Not necessarily *was*. More like *is*. Not that Childers would care for that. He was almost as much a sexist as Salmon, and very much married.

The ACC droned on. It was Resources and Costing by now: familiar themes.

Yeadings watched an invasive earwig labour its way along the window sill, clumsily circumnavigating the base of a ceramic plant pot. It made him think of the articulated buses Mayor Livingstone was inflicting on the capital, continental intruders clogging up London's maze of narrow streets.

'Value for money. Absolutely essential. Our first priority,' the AC insisted. He seemed unaware of having already used the expression elsewhere.

Yeadings continued nodding: toy dog in rear window of family car. Back at base things could be happening. He should be there.

CHAPTER TEN

A uniformed policewoman answered the door to DS Zyczynski and nodded her inside. The missing child's mother was crouched over her knees in a chair by the gas fire, staring into the flames.

'Mrs Bell?' Z asked, and introduced herself. The woman looked at her blankly.

'May I sit down? I'd like to talk to you. Is your husband here?'

Mrs Bell looked around. 'No, he's gone.' She stared defensively. 'Out.' There was no further explanation

'Never mind. I can see him later.'

Z took the armchair opposite. There was a red leather strap hanging over its right-hand arm with a shallow pewter bowl affixed. In it lay a half-filled pipe and matches.

'I'm so very sorry about your trouble,' Z offered. 'Finding Jilly is our top priority for now. I'm sure there will be news of her soon.'

The woman shuddered and looked away.

'Meanwhile,' the DS pursued, 'we'd like to have someone here with you to monitor any calls that come in. I believe you've disconnected the phone. Friends or neighbours who've noticed something may be trying to reach you. If so, we do need to follow up on them.'

Mrs Bell muttered into her hands. Z caught the final words, 'keeps ringing.'

'So let us deal with that for you. Look, I'm plugging it back in. I'll tell our technical team to come and deal with it.'

The woman raised no objection, so she rang through to make the arrangements.

'Now,' she said, 'how about you? Tell me how I can help.'

It was heavy going. All the questions were old ones and raised little answer. Mrs Bell was still too far into shock to be of use, so nothing new came from it.

Half an hour after Z's arrival Mr Bell had not returned. Outside, the evening drew in, dark and windswept. According to the WPC, Mrs Bell hadn't eaten. She had refused to have her doctor visit.

'Get some soup warmed up, fry some bacon,' Z ordered the policewoman, after surveying the kitchen cupboards and fridge. 'Maybe the smell of food will remind her she's empty.'

There seemed little more to be done, so she left, promising to be back later to speak to the husband. In the car she rang Area and asked to be connected to the Sussex force.

They took time finding someone familiar with the Winchelsea area, and when he came on there was little joy to be got from what he had to say. Major Trevor Barnes, late of the Royal Armoured Corps, had died the previous May at the age of eighty-seven, after a long illness in a Hastings nursing home. There was no known family, and his house, presumably put up for sale by his executors, was still empty.

So why, Z asked herself, was the elusive Ms Morgan driving around in a car registered to him? If the major had no relatives, had he, at eighty-seven and terminally ill, allowed himself the luxury of a popsy?

Sandy Craddock was feeling bad, but then he found he wasn't alone in that. Throughout lunch George Burford was pushing food about his plate and then shoving it away in disgust; not bad nosh, but the man was disturbed and barely trying to hide the fact. By the time coffee was being served he was openly fuming. Sandy went across on the pretext of borrowing the sugar bowl. 'Something the matter?' he ventured.

'Bit of trouble with the old ulcer,' Burford admitted, avoiding his eyes.

'Shouldn't you ask for a special diet?' He made it sound concerned, reached back for his own coffee and planted it, with himself, alongside the troubled man.

And what exactly, he asked himself, was it that troubled him? Anxiety over a wife he thought had gone off in high dudgeon, or something far more harrowing? Wasn't dudgeon also a word for the haft of a dagger? Sandy couldn't forget that black knife handle buried to the hilt under Rosa's left shoulder blade. George in dudgeon, and dudgeon in Rosa, but had Burford knowledge of that? Earlier he had mentioned skinning his specimen for the taxidermy class. A polecat, wasn't it? So what would a skinning knife look like?

'Are you skipping the next session?' he enquired.

'Suppose not.' Burford sighed heavily.

'I was wondering,' Sandy pursued. 'It sounds interesting.

Taxidermy, I mean. If it wouldn't be a bother, could I come along and take a shufti?'

'I don't see why not. Yeah, the tutor quite likes visitors dropping in.' Sandy's show of interest seemed to have lifted him somewhat from his downcast state.

'It's lab 2A. I'll be there about 2.15. Just have to pop up to my room first, check the wife's got back from her shopping trip.'

A shot of retail therapy lasting overnight? Sandy queried silently. Surely the poor sap couldn't believe that. Unless the couple had separate bedrooms. Or he was just covering up, playing for time before Nemesis caught up with him.

'Women are the very devil.' Sandy wasn't aware of having spoken aloud until Burford swung impatiently on him.

'It's not so much the woman as the money.'

He spread his hands hopelessly. 'She's the Queen Bee. It lets her treat me like something picked up on her shoe.' He looked shamefaced. 'I don't know I can stand it much longer.'

Sandy found himself literally blinking and put a defensive hand over his eyes. He wished the man hadn't said that. He wished even more that he hadn't forced it out of him, hadn't started meddling in the very first case. Wished he'd never set eyes on the Castle. On Fiona. No, cancel that last.

He had to get away, breathe some outdoor air, find himself again. This wasn't the person he was meant to be, the one who'd ploughed his single furrow at Hennigan's, valuing nothing more than good artefacts.

Out in the courtyard his eyes first registered the blue Mercedes, and he felt sick to his stomach. Behind closed eyelids he saw Rosa Burford's sprawled body lying alongside.

Yesterday she'd had life and breath, had – boringly – almost flirted with him, had fled in terror to his door in the night. It involved him. And against his natural instincts, but in semi-stupor, he'd let Fiona take over and complicate matters. Once the body again surfaced, how would the police discover who killed her, when all the evidence was tangled like this? The killer was someone from within the Castle, not abroad in the dark as they'd made it appear.

Normally law-abiding, he'd obstructed the police in the pursuit of their duty. He'd dropped into the proverbial hole. He had to find some means of climbing out. Perhaps that could mean interfering even further, following up his original suspicion of the husband. It was expected of him now to take some interest in taxidermy.

He gave Burford twenty minutes leeway, went back indoors and looked 2A up on the plan in the Castle's entrance hall. It was situated over the one-time stables in a detached block, and reached by an exterior iron staircase which clanged to warn of his approach. As he opened the gothic door the entire class facing him looked up enquiringly, spread along four lab workbenches. The smell in the enclosed classroom reminded him of the science block at his old school.

'A-ah,' he said foolishly, gazing around for Burford, who wasn't there. 'Er, George said I could come and take a look. Is that all right?'

A tall blonde in a long white coat like a doctor's moved towards him. She was blank-faced and smooth-skinned like one of those fearsome women in the toiletries advertisements who thought they were 'worth it'.

'Are you interested in taxidermy, Mr...?' she asked coolly.

'Er, Laing,' he said. 'Warren Laing. Yes, I am. Interested, I mean. As a spectator, that is.'

She gave a superior smile. 'Oh we wouldn't make you take part. A number of other observers have already braved us, if only to dine out on the experience later. Feel free to circulate. If my students can't supply answers to any of your questions, perhaps you will allow me to do so.'

Where do they breed them, these cold-blooded, managerial women? he marvelled. Here was one even more amazing than Fiona.

He ambled among the dedicated skinners, trying not to look closely at their victims. These were mainly birds; but what he took to be the outer portions of a squirrel and a Jack Russell terrier were also stretched over sheets of paper on the front workbench.

The dead birds were mostly suspended just clear of the benches and attached by fishhooks to three small chains connected by a ring to a pulley clamped to a stand. With the bodies winched into position, it left both hands of the operator free for snipping with fine scissors and teasing with tweezers or bone snips. The offal – and he thanked heaven for this – had in all cases been removed, but some grating sounds came from an area where a bowed bone-saw was gruesomely removing the inner solid frame of an anonymous mammal.

His only interest was, of course, the implements in use on the bodies. Beside him a small man with white side-whiskers started drilling holes into the bared skull of something resembling a deer. He looked up with a cherubic smile. 'I have to make three,' he explained, 'for screwing the trophy to its plaque later.'

Trophy, Sandy thought, and remembered with shame the moth-eaten tigers' and boars' heads that had passed without remorse through his hands at Hennigan's.

By then he had arrived at what must be Burford's specimen, a pelt of fine golden fur interspersed with sleek, longer hairs of warm brown. Pathetically pretty, even dead. Alongside, methodically ranged, were his tools, torn newspaper and paste for making papier mâché, Plaster of Paris, paint brushes, oil paint in a tube, a 3oz bottle of hydrochloric acid and another of linseed oil, a spatula, various sizes and shades of artificial glass eyes, a tape measure, a paint scraper, surgeon's needles, a spool of sewing thread, cotton padding, nails, tacks, and small drums labelled Borax, Hydrated Sodium and Asbestos Powder. The hoped-for knife was there too, its tip securely lodged in a slit cork. Beside it a tool roll was secured by black tape. He left it unexamined.

What Sandy had not expected was his enormous relief on seeing the knife. He had to admit then that something about Burford made the man almost likeable. Perhaps it was his initial surliness and reassuring social ineptness. Not a man eager either to please or impress; and humble in admitting his unmanly marital status. If his kit here was complete, none of it could at the same time be lodged in the corpse of his unfortunate wife.

Nevertheless, while he seemed now more a subject for sympathy, didn't all this autopsy paraphernalia prove that the man was a dabbler in death, some kind of necrophile? – and thus more likely to go beyond the acceptable bounds of husbandly outrage?

Whatever the truth, Sandy hopefully told himself, he had done enough investigation and felt absolved. It was now up to others to untangle how Rosa Burford came to be dead.

The moon hung over him, barely visible against a curiously lit sky, so that everything was white and painful to stare at. He closed his eyes and concentrated on the sea sounds that had preceded the vision. Mixed in it was whispering and, surely, padding footsteps. Then a voice, the exploding sibilants distorted into bird twitter. Someone was calling insistently, 'Sandy! Sandy, wake up!'

'What the hell was that old fart doing here? And what would he be doing sleeping with him in his, Warren's bed? Because he *was* in bed, certainly. The stiffness of his back told him that.

He tried to move to his side and found himself impeded. Muzzily his head began to pound. That was restricted too. It felt wound up in something. God, this was a bloody silly nightmare. And they were still calling for Sandy. Why should that loser have got in on the act, lodged in his subconscious?

Now his hand was being squeezed. Again the insistence on making Sandy Craddock come awake. 'Ugh,' he said, in protest. He opened his eyes and the moon was slowly transformed into a face; split into two faces.

'There,' said the young medic. 'I knew he'd come round if we kept at it. Try him with some water, Nurse.'

An obstacle was removed from his mouth. Glass clinked against his lips. Something cold ran over his chin and chest.

'Right, Mr Craddock,' said a female voice. 'I suppose you'll want to know where you are.'

Silly cow, he thought. I'm in hospital. That's plain enough. What I don't know is how I got here. What the hell have they done to me?

It was a case for lying doggo and not letting on. Without moving his throbbing head, he swivelled his eyes and made out quite a space round the narrow bed he was lying on. No curtains, so it could be a private room. Or Intensive Therapy. From visiting ITU at St Luke's he knew the style there was minimalist. That's where he was, then. Or some equally sterile place.

The medic was shining some god-awful light in his eyes, pulling the lids about, muttering about vital reactions.

He knew by now they were expecting him to speak. 'Uh,' he said again.

'Sandy,' the man said, 'on a scale of one to ten how's the pain?'

Mathematics, Laing reflected. His wits were coming back but that was stretching them a tad too far. Anyway, it wasn't exactly pain. It was a sort of floating giddiness. He must have been on quite a bender. Wasn't really over it yet. And this lot didn't sound all that sober themselves, calling him by the name of his pathetic half-brother.

Unless perhaps they'd some reason for the mistake. Was something of Sandy's on him when they brought him in? What about his own ID? Surely...

But it was all too much bother. 'G'nigh,' he managed, closed his eyes and was off again.

Sandy Craddock wandered into the television room a few minutes before the local evening news, dreading to hear of the finding of a body.

The main item covered the disappearance of a small girl,

snatched from her pushchair in the shopping precinct. House-to-house inquiries were under way and the public were urged to give assistance if they had seen anything suspicious in that area.

The regional MEP had stood up on his hind legs in Brussels and attacked France over its refusal to have the existing CAP provisions put under scrutiny. Well, what was new in that?

Sandy was about to wander off again when a fresh bulletin was handed to the newsreader. A further appeal was being made for witnesses to the Myron's Hill incident early on Wednesday morning, when a motorcycle had knocked down a pedestrian at the approach to Hennigan's Auction Rooms. The injured man, Alexander Craddock, who was an employee there, had briefly regained consciousness but was still in a critical condition at St Luke's Hospital.

Sandy shuddered. He didn't want Warren to fluff it, but when he came round long enough to make it plain exactly who he was, there could well be a hue and cry put out for the real Alexander Craddock.

CHAPTER ELEVEN

There had been neither sight nor sound of Fiona for hours. Sandy Craddock mooned about the grounds trying to make up his mind whether he resented or desired her. It was just like a woman to drag a guy into complications and then walk away when the situation got out of hand.

There was no adequate reason why he should still be here himself. It was more than time for the worm to turn. Perhaps he could wriggle even farther and right out of the hole.

There floated into his vision the outline of a post he'd almost collided with on his night walk. He realised now what the attached metal flag had been for. It was a bus stop. Which opened up the possibility of escape. He wasn't totally marooned here, reliant on Fiona for transport.

It had been just beyond the second village pub. If only he could find his way there again. But, even then, what chance of a regular bus service in this benighted part of the country?

Even as he balanced retreat against exploring the void for an alternative, he observed the maroon Jaguar drive into the courtyard, sneak into an empty parking space close to the wall of the dining hall, and douse its lights. He moved under the porch lamp to be better recognised, but went no closer. Let the lady make the advances.

She took her time getting out. Her expression as she neared him was one of calculated cool, which, knowing her now, he translated as disquiet for some reason. Guilt about going off without forewarning or explanation?

Apparently not. 'Where's the police presence?' she grated from the side of her mouth as they met up

'A-a-a-ah.' So she had assumed that the body, wherever she'd removed it, would already have come to light.

'There is no police presence,' he assured her.

This, curiously, appeared to increase her unease. 'Why not? Sandy, what've you done?'

That took some working out. To his mind, nothing he had done so far could have accounted for a police non-presence; even less than for a presence. 'Come inside,' he suggested, 'for some sorting out.'

She waited until they were in her room and she had wound herself out of the leather car jacket and a long college scarf which she proceeded carefully to roll up while he tried to assign the significant colours.

'Now,' she said, running her fingers through her hair, 'tell me where you've stashed it.'

He regarded her with dismay. Surely by 'it' she meant the body. 'I didn't. That is, I haven't. I mean, I thought *you* must've...'

'Not *someone else!*'

It now looked like that, because even Fiona couldn't be such a consummate actor.

They stared at each other. 'The husband!' she accused.

Not Burford, he thought. He had already half-acquitted poor George of the killing. Well, perhaps quarter-acquitted him.

But Fiona had her teeth into it. 'He must have gone out to the car for something before anyone else was about, found Rosa, and he's taken her off to dump elsewhere.'

'No,' Sandy argued, doggedly sticking to the man's defence. 'Why would he? There she was, outdoors, nowhere near his room, apparently been mugged, stabbed, whatever. Touching her at all would be too risky. There's this business the forensic scientists go for. If he'd used the car to transport her they'd be sure to find some—'

'Contact traces,' Fiona snapped. 'No need to explain. I watch *CSI* too, you know.'

'On the other hand,' Sandy said slowly, his brain barely doing more than marking time, 'who else would take such an unnecessary risk?'

Fiona flopped on to the bed and kicked her shoes off. 'Only the killer, whoever that is. Anyone else would have screamed the place down and run for help. That's the normal reaction to finding something grisly and unexpected.'

We didn't, Sandy reminded himself. Last night he'd been too stunned, almost pole-axed; and Fiona was like the proverbial cucumber. He shuddered at the treacherous fear that she might be more involved than he'd cared to imagine until now. And why should she be so knocked back by the body's disappearance? Wasn't it better to have it at one further remove from them? He put that idea to her and she chewed at her lower lip while letting the concept sink in.

'Suppose,' she said at length, 'the body never gets found. He'll have got away with it. He could say she's left him, gone to Australia. It's all been done before.'

'Eventually someone's going to query the story, when she

doesn't write back to friends. Maybe she has family. After a while they would be bound to get suspicious and contact the police. But anyway, I don't think Burford did it. I've been talking to him today. He's a decent enough guy.'

'Maybe people thought that of Crippen, and certainly of Dr Shipman.'

There was no dissuading her. Sandy decided to give up, watching her drop her legs from the bed, stand, stretch and, amazingly, complain, 'I'm hellish hungry, Sandy: missed out on lunch today. I could murder a steak. Let's go and mingle.'

'I can't do that sort of thing. Mingle, I mean. Especially just now. What are you smiling at?'

'Recalling something I read somewhere. "Low on social skills: no good at lying."'

He considered this. 'Yeah, I guess that's me.'

Nothing positive had resulted from police inquiries made in the shopping precinct, apart from two descriptions of Maisie Bell rushing from shop to shop in her desperate attempts to recover the child in the pushchair. As with many witness statements, they contradicted each other in the detail. People more often see what they expect to see than what is actually there: well meaning but useless.

Z, returning to the Bells' home, again found the husband absent. He had not been in touch all day although he normally carried a mobile phone in his pocket.

'Have you no idea where he might have gone?' the DS asked.

'Did you ask at his work? He's a plumber, see. At Bullen and Hardwick's. I know they've got a rush on at the moment, with all this cold weather.'

'They haven't seen him all day, Mrs Bell. Does he have any family he might have gone to, or special friends?'

'No.' Hunched in the same armchair, Maisie had let her tea go cold, the milk forming a thin skin on the surface. A framed photograph on the low table beside her showed her posed with Jilly and backed by a man with features not unlike a mastiff's.

'When did you last see him?' Z pursued.

That brought on a storm of tears. Eventually, her voice muffled in a handful of tissues, the story started to come out. He had left early that morning before she was awake. They'd sat up late the night before, watching some American film. It hadn't been all that good. And then it had taken her a long time to get off, so she'd overslept.

Lucky, that, with a three-year-old in the house, Z thought. 'Until Jilly woke you?'

Now there were racking sobs at mention of the child's name. Z felt she wasn't tackling this at all well and resolved to leave more questioning to the motherly WPC, who shortly saw her to the door.

'Bell can't be much of a family man, leaving his wife to bear all this alone,' she confided in an undertone. 'That is, if he's heard Jilly's missing, though we can't be sure of that. If he has, wouldn't you expect him to rush home?'

The other woman nodded. 'He's bit of a tartar, according to the next-door neighbour who dropped in some time back. She thought he might have gone off to do his worrying alone over a bottle. And, away so many hours, he's not likely to be of much use to her when he does get back.'

'That's assuming he's picked up the news from local

broadcasts. Otherwise he could be ignorant, simply have taken French leave, be skiving off work.' Either likelihood would be hard to handle, but came with the job, Z reminded herself.

In the car, her mobile burbled. It was Beaumont and he sounded tense.

'I'm at a derelict factory building in Slough industrial estate,' he said. 'Some kids, skiving off school, broke in and they've found a body.'

When Warren Laing next surfaced he was alone. It allowed him to take in his surroundings and think back to what had happened on the earlier occasion. While too weak to argue, he had been addressed both as 'Sandy', and as 'Mr Craddock'. For some obscure reason the hospital had wrongly identified him.

So whose mistake had that been? It was ironical when his whole intention had been to do a runner and turn up elsewhere as somebody else.

There had been some kind of road accident when he'd just crossed over by the auction rooms, on his way to pick up his new ID from Iggy Farrow at the printer's. Then, having collected his travel tickets, he'd meant to catch the nine-twenty-nine from the station and shake the dust of Thames Valley off his shoes for ever.

The auction rooms – that could account for the mistake, because it was where Sandy worked, and the hell of it was that they did look alike, colouring apart. But in that case, why hadn't the idiot spoken up to put matters right? Presumably it was because he didn't know of the mix-up. But as soon as he did learn that he was supposedly in ITU at St Luke's, he'd wise up to what had happened. And he'd blab. Then there'd be no way out.

So how easy was it to fake coma? He might manage to pull wool over the young medic's eyes, but everything here was checked by sophisticated machines. It would be as impossible to fool them as to cheat at computer solitaire.

But it seemed that the nurses had no way to measure his pain, except by asking him what level it had reached on a scale of one to ten. So, if he lay low, complained often, they should dope him down and not bother with demanding explanations. He needn't swallow the stuff, just lie there getting his strength back. Then seize a moment to escape.

So much ratiocination actually brought the pain on badly and he groaned. Nurse Halliday, who'd been fiddling with something on his peripheral vision, heard and came across.

'On a scale of one to ten,' she began.

'Eleven,' he said weakly, his eyes firmly closed.

Traffic clogged the south end of Farnham Road as it entered Slough. DS Zyczynski took a right into the Bath Road and followed directions Beaumont had given.

She would have missed the narrow turning except for the flashing blue light from a patrol car ahead. She pulled in behind it and joined the little group of uniforms at the rear of a hangar-like building where the main gates were being attacked by a burly constable with an enforcer. If Beaumont had already entered he must have done it by whatever means the trespassing youngsters had used. There was a formidable looping of barbed wire over the gates and jagged glass atop the walls. She hoped he hadn't been wearing a decent suit.

As the padlocked gates burst open she went in with a group of uniforms, waving her ID. Beaumont was waiting for her in the porters' lodge. 'SOCO?' he demanded.

'Are on their way. I've arranged to have electricity restored.'

'There's still light enough for what I have to show you.'

She followed him through cavernous rooms into a space lit by a circular glass roof three storeys above. Iron staircases surrounded a lift shaft up which Beaumont pointed.

The body hung against one side, the neck clearly broken by the fall.

'He was making sure,' Beaumont commented dryly. 'Went right to the top and used just eight feet of rope.'

Then jumped, Z assumed. 'Do we know who?'

'Can't tell till we go through his pockets, but who's your money on?'

Z wouldn't guess aloud but, confronted with the twisted features before her, she was reminded of the photograph of Maisie Bell with her husband and little daughter. This, surely, was the man she'd been looking for all day: Bell, knowing Jilly was missing, driven to more than drowning his sorrows as suspected. *Poor woman, losing a child and her man in the same day,*

By self-destruction or disposal at another's hands? Z asked herself. And if this was a suicide, experience warned her there could be little hope of finding the missing child alive. Bell could have known all along what had happened to little Jilly: something really bad.

'I've sent for the fire service and metal-cutting equipment,' Beaumont said. 'I want the rope complete, so they'll need to remove part of the stair-rail he tied it to. Then drop him in a sling.'

Z nodded. He was taking every precaution. They had to establish this wasn't a third party's doing. 'Police surgeon?' she asked.

'On his way. He can't confirm death until we get the body down, unless he's an athletic ape. Why can't these buggers give some thought to those who have to clear up after them?'

Because their minds were far too full to have room for it, Z thought, but swallowed the words.

It was cold in here, with a vicious wind blowing through which swept dry leaves and dust from overlooked corners. 'The kids who found him?' she asked.

'I meant them to wait for you, but Sergeant Willis packed them off to the local nick with a WPC. They've gone out by the back way: two boys, only nine or ten, and one of them had gone juddery. I didn't have time to reroute you.'

'I could stay on,' Z offered. 'You look frozen to the bone.'

'Thanks. I'll have to follow the body in. And get the exhibits listed.'

She drove to Slough police station to find that the boys were being given hot soup in the canteen. She eased in between them and opposite the WPC who produced her notebook with names and addresses.

'Is your mum at home, if I drive you there?' she asked the one named Barry.

It seemed she'd be at work until seven. 'But mine is,' Greg offered. 'He can come back with me.'

And that could perhaps cushion their reception: two likely

lads breaking and entering dividing the wrath between them. Z smiled. 'So, in my unmarked car, or one with flashing lights and a siren?'

One of them was for the first option, and one against. They compromised and opted for a lift with WPC Jenkins in a patrol car. Z waved them off and set off back to base.

Superintendent Yeadings was waiting for her. 'The dead man had Bell's credit card on him,' he told her. 'You've met the wife, and I want you along with me.'

The woman showed no emotion as he broke the harrowing news. She sat in the same hunched position in the armchair, dull-eyed and hopeless.

Yeadings waited while minutes passed. Then, 'And Jilly?' he asked quietly.

Slowly the woman stood up and walked to the door into the passage. At the foot of the stairs she reached out for support before climbing, and the other two followed behind.

The child's body, covered in a clean white sheet, was folded inside a drawer which she opened in a bedroom tallboy. An attempt had been made to clean off the blood matting her blonde hair where the left temple had been brutally stove in.

All the rooms had been cursorily checked earlier, but none of the drawers opened.

'It happened last night,' Maisie Bell said dumbly. 'It was all lies I told you.'

Yeadings put an arm round her shoulders and led her to the bed. She gave a little moan and curled up, hiding her face in her arms. Z picked up on his nod and went outside to phone for ambulance and SOCO support.

They stayed until the paramedics had taken the stricken

woman away. She said nothing more until being loaded by stretcher into the ambulance. Then she reached out for Yeadings's hand and hung on.

'He didn't mean to hurt her,' she pleaded. 'He was so awful drunk.'

CHAPTER TWELVE

In the car afterwards Zyczynski sat with her hands idle on the steering wheel. Feeling such horror and pity, she couldn't stay silent. 'What a terrible way for it to end.'

Yeadings looked levelly across at her. 'But it isn't the end. Not for that poor woman. Not for you either, Z. You have to go in and find out exactly what happened.'

He was right, of course, but for the moment she had had enough. It was as though she were physically engorged, unable to take in anything further.

'There is nothing worse,' Yeadings said in a low voice, 'than cruelty to a child. Perhaps that's what Roger Bell found he couldn't face up to. But for his wife…'

No end, Z thought. Yes, that was the unbearable thing: having to go on, after your life has been ripped apart, while you struggle to understand how in a split second the whole world has unbelievably changed.

Maisie Bell had staggered across the bedroom and collapsed, falling across the open drawer and her child's curled-up body. The paramedics had left with her, by ambulance for St Luke's.

She would probably be kept in overnight and assured of a good ten hours' sleep. Tomorrow, Z's own part was to go *in*, as the Boss said: penetrate this human tragedy and drag out the truth of every sad detail. She wasn't sure she was ready for that.

'You can drop me off,' he ordered, 'and go home yourself. Is Max there?'

'No. I'm expecting him back on Saturday.'

'Tomorrow's Saturday.'

Was it? She felt completely at sea. Well, if Max would be here tomorrow – but no, after talking to Mrs Bell, she'd have to go in to work and write all this mess up. There would be no free weekend for CID.

She drew up at the Boss's driveway. He got out and leant in at the open door. 'My best regards to Beattie, when you see her.'

'I'll tell her.'

Beattie would be on hand, of course, snug in her flat below Z's own: Beattie, once her lodgings landlady, and in bad times always her confidante. But police business wasn't for noising abroad. She wouldn't have sought out Beattie tonight, if Yeadings hadn't put it in her mind. Anyway, it was too late to disturb her.

Z glanced at the clock dial. The early dark had deceived her. It was only nine-forty. Too much had happened in the last few hours. So to Beattie she would go, for a mug of hot chocolate and gossipy comfort. Then a steaming bath with lavender essence; finally bed, and hang on to the thought that tomorrow dear Max would be back, even if she wouldn't have access to him.

The young medic was on call, stretched out in a small cell off the corridor allocated for such sleeping requirements as emergencies allowed. For the moment all was under control, but before throwing his shoes off and himself to the horizontal, he had been to check on ITU. If there was a run on beds in there overnight, he might need to transfer Sandy Craddock into High Dependency.

He found the man asleep, pulse and temperature reasonable. 'Still had no visitors?' he asked the nurse who had relieved Halliday.

'Actually, he did. I was going to ask what you thought I should do.'

'About his visitors? No reason he shouldn't see family members. Provided they're not rampageous, of course.'

'No, it was just this one man. I caught him in here, at his bedside. Like a workman, in rough clothes, and he couldn't explain himself. Or wouldn't. Just waved his arms about a bit and took off.'

'How odd. Did you report him to Security?'

'No. Should I have?'

'Under the circumstances, I think you should. The police seem to think it wasn't an accident. The biker intended to run Craddock down. They still haven't questioned him about any enemies.'

The nurse sighed. 'As if I hadn't enough to do.'

'Yes. Well, they could have left an officer to sit by him if they're all that concerned. No doubt they'd give the same excuse that we do: thin on the ground; too many Chiefs and not enough Indians. If you like I'll give the local station a buzz and warn them someone questionable's been in.'

The duty sergeant rang the uniformed inspector who dug out a constable from the locker room. He'd been on the point of heading for the pub. 'It's possible there'll be a move against that biker's victim in St Luke's. A dodgy-looking type's been seen there already and could give no account of himself. I want you at the bedside, or at very worst in the corridor outside. While you're there get a full description of the intruder.'

'Ma'am, I've been slogging around on house-to-house, all relief.'

'Then you'll be glad of a sit-down. And approved overtime. Only don't nod off. You may get the chance for some heroics.'

'Sarcastic cow,' the PC muttered, dialling his current heart-throb as soon as he was clear of the building. With the pub date cancelled, he consoled himself with money saved and overtime on the plus side.

George Burford knew better than to make a fuss. One thing Rosa wouldn't stand was being checked up on. Nevertheless he was uneasy about her failure to return. He had satisfied himself that she wasn't anywhere in the Castle's main building. Now he was doing a round of the other blocks in case she'd shown a sudden desire to change courses. His brief look in at the taxidermy class earned him a raised eyebrow from the woman tutor and the odd grunt of recognition from students barely raising their heads from the intricacies of boning and skin-preparation. 'Back soon,' he promised and again made off.

That she hadn't taken the car didn't surprise him. Rosa often preferred being driven to taking the wheel herself. And since she hadn't noticeably been cultivating anyone to provide that service, he assumed she must have rung for a taxi. With this in mind he presented himself at the office to find out.

'I like to pay for extras as we go along,' he explained. 'So would you let me know what phone calls and taxis you have on our tab. The name's Burford, Rooms 27 and 28.'

'Yes, sir, I'll just bring it up.' The girl tapped her keyboard and swung the screen towards him. 'Shall I include the bar expenses as well, sir?'

'Not for the moment. Just the—'

'Phone calls and taxis. Yes, sir. Here we are. Your account's clear, sir.

'You mean – nothing?'

'Not a thing, sir. Was there anything else?'

'No. No, that's fine. Thank you.'

Poor old sod, she thought as he walked dejectedly away: checking on the wife. He should realise she'd have used her own mobile if she was up to any funny business.

Burford proceeded to the bar to look up that chap who'd said he was in the same life class. He found him in the process of collecting half a dozen cans of fruit juices and mixers. 'Don't suppose you've seen anything of the wife this evening?' he enquired.

'Er.' Sandy was caught open-mouthed.

'Rosa,' said the girl with him brightly. 'You know Rosa. She's the one who lent you her pastels.'

'Oh, *Rosa*. No, I haven't seen her all day, I'm afraid.'

'That's what everyone says,' complained Burford. 'It's a bit worrying. I don't really know what to do.'

'When did you see her last?' Fiona asked.

'It must have been yesterday evening, after dinner. She said she wanted to dance, but, quite honestly, I was tired: been standing over my work, and I fancied putting my feet up, in my room. Do you think I ought to…?'

'Ring the police?' Fiona suggested.

Sandy stared at her. She'd been the one against that all the way.

'Well, I don't know about going that far. Maybe if I got the office to page her'

'Good idea. Then if that doesn't produce her, you'd have good reason to make it official.'

'She won't be very pleased if I embarrass her.'

'Just to be on the safe side,' Fiona persisted.

'Right. That's what I'll do, then.'

In the half-empty Area station, Uniform Inspector Jane Drummond was clearing her desktop ready for going home. If Harry had picked up the pork steaks, they could have them with creamed potatoes, grilled apple slices and frozen peas. She'd do a quick cook-up and leave filling the dishwasher for later, while both curled up with mugs of camomile tea to watch the costume serial on TV.

She had already changed into civvies in the loo and only returned to her office for her shoulder bag from the locked drawer. When the phone shrilled it startled her. She sensed it was trouble. She lifted the receiver, ready to stop any nonsense. The duty sergeant sounded prepared for a rebuff.

She listened, assuming an attitude of exaggerated patience, then cut him off brusquely. 'Did you ask how long she's been missing? I mean, unless she's a minor, I just don't—

'Oh, I see. Well, it's not my relief. I shouldn't be here anyway. Why don't you put this through to CID? No? Well, there should be someone there. Then you'd better ring DCI Mott at home.'

* * *

Paula Mott straightened and rubbed at her aching back with the oven glove still on her right hand. The layer cake hadn't risen too well: not beaten enough, she supposed. But the lamb roast was spot on, just the way they both liked it: crisp outside and sweetly moist at the centre.

She was no cordon bleu cook, and the fan oven took some getting used to. Her bachelor flat in Pimlico had boasted no more than a hotplate and a microwave oven, both under-exercised because mostly she'd eaten out with colleagues: one of the benefits of professional life.

Well, once the baby had arrived, and after minimum maternity leave, it would be that way again. She'd given Goodman her word and he would see to drawing up the paperwork. It remained now to get the message across to Angus. While he finished soaking in the bath, she slid the roast to rest in the oven's warm compartment.

So, what would be the best moment to break her news to him? Not while he carved, certainly. And waiting until he was replete – like a goose stuffed to *foie gras* level – was too crudely obvious. Drop it in, perhaps, while they both were busy with knives and forks, on their second glass of Chateauneuf – 'by the way, I went into Aylesbury today; ran into Oliver Goodman. You know: of Ellis, Knowles and Goodman.'

The phone rang across her imagined machinations. She accepted the call. It was for Angus: work, of course. And this was his free Saturday evening. 'Hang on,' she demanded, and took the phone into the bathroom.

Her husband was rubbing himself down, his lower limbs

white against the teak tone of his torso. He was far too lean, she thought. Thank the bloody Balkans for that. 'For you,' she said shortly, handing the phone across.

'Mott.' He was scowling, as well he might. 'Where's this?' he demanded. He listened while someone at the other end filled him in on the disappearance of Rosa Burford. 'Already been gone over twenty-four hours? Why didn't the husband worry earlier?'

Apparently there was more explaining to do, while Angus rubbed at his streaming legs and made a grimace of disgust to Paula. 'Leave it with me then,' he ordered, and rang off.

'A missing woman?' she assumed. 'Can't Zyczynski deal with it?'

'No. She has as much as she can handle, with that dead child. It'll have to be Salmon, because I've no intention of turning out tonight.'

'Just as well. Dinner's ready.'

'It'll have to go on hold while I chase him up.'

'Can do, I suppose.' If she felt peeved it wasn't on account of the delayed meal so much as for the putting-off of her admission. And it was getting to look more like guilty confession the longer she groped for the right words.

The calabrese would be spoilt. They both preferred their vegetables al dente, but Angus appeared to be on a phoning marathon and getting more tight-lipped at every snapping encounter. Finally, 'So, it'll have to be Beaumont. Get him to ring back.'

Paula watched him get a grip on his temper. 'There must be something in the local water. A child goes missing, next a woman, now Salmon wiped off the face of the earth. He should be running this, not me.'

He tried to switch off, managing to compliment her on the excellent roast parsnips.

She appreciated the effort. Perhaps he wasn't too rattled after all, but she must feel her way warily. 'Yes, they're always better after a sharp frost. Or so the greengrocer tells me. I got them in Aylesbury.' She paused and glanced up brightly. 'You'll never guess who I ran into there.'

Angus barely raised his eyes from his plate. 'You're obviously going to tell me.'

'Oliver Goodman, of Ellis, Knowles and Goodman. You remember Oliver? He was at King's with me as a student.'

'You were with him when we first met.' He remembered well enough. He Mott, and she Musto; they had been seated alphabetically at the degree ceremony to receive their LL.Bs. Goodman was the too-slick, moustached guy with the silvery-gold hair who'd put her in a taxi afterwards. But not before he, Mott, had extracted her telephone number while they were seated alongside.

He hadn't a lot of hope at that point, but he was compelled to pursue her. It had taken only the length of the awards ceremony for him to know she was the only girl in the world for him.

Goodman had looked like the opposition, having known her for years, while Angus was then a stranger, having won his degree the hard way, as an external student, still working his way as a Plod with Thames Valley force.

Paula had outshone him academically and gone into chambers at Middle Temple, entering pupillage with an eminent QC. She'd made a name for herself at the Inns of

Court while still a junior. And he'd won her, courting her determinedly over the years until their marriage eight months back. Physical distance had always been imposed by the demands of their jobs, his last stint in Bosnia being the most unbearable. Now, finally, with their baby only months away, they could be truly together. And then Goodman had to turn up again.

'So how's the world been treating him?' Angus wielded his fork to push a strand of dried rosemary to the edge of his plate.

'So-so, it seems.'

'That figures. He struck me as a so-so sort of person.'

'He never needed to be outstanding. With Daddy the junior partner, his future in the firm was assured.'

Angus waited. There was surely more to come. Her voice hadn't dropped at the end as if closing the subject. 'And?' he quizzed her.

'He qualified as a solicitor, not happy on the court side. They're looking for fresh blood to balance the practice: a barrister, someone young, but with experience.'

Angus let a silence build. He had heard quite clearly what she left unsaid.

'So I said I'd consider it. He'll be sounding out the partners.'

Angus drained the last of his wine, folded his napkin and slid it into the monogrammed silver ring his godfather had given him as a bawling infant. Tonight he wouldn't need a dessert.

'Goodman must have noticed—' he suggested.

'The bulge. Of course. He sent his congratulations.'

'And despite that, he thinks you would want to get straight

back into harness?'

A flush came to Paula's cheeks. She had to check an instinctive rejoinder that there was a choice of harnesses. She wanted this baby. It was the most marvellous thing that could happen. But she didn't know that she was cut out to serve its every physical need, day and night, for the next eighteen, twenty-odd, years. And the truth was, she did need the courtroom drama, the working out of a case, the battle of wits in saving a client.

'As defence counsel,' Angus said sombrely at last, knowing that the silence had gone against him. 'We discussed once how, if you resumed as a barrister, you could join the Crown Prosecution team locally.'

'*Defence* is what I do, Angus. It's my forte. I've built something of a reputation.'

'And you'd be quite a feather in the cap of Ellis, Knowles and Goodman. I appreciate that. But you do realise, don't you, Paula, that it puts us in opposite camps? I could work my guts out putting together a police case for the CPS, only to face you doing your damnedest to pull it to shreds and get my suspect off.'

CHAPTER THIRTEEN

Beaumont eyed George Burford warily. His story was weak. Either the woman had done a runner in the past or she hadn't.

'Well, not exactly,' was of no use to anyone. When Beaumont's own wife had gone off there'd been no doubt about it: torrents of angry tears, complaints of frustration, slamming doors, a mad urge to 'make something' of her life. Nothing of the kind with this one, it seemed.

'Twice she's taken holidays on the spur of the moment, and rung me up when she's got there. So that I wouldn't worry, like.'

And this time he was worried; or a good actor.

'You say it was her idea for both of you to come here and follow courses?'

'Yes, we'd done it for two or three years. Someone sent her a brochure. She paints as a hobby; and I need someone to help me with stuffing three polecats I caught in Wales. I'd not done taxidermy before. It seemed a good opportunity.'

'But it seems you both gave up when you'd hardly begun. So what went wrong?'

'I wish I knew. The first day went all right, I think. She's always got on with her tutor, and took a liking to the chap at the next easel. She's very outgoing; mixes well for the evening social stuff. I really thought she was enjoying herself.'

Probably more than he did, poor sod. He struck Beaumont as morose, though that might be due to his present uncertainty.

'You know, sir, we can't prevent adults taking off if they get the idea they want to get lost for a while. They're supposedly responsible for their own actions, so unless you have any reason to suspect that the circumstances are suspicious, I suggest you simply wait until she chooses to get in touch, as she's done before.'

'But this is the second night she's been gone, and no word. Besides, she didn't take any clothes with her. I know what she brought here and it's all in her room; even her nightclothes and overcoat. She must have gone off in that flimsy bit of frock she had on when I saw her last in the bar. They'd cleared a space and she was dancing with some friends.'

Beaumont scratched at his chin. Presumably she'd have left that night in one of their cars. Even then you'd expect her to put on a coat. Outdoors it had been a degree or two below zero. 'You'd better show me her room.'

It was a double, and Beaumont wondered why in that case they hadn't shared it. It struck him as needless expense, unless one of them was a champion snorer. Or they'd both come here with a spot of extra-maritals in mind.

'Did you recognise the partner she was dancing with, sir?'

'No. There was just a mob of them, all waving their arms and shaking their heads like teenagers. You know how it is nowadays. Not proper ballroom stuff.'

And drinking, Beaumont supposed. She sounded an independent sort, with Burford as the wake she trailed behind her.

He looked through her wardrobe. The dresses and trouser suits were of good quality, on the flashy side and made for a woman of generous proportions, the three-quarter coat a black mink. There was certainly no lack of money here. He'd already satisfied himself that Rosa had carried cash and at least one credit card on her person. 'Would you have a recent photograph of your wife, sir?'

Burford couldn't produce one, but explained that on the first evening someone with a camera had taken several shots of groups dining, and they were on display in the entrance hall. They went down together to examine them, Burford pointing out people he recognised, including their respective tutors and the man Rosa had befriended because he hadn't brought proper art equipment with him.

'One of Rosa's lame dogs,' he offered. 'I've seen him mooning about this last day as if his heart's not in it.'

So why come on an art course at all? Beaumont wondered. He wrote down the name written under the craggy face in a group photograph: Warren Laing. Not that he could be important, being still here after La Burford had disappeared. Besides, the camera had caught him with eyes fixed on the attractive dark-haired girl laughing alongside.

'Pretty girl,' the DS commented, and purely out of male interest wrote down her name too. Rosa herself wasn't in the same league: a big, bosomy woman, florid, a once-babyface gone droopy. Bags of go in her; he didn't doubt she was a party animal.

'I'll take a look at your car, sir, before I leave. No need to come out in the cold. Just let me have the keys and say where it's parked.'

But Burford insisted on accompanying him as he opened the Mercedes's doors and shone a flashlight inside. The interior was immaculate, with a tartan wool rug tidily folded on a rear seat.

'Well, that's it,' Beaumont said. 'Give me a ring tomorrow, sir, if the lady gets in touch. I'm sure you have no cause for real concern.'

'Right,' the man said lamely, unconvinced. He started back towards the Castle's main entrance but stopped and turned, a hand raised to detain Beaumont as he made for his own car. 'Oh, there's one thing I didn't check on. We left some stuff in the Castle manager's safe. Cash, you know, and her jewellery. Maybe I should take a look.'

Beaumont stood undecided. Why not, since he was here anyway. They trudged back together, made enquiries and located the manager who held the necessary key.

'But Mrs Burford signed for the velvet case and took it away with her yesterday evening, sir,' the man said defensively.

'Oh,' Burford said, 'I didn't know. That would be her jewellery case.'

'I understood she wasn't sure then exactly what would go best with her dress, sir.'

'Valuable?' Beaumont demanded. When the man nodded he drew a long sigh. 'In that case, we need to make a more thorough search of her room.'

When they found nothing, it seemed serious enough for Beaumont to ring Angus at home and report the case as a possible aggravated burglary. Burford hadn't been able to describe his wife's jewellery in any detail, except that she had a lot and had brought it with her as a safety measure. There had been several break-ins recently in their neighbourhood and for just these ten days they hadn't employed a house-sitter.

'But it seems she didn't return the case to the safe after she'd chosen what to wear,' Beaumont had pointed out. 'Do you recall which pieces she had on at dinner that night?'

The man had to think about it. Rosa's appearance had not been at the front of his mind. Eventually he recalled, 'Diamonds. She was wearing a necklace and matching earrings: pretty gross, actually, like chandeliers.'

'And on her hands?'

'The usual, I suppose. Four or five rings: a solitaire, one with a band of rubies, an eternity ring, an emerald one. And her wedding ring, of course.' Beyond that he couldn't give any description.

'Missing woman, missing jewellery,' DCI Mott had summarised unsympathetically when told. 'Most likely she's gone off weekending with someone and taken the stuff along to impress. See who else is missing. But there's a long chance it's a snatch, in which case we wait for the ransom demands. Nothing more you can do tonight, but I'll warn the Boss, just in case.'

And there it rested. Two hours later the phone disturbed the Motts as they prepared for bed. The night duty officer reported that DI Salmon's Vauxhall Vectra had been identified at the car pound, having been clamped and loaded after overstaying in the town's east end. It had not been possible to contact him by mobile or landline.

'Right, I'll deal with it,' Angus said shortly. 'I need to know exactly where it was found parked, street and house number.'

The information was less than ten minutes in coming. Meanwhile, Mott had dressed again, while passing on the gist of the problem to Paula who seemed amused.

'A woman, a DI, and a load of gems, all gone missing at once. It's obvious: the fulsome Rosa has bewitched our hero and they're riding off into the sunset together.'

'It isn't funny, Paula.' Actually the image of the unpalatable Salmon in thrall to a buxom charmer was hilarious, but he wasn't in the mood to enjoy canteen humour just then. Something could have happened to the poor sod, and it was his, Mott's, fault that the DI hadn't been checked on earlier.

He drove to where the Vauxhall had been abandoned. It was in a small lane off a one-time council estate, now mainly owner-occupied, and just four houses short of the address Z had visited a couple of days back. Wasn't this where the man lived who'd been run down by the biker? So, was it coincidence or connection?

Mott sat on in the car, running his memory back over recent reports. Z couldn't gain entry to Craddock's house. The keys didn't fit. Salmon's last-known intention had been to follow up at Hennigan's auction rooms. Maybe they'd held a spare key and the DI had carried on here afterwards. In which case, something bad could have happened. A man worth running down in broad daylight might also merit having his house booby-trapped, as the attacker's belt-and-braces insurance.

So, softly, softly; and ring in to Control so that somebody would know what he intended looking into. There had been too many disappearances already in this freak week.

There were no lights on in the house, which was to be

expected. Mott walked round to the rear and tried the kitchen door, which opened to the touch. He used his flashlight to make his way through the lower floor. Nothing appeared disturbed. He started up the stairs and halted midway. There was a sound of scratching, like rats, and a muffled voice. God, had the wretched man got himself locked in a cupboard?

It went silent again. Nothing was amiss in the bathroom or the small bedroom over the hall, but a familiar well-worn brown leather car coat lay on the floor by the next door. In the larger bedroom Mott marvelled at the Aladdin's Cave, flashing his torch over the collection of chinaware and bric-a-brac, the impressive shelves of books.

On the landing he heard noises again. They seemed to come from overhead. 'Salmon,' Mott called, 'is that you?'

A muffled bellow came back.

'Hang on, then, while I find some way to—' There was a steel rod leaning against the bedroom doorpost. It had a hook at one end and a rubber ferrule at the other. Mott reached up with it and prodded the trapdoor over his head. As it swung down he barely escaped it scalping him.

'Don't!' screamed Salmon, his voice coming hoarse but close enough now. 'Don't attempt to come up!' As he spoke an aluminium ladder extended itself towards the DCI's feet. There was a flurry of movement and Salmon's ashen face appeared in the gaping square above, to be replaced by his backside, then a tentative boot reaching for the top rung. Mott held the ladder steady as the man came clumping down.

They came face to face, and now Salmon's cheeks were heavily flushed. 'Well?' Mott asked.

'It's a dia– diabolical trap, that's all.'

'So what's up there?'

'He's set up a sort of office: computer, printer, fax, the lot.' Salmon fought against admitting how he'd set the trap for himself, but Mott was waiting and the silence had to be filled.

'He's some kind of electronics nerd. It all works off the computer. Once you try to log on, the lights go out, the ladder comes up again and the trapdoor closes. There's no way of getting out.'

'You tried to break into his system.'

'It's protected. You need the password,' Salmon croaked.

'So what's in his computer that needs all that security?'

'That I'd like to know, but it'll have something to do with all that clutter in the bedroom. He'll have been stealing from Hennigan's and dealing on the Internet.'

'How long have you been up there?' Mott demanded.

'Nearly thirty hours, in pitch dark. I'm starving; had nothing to drink. My throat's like sandpaper.'

'Lucky your car got clamped, or you could have been there ad infinitum. I know you want to get home, but I have to take a look for myself. Stay down here, in case of any more nasty surprises.'

He climbed up into a well-lit loft equipped, as Salmon had said, with modern office furniture. At the far end a number of sealed cardboard cartons were stacked as if ready for dispatch, and among stationery in a drawer of the work station he found books of sticky-backed labels with the printed heading 'Deco Artware Int.' but bearing no return address. Cautious fellow, Mott reflected; but at least he'd left a trading name to be followed up. He tore off the top label and slipped it into his pocket. He would have liked to open one of the cartons, but as yet the man's activities didn't justify a full search. Officially he was, after all, just an RTC victim. Salmon's intrusions could prove embarrassing if the man cut up rough. But maybe he need never know his retreat had been penetrated.

'Right,' Mott said, having descended and watched the ladder dispose of itself at the press of a button. The light above was extinguished and the trapdoor silently closed. 'You'll need a lift home. I'll drop you off at an all-night caff if you prefer, but I imagine your wife will be half out of her mind at your absence. I'm surprised she didn't ring in and complain at your excessive hours.'

'She knows better than that,' Salmon grated, picking up his car coat, shaking it and reaching inside for his mobile phone.

So he was as hard on women at home as he appeared to be at work. Yeadings had warned about that: a bit of a misogynist.

It was still dark as Nurse Melua came off duty. It was her lot always to be heading for bed when early workers were starting out for the new day. Dog-tired as she often was, she felt she was one up on the other pedestrians as she passed them, walking home.

This morning she'd dropped into the staff canteen for a bacon sandwich and a decaff coffee, to save time and energy when she got back. The timer would have switched on her electric blanket, and all she'd have to do was drop her clothes off, shower and turn in.

It had been a hell of a night, with two new patients for ITU, which meant a lot of phoning around for substitute beds for two of her charges. Finally Old Biddy Martin had been moved to Higher Dependency and Craddock squeezed into a side ward in Surgical. She wasn't happy about either of them. Biddy wasn't going to get better wherever she went, and it had upset the poor old doll to be shifted from what had become familiar ground. And Sandy Craddock was what she'd call a wobbly one, seeming better at one moment and then sliding back, semi-comatose, at the next. She had a nasty feeling she might find him back in ITU when she came on duty in two days' time.

By then there might be a bed come free. She wouldn't give much for the chances of the new RTC admission, once she returned from emergency surgery.

She crossed to her own side of the road, approaching the building site for the three-storey block of retirement apartments. Generous window frames had appeared in the front elevation since she passed the previous morning. Several workmen in hard hats were assembling by an articulated lorry loaded with vast steel roof beams about to be unloaded.

'Morning, love,' they chorused, as they often did.

'Good morning. It looks like the weather's keeping fine for you.'

One of them came towards her and she was afraid he was going to get fresh, but then she recognised him. 'Excuse me, miss. *Nurse*, isn't it?'

'Yes.' This was the intruder who'd sneaked in to Craddock's bedside while she'd gone to the drugs cabinet.

'I bin wondering about that Mr Craddock. How he's getting on, like.'

'Are you a relative?' The question was almost automatic: patient protection and all that, particularly important in the case of someone who'd been attacked.

'No. Nor a friend, really. I just used to see him set out every day and jog right round the triangle. Then later, driving his van. You notice a lot from up there.' He gestured towards the giant crane in the background.

'There's not many look up, but he always did. Waved one day, and I got to wave back. We kept it up. Sort of mates, without meeting.' He grinned apologetically. 'Bit of a loner, like me, I thought.'

Maybe he was all right. He wasn't as pushy as his actions had suggested. She remembered how her sudden return to check on Craddock had caught the man off balance. Struck dumb, he'd just gesticulated, turned tail and run. And now he seemed harmless. She was sorry she had notified Security.

'He's in the best place,' she said, regretting again that he'd been moved from her care. 'We shall do everything we can for him. You don't have to worry.'

'Nasty business, him getting knocked down like that.'

'Did you see it happen?'

'No, I was busy operating. Saw the crowd afterwards, and the ambulance.'

Operating, as if he was a surgeon! She almost laughed. 'So how did you know who he was, seeing you'd never met?'

'His van has Hennigan's name on the side. And then I read the bit in the *Argus*. Had to be the same chap.'

His grin made her think of a large, bashful dog. 'Got to get up top,' he excused himself.

She smiled back and started moving away. Maybe she'd look up some day and catch him watching her walk to work and back. And even wave.

CHAPTER FOURTEEN

I wish I were triplets, Z thought: this multi-tasking is a curse. I really should get myself cloned.

An evening spent listening to Beattie's cheerful irrelevances had soothed her on the surface, but next day's need to follow up the killing of little Jilly left a leaden dread at her heart. She felt a deep need for being with Max.

She rose early and looked into the next-door apartment, where everything was in order. Why shouldn't it be? It was comforting to see his things just as he'd left them. She checked the refrigerator, saw that Beattie had stocked it amply, fixed her note to him under the magnet shaped like an Egyptian felucca, and left for St Luke's.

Maisie Bell had been given a small room off the corridor next to the Psychiatric department and was still in a controlled sleep. She was expected to be discharged after counselling later that morning. Z decided to keep in touch and see her at home; or wherever the poor woman found refuge.

Sandy Craddock, she learnt, was breathing without a ventilator and had been moved to the Surgical Wing, but that didn't imply anything more than juggling with beds. Like many hospitals in the south-east, St Luke's was understaffed and pressed for space. Unsure whether she might be allowed to see Craddock, she knocked at Surgical's staff door and showed her warrant card.

'Well, if you're really quick,' the senior nurse told her. 'Doctors' rounds will be starting any minute now. You won't upset him, will you?'

'I'll go gently. It's purely routine, to see if he's remembered anything to help us find his attacker.'

The patient was on his back, propped up by pillows, a handsomely hawkish man whose toes reached to the bottom rail of the bed. 'Are you for me?' he croaked as she came close. 'How could I be so lucky?'

Lucky he didn't look, with his shaven head half hidden under cotton padding secured by surgical tape. His plastered left arm was extended to a clamp by the side of his bed and he appeared to have difficulty breathing as he spoke.

'DS Rosemary Zyczynski,' she informed him, flashing her card. 'I'm hoping you can fill me in on some details about your accident.'

'Is that what you're calling it? The copper who sat by me suggested something else.'

'We're keeping an open mind. What's your opinion?'

'Haven't an enemy in the world,' he gasped. 'I'm a really likeable chap – when you encourage me.' He managed a leering smile.

Z had trouble not smiling back. This one wouldn't need any encouragement, even in his injured state.

'Let's stick to what happened.'

'Wish I knew. I remember voices, being wheeled somewhere; lights overhead. Then I was here; or somewhere similar. Nurses: not as pretty as you, though.'

'Nothing earlier: the impact?'

'Mercifully, no.'

'You'd just crossed the road to the auction rooms. Do you remember that much?'

He appeared to consider this. 'Yes and no. I mean, I do it so often, every day. How can I tell which time it was?'

'Do you know anyone who rides a Yamaha trail bike?'

'Is that what it was? No.' He sounded exhausted. She felt she could let it go at that, except, of course, for an enquiry about relatives or friends.

'Mother's abroad. Don't want her notified. No need for next of kin, because I'm not going to fluff it.'

'You're sure there's nobody else we need to inform?'

'Not that I'd care to contact. I'm a particular sort of fellow.' Again he smiled, watching her under drooping eyelids. His voice was weakening. She patted the bed beside his uninjured hand. 'I'll leave you in peace then.'

'Will you come again?'

'Who knows? Get better soon.'

Back in the car park, she phoned Max's number at the flat, but there was no answer. There was nothing for it then but to return to base, write up her negative reports and see what next she was tasked for.

She found Beaumont in the CID office concluding a phone call. He didn't look overjoyed.

'Bad news?'

'The Burford woman hasn't turned up or been in touch. I'll have to go out to the Castle again, and I didn't get any breakfast at home.'

Avoiding the family, Z guessed. Since his wife had opted to

return, there was a state of something like undeclared war between them. And the teenage son wasn't helping.

'I don't suppose...' he wheedled.

'I could do what? There are enough cases to chase up without taking on—'

'Printing out my yesterday's notes, while I punish an egg and bacon ciabatta?'

She sighed exaggeratedly. 'I guess so, if your writing's legible. But I'll not be held responsible for any facts in the report.'

'You're a star, Z.' He pushed his notebook across, waved cheerfully and made for the door.

Z booted up her own computer and began reading through the notes. Almost immediately a name jumped out at her. *Warren Laing* – the very man she'd tried to chase up as a possible relative of Sandy Craddock. And, below that name, another that surely proved the link: *Fiona Morgan*, girlfriend. They were staying at the Castle, cited as witnesses. Although Craddock had absolved her from contacting his half-brother, Z was curious about the maroon Jaguar, still registered to the late Major Trevor Barnes. Even if the transfer had been legitimate, the car's papers had yet to be amended.

Z rang down to the canteen and informed DS Beaumont of the coincidence. 'Well, bless my whiskers,' he replied, in one of his new, mixed-company expletives. He engaged teeth in ciabatta and swallowed noisily. 'You'd best look slippy with that printout then, so you can cummalonga me.'

They travelled independently and had difficulty finding a parking space in the Castle's forecourt. Classes had recommenced and Zyczynski was escorted to the life studio.

'Would you please wait here,' the principal said prissily, halting at the door, 'while I see whether it's convenient.'

As if a nude would shock me, dead or alive, Z marvelled. Perhaps her face betrayed her, because the man lowered his voice and confided, 'Sometimes the models are offended by visitors arriving.'

She waited until a tall, lean-faced man followed him out. There was no mistaking that he was related to the one she'd seen earlier in a hospital bed. They were almost identical. 'Warren Laing?' she asked. 'Did you know that Alexander Craddock is in St Luke's hospital, seriously injured in a road traffic collision?'

His jaw dropped. 'I – er, that is – Sandy. How's he doing?'

'You haven't been to visit him?

'We're not that close. I mean, we're half-brothers but brought up apart. Different fathers.'

He wasn't good at answering the questions asked, but had the grace to look ashamed. 'I did see a bit in the local press, but it mentioned ITU. I thought he wouldn't be up to having visitors.'

Behind him the door reopened and a girl came through. She was barefooted and wore a red silk bathrobe. Dark-haired and cool-mannered, this could be the one caught by CCTV as she drove out of Belvoir Court underground garage.

'Ms Morgan?' Z suggested, hoping she might prove more helpful than the man.

Fiona took over. 'This is about Sandy, yes? What's the latest news?'

Z explained. 'I've just come from seeing him. He's in Surgical 3A at St Luke's, if you wish to visit.'

'Oh, that sounds like an improvement. Warren and he don't hit it off, but I'm quite fond of the old weirdo. I'll certainly drop in with the proverbial grapes, now he's on the mend. Thanks for coming, though I suppose you're really here about Rosa having gone off.'

'Can you help us with that?'

'Not really. We both guessed she was taking a break from the husband. He's a dry old stick, and she seems to expect a bit more out of life.' She glanced at her wrist, although she wasn't wearing a watch.

'Look, I have to get back. They allow me just ten minutes' break and I'm dying for a coffee. Why don't you come in and talk to the others?'

Nobody was as forthright about the missing woman as Fiona Morgan had been, but the general feeling was much the same. The Burfords were not that close as a couple, Rosa making it plain that she held the purse strings and made all the decisions. This left George to find solace in stuffing dead animals culled from their property in North Wales.

'Would you say,' Z pursued, 'that she was perhaps a little free with her favours?'

She heard someone behind her snort. 'She could be a ruddy nuisance,' protested a pink-faced man with a white, military moustache.

A wandering wife, Z concluded. That had given rise to Beaumont's cynical supposition in the canteen: 'Maybe the old tosser's marked her down for his next taxidermy subject.'

With such a crowd of characters at the Castle needing to be questioned and have their alibis checked for two nights back, there would be a lot of manpower tied down here during the next few days.

For herself, she knew she hadn't fully discharged her duty to the man in Surgical Ward 3A. Once she'd spoken to Mrs Maisie Bell, she would have to come back and wring any secrets of Craddock's private life out of Laing and Morgan. If the attack had been a deliberate attempt on his life, then those two might, even unknowingly, hold a clue to whoever was behind it. And the question of the maroon Jaguar could also be left for then.

She rang Beaumont to say she was leaving and drove back to St Luke's. Mrs Bell, she was told, had been given a lift by her next-door neighbour and would be staying over with her. Z went back to Area to collect DC Silver.

The street, normally a rat-run at rush hour, was suspiciously quiet, as though out of agreed respect. There was a little pile of flowers in plastic wrappings beside the door. As soon as Z drew up she saw curtains twitched at the house farther on, and a woman came out on the steps to beckon her in. 'I recognised your car,' she said. 'From when you were here before.'

'How is Maisie?'

'Stunned. She doesn't say anything or cry. Won't eat, and lets her tea grow cold. I'll make fresh now you're here. I've built up an open fire, but she's still shivering.'

Z found her slumped on one end of a sofa, with a rug across her knees. In an armchair opposite a curled-up cat raised its head to give a baleful stare and then sank back to sleep.

'Hello, Maisie,' Z said, sitting beside her. 'I was here last night. Do you remember me?'

The woman nodded.

'We need to talk.'

There was no response.

'You put her there, didn't you? Made her comfortable.'

'My baby.' She started rocking over her knees.

Z took her hand and squeezed it gently. 'She looked lovely.'

Tears started silently running down the woman's cheeks. 'I didn't know what to do. I said all that about the shopping and that, just to give us time. But I knew in the end it would all come out.'

'She didn't go with you there?'

'I'd sat up all that night. He'd gone quiet, he was so drunk by then. And I thought if we said she'd gone missing everyone would be so *sorry*.'

'They'd look for someone else to blame? And the buggy – you hid that in the skip behind Sainsbury's?'

'Just before it started to get light, I made him take it away somewhere. He'd gone all helpless, hardly knew where he was. When he didn't come back I knew I'd have to make something up. So I went out early and sat in the park until the shops opened. It was like being in a play. Out shopping, I even thought she—'

'Jilly?'

'—was with me. I could see her in the buggy, under her little blanket. Only there wasn't even any buggy, was there? And then, suddenly, I knew what had happened. I knew how awful it was. My Jilly wasn't there, and I couldn't go on any more.'

Now that she had opened up she seemed unable to stop the words stumbling out. 'They all kept asking questions, but I kept to my story: someone took her. Some awful man. I wanted to believe it, except that he might have hurt her.'

The neighbour came in with a tray. 'I've put something in it,' she said and went out again. Maisie was unaware of any interruption. Z lifted one of the steaming mugs and closed the woman's hands around it, for the comfort of its warmth.

'When he'd gone I took her upstairs and made a little nest in a drawer. Private and quiet, where she couldn't be hurt any more. Then you people came and I thought maybe he wouldn't ever dare come back. So I showed you.'

She bowed over her lap and Z thought she might be falling asleep, so she removed the mug of tea in case it tipped and scalded her. It wasn't certain that she even remembered her husband's body had been recovered. There would be time enough later to question her about his part in the tragedy.

'That's enough for now, Maisie. We'll leave you to get some rest, but we'll talk with you again soon.'

She nodded to Silver who put away his notebook and stood, looking helpless. Then, on a fancy, he lifted the sleeping cat and set it gently on Maisie's lap. Her arms went protectively round it.

Warren Laing, in his Sandy Craddock persona, woke from his post-lunch snooze to find a visitor sitting by his bed. She was another attractive young woman, with windblown fair hair, a snub nose and large wire-rimmed glasses.

'Hello, Sandy,' she greeted him. 'Everyone at work sends their regards and best wishes. We've done you a monster card, and half the clients wanted to put their names on it too.'

That settled who she must be: one of Hennigan's staff. He watched her prop the envelope against his water jug. 'You'd better open it for me. I'm a bit short of hands at the moment.'

'So is Charlie. That's what's bothering him. He's moaning to have you back as soon as you're well enough. Which might cue a demand for a rise, don't you think?'

She plucked the envelope back and began to tear the flap off. 'Did I ever,' Laing asked, 'tell you how pretty you are?'

'Good God, no!' She looked startled. She regarded the bandaging on his head, wondering if there was brain damage.

'What's the matter?' he demanded.

'Nothing really. I was just wondering – why you'd dyed your hair.'

'My hair?' He ran his free hand across the little tufts left unshaved above his ears. 'Oh, that. Vanity, I suppose.'

She gave him a direct stare. 'Well, that's a first, if you like!'

CHAPTER FIFTEEN

DCI Angus Mott hung his parka on the mahogany hat tree in his new office and instantly the walls closed in. The restriction made him feel older, almost middle-aged: a parallel with Yeadings who always resented the need to direct operations from behind a desk. It was small wonder that the Boss sometimes broke out and defied protocol. So what was sauce for a superintendent, should be sauce for a chief inspector. Angus decided to drive out to the Castle and see what waves Beaumont was stirring.

He found him in a small room near the secretary's, which had been ceded for interviews. One advantage was that it overlooked the forecourt, so the DS was forewarned of his approach and had the used coffee mugs discreetly removed. He was sitting alert and upright, about to question a tall, rangy man who struck Mott as faintly familiar.

He recalled a ringed face from a group photograph in the *Argus*. This almost identical man, Warren Laing, was half-brother to the one run down by the biker. Craddock had worked at Hennigan's, and it was outside the auction rooms that the attack had occurred.

Mott settled to listen to Beaumont's line of inquiry. It concerned, of course, the disappearance of Rosa Burford, but the man's family link with another crime was clearly setting the DS's antennae aquiver. 'You were working alongside Mrs Burford,' he reminded the man. 'How well did you know her? When did you first meet?'

'I didn't know her,' Laing said shortly. 'I saw her across the courtyard when they arrived. She was clutching a pillow. Then she turned up in the studio and had her easel planted next to mine. We weren't connected.'

'Your tutor seems to think otherwise. You appeared on familiar terms. She had taken up her place while you were still helping with the other easels. You were the one to join her. Not the other way about.'

Thank you, Gordon, Sandy thought, running a hand through his hair. The tutor seemed to have taken against him from the start. Or was he being paranoid?

'Mebbe it was like that. I just had to fit in where there was a space. She was an expansive sort of lady. I was just being polite. And later she lent me some pastels. All I had was charcoal.'

Beaumont leafed through some statements, to unnerve the man with waiting; or perhaps to assume gravitas.

'Her husband, George Burford – when did you first meet him?'

'I noticed him too when they arrived, then later I ran into him in the bar. He was at a loose end and I'd given up on the drawing, needing a break. We stood each other a round, talked a while.'

'What about?'

'I don't know. Just talk, as you do with strangers. Certainly not saving the planet or comparing our love lives.'

Now he was reacting with sarcasm as Beaumont warmed to the chase. 'What made you choose the life class, if you weren't all that keen?'

Laing looked uncomfortable, uncertain whether he should confess that Fiona had hustled him into it. 'It was something I'd never tried before. It seemed a good idea at the time.'

'Mrs Burford was an enthusiast. I understand she'd been attending the annual course for a couple of years. Perhaps you knew that, and saw it as an opportunity to make her acquaintance.'

'Look, I've no interest in the woman. I came here because I knew the model, Fiona. We're sort of friends.'

Beaumont had gone wooden-faced. He spent half a minute staring into Laing's eyes before he fired his broadside. From the bundle of statements he extracted a scrap of sketch paper which he placed in front of him. Mott leant close to see the drawing. It was in pastels, showing a collection of gold rings set with gemstones, but enlarged about four times.

'This was found when the studio was being cleaned; on the floor by your easel. Can you explain what it is?'

Laing's jaw dropped. It took a moment for him to answer.

'I was doodling. She wore a number of rings. I'm better at drawing objects than people. I guess I was feeling a bit down because I couldn't do justice to the model.'

'And you have an interest in jewellery.'

'No more than most.' He sounded defensive, and his face had flooded with colour.

'And your full-time occupation, Mr Laing?'

Again he seemed momentarily tongue-tied. 'I – er, I'm a property manager.'

'Really? Well, thank you, Mr Laing. That will be all – for the moment. I should like to take a look at your room if you would show it to us now.'

It shook the man. He seemed about to refuse, when Mott interrupted. 'We can always come back with a search warrant if necessary. In the meantime, of course, you would need to stay under observation.'

Fearing the carpet might still show dampness, Sandy was appalled, but he didn't try to call their bluff. 'I guess I've no choice. You'd better have my key.'

If he had been a serious suspect Beaumont would have handled him differently, held back for a warrant and called the specialists in to take the room apart. Mott guessed the DS was getting a kick out of upsetting the man and savouring petty power. He could also be putting on a show for his, Mott's, benefit. The Boss had already warned of rivalry between Beaumont and Z. Although the promotion slot had been filled for the moment, Beaumont could still be fighting his corner.

They went up to the second floor of the residential block and Laing unlocked his door. 'I don't know what you expect to find,' he said limply, standing to one side of the double bed while the other two made a rapid examination of wardrobe and drawers.

'Is this your suitcase?' The Samsonite was monogrammed in gilt: W.H.L.

Sandy, as Laing, nodded, hoping they'd not ask what the second name was. He hadn't known there was one.

Mott asked to see inside, and he opened it for them. After raising the window sash and staring out, Beaumont came back to the bed and upturned the mattress with a mighty heave, spilling bedclothes over the carpet. He ran his hands over the exposed springs and peered underneath.

Sandy clenched his teeth, recognising it as a gesture of contempt. This puppet-faced policeman appealed to him less at every minute. 'Is that it?'

'For the present. I may need to question you again. Don't leave here without informing one of my men of your intentions, Mr Laing.' They left him to put the room to rights.

'So what was all that about?' Mott demanded as they descended the staircase.

'The tutor, Gordon Beasley, was quite insistent that something was going on between Laing and the missing woman. The model he arrived with is a really dishy number and, considering Rosa Burford's photograph, I'd say he'd need his head examined to look elsewhere, especially with the girl posing in the same room. So there had to be some other motive for picking the woman up. If Rosa's really loaded, it could be her jewellery that attracted him. And since it too is missing, we could be looking at something grimmer than a bored wife gone off with someone she fancied in the bar here.'

'Your report mentioned her dancing in a group that last evening. Have you got prints of the photographs taken then?'

'They should be in the package handed me as I started on Laing. I haven't opened it yet.'

'I'd like to see them. And then have a few words with the model. Maybe Laing and she share some private agenda. If Laing strengthens as a suspect, we should pencil in this Ms Morgan for collusion. I know Z has some doubts about her car's registration.'

* * *

DS Zyczynski had gone to call again on Maisie Bell, who was now back home. The Scenes of Crime team had finished in the house, and at the morgue the child's body was scheduled for post-mortem examination next morning at High Wycombe.

Z found Maisie tearful, but more than ready to make excuses for her wretched married life.

'He never meant to hurt me, but he couldn't seem to help himself. When there was just the two of us he'd flare up at something silly I'd done, and then, next day, he was so sorry, begging me to forgive him. He'd never, ever, do anything like that again. But he did, you see. He kept on.

'And Jilly, poor little soul, she used to get so frightened when he shouted and started to thump me. I knew sooner or later he'd have a go at her, but I was always there, see? To protect her. And I think he knew social services would be on to him in a flash if any marks showed up on the poor little mite.

'He really did try to be a good dad, bought her this silver scooter thing for Christmas. It cost more than we could really afford, and she wasn't big enough to use it properly. That'll be why she left it against the wall outside while she tried skipping with her new rope. And a bigger girl went off with it. I saw who it was, but I didn't dare say. They're not nice people, live at the end of the terrace and they've got this terrible fierce dog.

'Well, when he got back from the pub he saw it wasn't in the hall.' She stopped, fearful of going on.

'The scooter?' Z prompted.

'Yes. So I had to say some other child had borrowed it. And I didn't dare admit it was stolen. He'd have gone down there and laid into them. I couldn't have him start a war with the neighbours. But anyway, he guessed.'

So, instead, he'd taken it out on his own family.

'He became violent?'

'He said Jilly shouldn't have allowed it. He pushed me down and went for her, shook her like she was a rag doll. And such shouting! – that she was an ungrateful little shit who didn't deserve a decent home or Christmas presents. And then...'

She paused to take breath.

'...and then he picked her up by her legs and swung her...and her head hit the doorpost.'

Maisie sat crouched over her knees, fists balled against her ears, her eyes screwed shut. 'I keep hearing it. Over and over and over.'

The policewoman Yeadings had sent came through from the kitchen and took the woman in her arms, murmuring her name. They rocked silently together and Z knew it was time to leave. She passed the smudged red-brown marks that someone had inefficiently tried to wipe off the paintwork, and blundered out into the last of the daylight.

DI Walter Salmon had been granted a day for recuperation, but turned up for work just before two in the afternoon. For reasons of marital strategy he hadn't stayed home for a midday meal, so headed for the canteen, queued for lasagne and carried his tray to a corner table away from the crowd.

But the story of his imprisonment in Craddock's loft had been too rich not to leak out and be traded among the uniforms, so he was miserably aware of grins directed towards him from other tables. CID members from his own team were noticeably absent, and omission from current tasking reminded him how demotion from Acting-DCI cut him off from the reunited quartet headed by Yeadings, leaving him as disgruntled outsider. From established custom, Mott and his two sergeants were still a closed triple act. In assuming his new rank Mott should route all instructions for them through his DI.

It wasn't his own fault that the recce on Craddock's house had turned into a disaster. If that imbecile Beaumont had been available when needed, Salmon would never have gone there on his own. It would have been Beaumont stuck up in the loft, and Salmon standing by, to get him down and save the day.

He wiped his plate clean with the remnants of his roll and downed his mug of over-strong tea. The scrape as he pushed back his chair failed to cover an exultant voice from the nearest table; 'trouble is, once you've worked your way up the ladder, you still have to deal with what you find up there!'

The burst of ribald laughter that followed, accompanied by beating on the table, assured that Salmon's hurried exit should leave him red-faced until he made it to his office vowing, whatever the drawbacks, to find some alternative place to eat.

There was no pile of reports waiting for him to approve or edit. He reminded himself that officially he wasn't there: their absence was not intended as a rebuff. If he wished to be involved in current cases he should get along to the Analysis Room and look at the new charts.

The place was deserted. Only a photograph of the missing child was left attached to the wall. It appeared that the room had been stripped. Next door in the Incident Room two uniformed women remained, logging data in their computers.

'What about the missing Bell infant?' he demanded.

'Case closed, sir,' one said looking up momentarily.

'She turned up, then?'

'The body did,' said the other WPC stiffly. 'Also the father's, hanged in a disused factory in Slough. Seems he did it. A row over a stolen scooter.'

Told boldly like that, it didn't seem much, but Salmon felt suddenly limp. Not a parent himself, he had an almost superstitious fear of small children. Or fear for them; because he had once fathered a premature boy who hadn't lived through his first day and, no matter how many years had passed since then, he could still see the pathetic little jaundiced body.

He didn't feel he was quite up to reading through the details of what happened. But there was another, minor, case he could chase up: a hit-and-run biker incident which might, or might not, have been attempted murder. He could pick up something on that from his own computer.

Almost at the door of his office he was hailed from behind. 'Inspector, there you are!' Someone was actually looking for him: Superintendent Yeadings, no less.

'Sir, I've just heard about the Bell family.'

'Yes. Grim, isn't it? I've the unenviable job of talking to the press. You can come along for moral support. If they direct any questions at you, just pass them back to me.' He darted a glance at his wrist. 'Actually, there's time for coffee first.'

Salmon fell in behind, almost humbly grateful. At last he was needed. And although he was a tea man himself, at present he'd willingly endure what he considered a tar-flavoured brew produced by Yeadings from his prized machine.

Once in the superintendent's office he endeavoured to make conversation. 'Has anything turned up about the biker, sir?'

'DS Zyczynski will be following that up, now that the Bell case is closed. Beaumont is at present questioning students and staff at the Castle regarding Mrs Rosa Burford who has possibly decamped together with her entire collection of jewellery. There's a lesser possibility she may have fallen foul of an opportunist, and present us with a kidnap case.' Yeadings was fiddling with a filter paper and seemed happy to continue his chatter.

'We haven't had one of those for a number of years. Two thousand and two, that would be: a teenager taken abroad by his Iranian father in a tug-of-love, as they call it. Quite a legal and political wrangle in the end, but it did provide me with a memorable trip to Isfahan.'

Salmon nodded. So he could assume the matter was favourably settled. 'And the DCI, sir?'

'Is doing what DCIs do, Inspector: keeping all the balls in the air and the plates still spinning. You know how it is.'

Salmon did. And he'd have given a lot to be doing just that again, in a slightly larger office that boasted a carpet.

CHAPTER SIXTEEN

Z printed out her report and logged off. Working through
Saturday was no novelty, but this one had held such enticing
alternatives, and Maisie's story had taken out what sunshine
remained in the day. Now at last she was free to get home, to
Max returned from his most recent trip, eager to see her and
make up for the weeks of separation. Or, if he was detained in
London, at worst she could get one of his favourite meals
prepared, to save good talking time later. Or loving time.

Clearing her desktop, she looked up to find DC Silver
grinning in the doorway.

'The Boss is soothing the Salmon's ruffled scales,' he
claimed. 'He's taken him along to scowl at the press. Did you
get the message from Angus?'

'No. Were you meant to pass it on?'

'There was a note on your desk'

'Then it's gone in the drawer or the bin. Was it important?'

'Freudian "accident", Z?'

She guessed so, but when had Silver been mugging up on
psychology? 'You'll do yourself serious damage with all that
networking. What did the note say, or must I go through all
my papers again?'

'Something about following up on the car.'

'You're sure it wasn't "bike"?'

'Definitely car. A Jag, no less.'

'What, *now*? I've finished for the day, and it's been a bloody long one.'

Silver grinned. Z swearing – that was something new. And she looked really miffed, probably missing out on a hot date. 'Ours not to reason why,' he droned sanctimoniously.

'Right.' She set her jaw. 'The Castle it is, then.'

She found dinner there had been brought forward an hour to allow for some form of entertainment later. Fiona Morgan was seated at the tutors' table and looking quite ravishing in a décolleté olive green sheath which complemented her creamy skin and dark hair.

Zyczynski looked around for Laing and saw him in an apparent sulk among a crowd of middle-aged couples at a table close to the small jazz combo who performed at one end. They played with happy abandon and varying skill, so she assumed that Trad must feature among the Intermediate courses.

Fiona had just finished her starter and was getting involved in a conversation with the principal across the table. Having no intention of politely waiting for the meal's end, Z marched across, leant towards the girl and said, 'I'd like a word with you, Ms Morgan.'

Fiona smiled easily. 'Sure, later.'

'Now. Here, if you really wish. Or we could go outside for a moment.'

Their eyes locked and a faint flush started up Fiona's neck. 'If you really insist.' She was getting some curious looks from others who had overheard the exchange. She placed her napkin on the table beside her plate and rose, following Zyczynski out.

In the hall she turned on the DS. 'I don't know how I've deserved being treated with such discourtesy.'

'There's no call for embarrassment. I'm sure you'll be able to reassure your friends. I merely have a couple of questions to ask you: regarding the car in which you drove here – a maroon Jaguar – do you own it?'

'Oh, that!' A note of relief escaped her. 'Well, yes and no. Strictly speaking the Jag is my twin sister's. Sister, deceased.'

Z couldn't miss the defiance there. 'I'm sorry.' She softened her tone.

'Marty left a will, which hasn't yet passed probate, but everything she owned comes to me, apart from some small gifts to friends. I suppose you're going to say the car's being driven illegally, because she can't sign the change of ownership paper.'

Not being in Traffic Division, Z hadn't the remotest idea how the law stood on that. 'I should like her name, please.'

'Martine Gillespie. Different surname, because she was once married. And officially divorced: no offspring.' Now she was being openly contemptuous.

'And apparently your sister also failed to register ownership of the car. What was her relationship, Ms Morgan, with Major Trevor Barnes of Winchelsea, Sussex?'

Fiona was left open-mouthed, but only for a second. 'They were lovers. I never met the man, but I understand he's dead also.'

'So, if I make inquiries, shall I find that his will too is awaiting probate?'

'How should I bloody know? You can just go and stuff your inquiries, and I wish you well!'

'In the meantime,' Z warned, 'it would be unwise to use the car while ownership is in doubt. Thank you for your time, Ms Morgan. Enjoy the remainder of your meal.'

She turned to find Warren Laing bearing down on them, his face like thunder.

'Anything I can help with, Fiona?'

'No. Just officialdom,' the girl said airily. 'A bit of a hiccup over the car.'

He clearly didn't understand.

'Nothing to bother your pretty little head over,' she assured him, put her arm through his and led him away.

'Mr Laing,' Z called, detaining him. 'I've been trying to find relatives to visit Alexander Craddock. I thought you should know he's conscious now, and his only other relation, his mother, lives abroad.'

'Right.' He sounded ashamed. 'I'll trot along to see him. Maybe tomorrow.'

'We both will.' Fiona assured her sunnily. The girl's moods were like an April day.

From her car Z rang through to Max's flat, received only a recorded response, and tried her own landline with the same result. She hoped he hadn't grown tired of waiting for her return and gone off for a meal elsewhere. What a wasted evening! She'd achieved nothing beyond giving the impression of a real old warhorse.

Fiona Morgan had reason to resent her dinner being

interrupted. She seemed a girl of some spirit and in a relationship with Laing. It was unfortunate that so many people had been dying around them or getting run down.

She doubted that Fiona would wean herself off use of the Jag. It might be an idea to turn up tomorrow and drive them to visit Craddock at St Luke's. She went back and made the offer, which was accepted by Laing and reluctantly agreed to by the girl.

And now nothing remained between her and home, however empty it might prove on arrival.

Sandy Craddock sat cross-legged on Fiona's bed watching her apply fresh lipstick

There was an obligatory interval for the dining room to be cleared for dancing, and he intended using it to get some clarity into their situation.

'If the body doesn't turn up soon...' he began.

'The course will end and we'll be on our way before trouble breaks out.'

'And Burford, poor devil, will continue thinking his wife's walked out on him. Whereas we know she didn't. He has to know the truth.'

'Sandy, don't you know it's almost always the victim's nearest, if not dearest, who does the killing? George Burford's putting on a good act as the ill-done-by spouse. He even admits she was the loaded one and he only featured as wallpaper. What's the betting he's taken out massive life insurance on Rosa?'

'You're missing the point. Murder's been done. It was brutal, and I don't believe the poor cow deserved to end like that. You saw her. How can you be so flint-hearted? You may think Burford's guilty, but I don't, and anyway it's up to the police to sort it out. God knows there are enough of them hanging about looking for clues. You can't walk through the grounds but one pops up from behind a bush and starts stalking you. There has to be some way we can put them on the right track.'

'And what track is that? Where's the body gone? Our guess could be no better than theirs. Burford has dumped it somewhere. Sandy, I'm not being callous. It's just the only way I can cope with all that's been happening lately. Being flip, I mean.

'I do agree that it's really rotten, but none of it's our fault. We both have enough to bother us without this, and the only hope is to carry on as expected, and then clear out at the end.'

She came across and leant against him, running her hands over his bowed shoulders. Almost automatically his arms went round her and he pulled her close. 'Poor love, you have had it rough. I'm really sorry about your sister too.'

She was silent for a moment, gently rocking with him; then she pulled free. 'I've told you about that. Now it's your turn to come clean. What are you running away from, Sandy?'

He opened his mouth but stopped short of denial. 'It's a long story.'

'We have time enough. Was it something illegal?'

'I'm not sure, actually. It was a mistake. I'd been doing very nicely up till then.'

'At what? This is something to do with the auction house you worked for, isn't it?'

'Sort of. I used to pick up things, became quite a collector in small valuables. It was all above board. Charlie Hennigan approved. When something didn't reach the right price he'd take a nod from me and that would go on my account. Then I'd sniff out the wider market and offer it on the Internet. I worked up a good name on eBay. You know they regularly check back with buyers to make certain nothing shady is going on?

'Well, after a while I thought I'd set up a website of my own, and that began bringing good money in. Then there was this collection of jade and turquoise.'

'Which you bought in good faith?'

'I didn't know much about jade's value, but Charlie was sure it was kosher. Nobody would go near the reserve price, so that's when Muggins walks in and is set to make a killing.'

'Go on. Did you get lumbered or did you pass it on?'

'I divided it into lots and offered them at what seemed a reasonable price for the real thing. And most of it sold. Then I started getting complaints. So I had an expert value the remaining stuff. One third of the jade was rubbish, and nearly all the turquoise. So I fled the website.'

'And?'

'Not before I received a couple of threats on my life. The last one said "I know where you live!" So when Warren was run down right outside the auction rooms, I knew it had been meant for me. And the poor devil could have been killed.'

'So it weighs on your conscience.'

'Which is why I don't need extra guilt over what we did to Rosa.'

'I don't feel guilty, but then I'm not a nice person like you.' She squeezed him round the waist, snuggling her head against his chest.

'It might help you to know that Warren Laing is no saint. There could be a dozen things in his life which merit him being run down by that biker. I told you from the start: your half-brother is a shit of the first water.'

'You don't know that.'

She looked up at him. 'I know enough. He and Marty were running a nasty little con game between them. Unfortunately some of the fallout looks likely to affect me: over the Jag. I could be in trouble there. I'm not going into details, at least for the present, because I don't want to blacken my sister's name. She was a bit of an innocent in this, led astray by sheer greed. She would have been all right if men hadn't fallen in love with her wholesale. I guess it went to her head. She'd trained as a nurse, and specialised in geriatrics. You can't get much nobler than that.'

'But the car – that's what the woman detective was asking about?'

'On our twenty-first birthday we each made a will, leaving everything to the other. Not that we had any intention of dying. At that age you're immortal. It was pathetic really. Maybe it made us feel grown up. Anyway, neither of us has had any reason since to change what was written. So the Jag should really be mine – if only she had a right to it in the first place. It all seems so petty, but now I'm afraid the police may check back and the whole scam will come out.'

Sandy sat gently stroking her hair, his mind on what she had told him days ago about her sister's death by drowning. 'Is there a connection,' he asked, 'between Warren Laing and the Cyprus thing?'

'I think there has to be, but the difficulty is that he has a cast-iron alibi for when it happened, and the victim of their scam is dead too.'

Sandy continued brooding. Just a few days back he'd had no reason to consider death's intrusion into life; and now suddenly it seemed that strangers had been dying all around.

Fiona moved apart as distant music reached them. 'Listen, the band's started up again. Let's go. We need to forget all this and dance our legs off.'

As her car swung into the driveway Z scanned the upstairs windows. All at the front were in darkness. She let resentment build against the Job. She was sure Max had been here and gone off again, convinced that she'd stood him up after texting back a promise to be waiting on his return.

She should have expected Murphy's Law to be in operation. Thames Valley offered no guarantee to keep CID's weekends inviolate.

Desolated, she drove behind the house, garaged the car and rapped at Beattie's kitchen window. 'When did Max arrive?' she demanded when the old lady opened up.

'Oh duckie, he didn't. I'm sure he'd have looked in, otherwise. What a disappointment. Come in and have a cuppa.'

'Thanks, Beattie, but I'd better not. There may be a message on my phone to explain the delay. It's been a pig of a day at work, and I'd not be the best of company in any case.'

'Well, don't worry, love. I'm sure he'll turn up bright and early tomorrow.'

The red light on the phone was blinking as Z let herself into her hall. She snatched it up and heard Max's voice with a confusion of background noises. A public address announcement swamped his first words. He stopped and started again.

'Rosebud, I'm hung up at Marrakech. Their air traffic control system's down for some reason. No panic. We'll be transferred to another flight eventually. You can't be more impatient than I am. I love you, darling.'

His voice was replaced by a mechanical one recording the time and date. Max had been making the call at 8.40 p.m.

So perhaps he'd catch a plane tomorrow, as Beattie had said. Today hadn't been such a total waste of time then. And she hadn't meant it, cursing the Job. What would she ever do without it to fill the days of his frequent trips away?

At home, Angus Mott glowered in the direction of the television set. Lounging beside him on the sofa, Paula knew that he was blind to the programme. His eyes had glazed over as he allowed a fine head of steam to work up inside. Sooner or later, despite his enjoyment of the rather good dinner, there would issue a burst of spleen to cover his wounded male pride.

And none of this was necessary because he had his life; she had hers. The baby would have his or her own. They could surely all come to some accommodation on this?

It wasn't as though any change would be immediate. There were another six weeks before Bulge became a vociferous and demanding baby, and then she would dutifully serve her full sentence of maternity leave. Then again, this arrangement with Oliver Goodman wasn't set in stone. He'd seemed pretty sure the partners would jump at the chance to invite her in

Chambers, but it was tentative. He had yet to consult with them, and he could have been jumping the gun.

Perhaps it had been a mistake to spill the possibility to Angus so soon, but her intention had been to keep everything open between them. And as a result, although he was rumbling like Vesuvius on a bad day, the atmosphere between them had gone several degrees cooler.

'Would you rather we change channels?' she asked, waving the TV control and hopeful for some interaction.

Mott grunted. 'They all seem as bad as each other.'

'Well, how about *CSI* on 5? You usually enjoy picking holes in their MO.'

'Those squeaky women dripping all that loose hair over sterile samples! And I'd put money on it that their High Sci equipment isn't standard for the rest of the US.'

There, Paula told herself: a little discharge of grumble. She supposed a baby's burping would have much the same beneficial effect.

CHAPTER SEVENTEEN

Rosemary Zyczynski slept badly, waking three times, and unable to find a comfortable corner of the bed until she had crept along the corridor to see whether Max had returned. Each time, losing bed-warmth, it had taken longer to drop off again. All of which was stupid, she knew, because the hold-up was at an airport, and there was limited night flying. Even when he reached Heathrow he could go straight to the flat he still kept on in London.

She arrived at work edgy, to find Salmon loudly complaining about his sergeants' failure to respect the chain of command. Beaumont was doing his wide-eyed head-nodding act, which always raised the DI's temperature an extra degree or two because he knew it would be followed up by an innocent-sounding put-down.

'You're right: that's vital procedure,' the DS agreed. 'It raises all hell when it's broken and someone goes AWOL.'

Angus Mott waited for the pantomime to be over, silently admitting that Salmon had walked into that one, but Beaumont was wasting valuable briefing time. Yeadings, called away to Kidlington from his normal Sunday gardening, had been in early and left computer instructions for his team. Mott made short shrift of allocations, aware that the Boss would be enduring lofty verbalising over the stalemate in their current cases.

'Yesterday's new hit-and-run victim has now been identified. She is not as we'd hoped the missing Rosa Burford, and no suspicious circumstances are involved. There is no progress in tracing Mrs Burford's whereabouts and I don't have to remind you that as the days pass it becomes more likely that she has run into some kind of trouble.'

'Unless she just doesn't want to be found,' Beaumont said, half under his breath.

'You have a theory worth airing?' Mott invited.

'Just that she may be doing a rerun of the Agatha Christie charade; lying low and letting hubby suffer; turning up in a few days' time with convenient amnesia.'

'To date she's made no withdrawals on any of her credit cards. All of the companies have been notified and an alert issued. Jewellers in the south-east have received a description of the rings, necklace and earrings she was wearing for her last evening at the Castle. A member of the art class there has provided quite detailed colour sketches which we have photocopied. The husband has contacted their insurers for duplicate photographs of her whole collection, which appears to be considerable. Copies will be delivered here this morning by Sunday courier.

'Records of legitimate taxi services have been scoured for a connection with her departure, with nil result. God knows how many illicit firms operate, or acquaintances she might have called on to give her a lift. Whatever way she left, the CCTV camera for the Castle's courtyard failed to pick her up. Film had unfortunately run out on the one beside the main exit. Dog-handlers are being brought in today, with divers on standby in case we need to check the river. Further searches of all the buildings will be completed today. As ever, we're between a rock and a hard place: limited finance and pressure for results.

'As follow-up to Wednesday's biker incident, a check on all likely machines licensed within Thames Valley is almost complete. Alexander Craddock is recovering, but so far has not remembered anything vital. DI Salmon, together with the Area's computer specialist, will return to the Craddock house and further investigate the man's unusual approach to security. Craddock's dealings on the Internet may prove small beer or even legitimate, but they could lead to whoever made the attempt on his life. Or, at least, to a reason for it.

'Incidentally or not, the keys found on him were not for that house, which implies he has access to an alternative address. We need to know whether there's a girlfriend. If anything questionable is found on his computer, we shall have to follow up where that leads.'

'Do we have a warrant to search?' Salmon demanded, covering their rear.

'It can be obtained, but working on the assumption that the man's life could still be threatened, a search can be regarded as protective. In which case, no serious complaint is expected.'

That's iffy, Z thought. Since Angus's stint in Bosnia he'd become less rigid about doing it all by the book.

Mott ploughed on. 'DS Beaumont, for you it's back to the Castle for in-depth interviewing of every person present during this course period. In only another week classes end and the students disperse. In view of nil progress so far, you need to turn up something promising on the Burfords PDQ.

'DS Zyczynski, you said you expect to take Laing and Morgan to visit Craddock at St Luke's. I'm not sure we'll get anything useful out of that, but it will give you an excuse to deliver them back to the Castle, where you can help out DS Beaumont with the interviews. And don't overlook the Major Trevor Barnes angle. You're probably right that there's something dodgy about the Morgan girl. Dig into her background while you have them along with you. She sounds a bit of a motor-mouth, so she may actually let out more than she intends.

'I shall be in my office until 2 p.m., where you can all reach me by landline. After that, use my mobile number. Since DI Salmon will be off piste at the Craddock house, you may overlook chain of command on this occasion and ring me direct.'

'Right, guv,' Beaumont said for them all; and, exiting past Salmon, murmured solicitously, 'Mind how you go with that ladder, sir. We're none of us getting any younger.'

Z found Laing and Morgan lingering over a breakfast of croissants and coffee in the dining room, having found a rare spot of winter sunshine. Light streaming through the stained-glass window dappled them and their table with reds, purples and blues. They had exhausted all topics of conversation and simply sat back enjoying the warmth.

Laing was the first to see her and lurched to his feet, pulling out a chair. 'Morning, Sergeant. Coffee?'

Fiona laid the back of a languid hand against the cafetiere. 'It'd be no trouble to order fresh.' Her tone was little short of insolent.

Right, madam, Z thought and picked up the challenge. 'How pleasant. I'm sure it's better than we'd get at St Luke's.

'And with quite decent china,' said Laing as though it mattered to him.

Z looked at him. She hadn't quite decided yet if he was the innocent she'd first thought him. Maybe he just seemed so in contrast with the girl. This could be an attraction of opposites. And there certainly was attraction there: she could sense it in the tautness between them, as though each tried to resist the pull. Perhaps they hadn't known each other long. It wasn't the resistance of a too-long-tied couple.

She remembered being at this stage once with Max, a sort of light verbal sparring to draw a spark from the other and to find out more.

'You're not from around here,' she said, facing Fiona.

The girl's eyebrows shot up. 'Really? So I haven't managed to adopt local manners and accent? You're right, though. I was born in Malawi on a tobacco station and lived there until I was eight. Then my parents decided Africa wasn't suitable for bringing up little girls and we were sent to boarding school in Bournemouth. Later they returned to England and settled in Suffolk, so Marty and I spent most of our holidays there; unless they took us abroad. So I really don't know where you'd say I come from.'

This was drawled as from a great height. Z smiled at the intended put-down.

'So how about you? Are you local?' the girl demanded.

'I lived and went to day school in Woking until my parents were killed when I was ten. My widowed Granny Zyczynski couldn't afford boarding school for me and she hadn't long to live herself. I was sent to my maternal aunt in Aylesbury, which wasn't a very happy arrangement.'

'Rotten luck,' said Fiona, almost sounding sincere.

'I didn't mean it as a sob story. The good outcome was that it toughened me up.'

'Is that why you joined the police?' Laing asked.

'It could have something to do with it,' Z admitted. She smiled grimly, reliving the cold anger with which she'd vowed to do all she could in the world to fight back at the aunt's abusive husband. She could now recognise a career in collaring criminals as mental transference.

'So that's us done and dusted,' she said, turning to Laing. 'I already know that you have a half-brother. Your surnames are different, so it would be your mother you share in common.'

'Alicia, yes.' He had to be careful here to sort the right story. If he was Laing at present, he was the legitimate son, and his respectable father was dead. The supposed Craddock, currently injured at St Luke's, was the anonymous man's offspring, but he could hardly call him a bastard. Best to leave that unexplained. 'I'm the younger one,' he lied firmly, and hoped it sounded final.

They appeared in no hurry to visit Craddock, and Z was content to sit here relaxed – all chummy-like while the waitress delivered her coffee – and let the conversation take its course. Both had a certain amount to explain, and this might be a chance for it to come out of itself. She closed her eyes against the sun and let a useful silence build.

Eventually, 'Are you going to do anything about the car?' Fiona felt forced to ask.

'I'm not sure it's my business to. You'll need a lawyer's

advice. He may even decide a certain laxity is permissible and you can drive it while ownership is in doubt. But cover yourself, in any case.'

'If I leave it here indefinitely it could be clamped and towed away.'

'Or, at worst, torched by the local riffraff,' Laing warned.

'So why not contact Major Barnes's executors and get provisional permission to protect your late sister's intended property?'

'I suppose,' she agreed sulkily.

Laing hadn't volunteered anything personal, and Z decided further questions about occupation and background could turn him hostile. 'So, how about moving on?' she suggested, and downed the last of her cappuccino.

They stayed silent as she drove, Fiona having opted to sit up front, leaving Laing in the rear. Arrived outside the surgical ward, she stood across the doorway as if barring it to the detective.

'I'll just go and see how he's getting along,' Z said equably. She nodded towards the notice to visitors, reminding them to use the washing facilities before approaching any patients.

'Let's do that, since they've given us permission to visit out of hours. There's an MRSA scare on.'

They parted company and met up again inside. She waved the other two across to where Craddock was propped against his pillows and wearing a radio headset. He removed this as they approached. *Wary*, Z registered. He reminded her of a racehorse led out on to ice. She could almost imagine his ears flattening back under their gauze padding.

She nodded to him, then stood back to observe the other

two, keen to pick up on their reactions. Laing's face had tautened. She was particularly aware of the quirky quiver of his eyebrows. Accustomed to interpreting the Boss's furry caterpillars whose broadcasts ranged from storm signals to proof of approval, she registered the man's apprehension. His eyes, too, flickered uneasily towards the other man's, and quickly away again. The half-brothers were not happy about being brought face to face.

The girl thrust herself forward. 'Mr Craddock, I'm Warren's friend Fiona. How are you now? We've been so worried.'

Why so insistent? Z wondered.

Craddock opened his mouth, closed it, smiled weakly and permitted her to squeeze his hand.

Z stared from one of the almost identical, gaunt, beaky-nosed men to the other. Even their expressions now were the same: relieved, almost grateful. As if Mummy had just arrived in time to prevent some odious child from snatching away a treasured toy.

'Look, I'll leave you all to talk,' she offered, and moved away to watch them from beyond the glazed door.

With her removal, there were glares all round, and then the talk burst out, each trying to hog the stage. A lot of demands, explanations, excuses. Clearly Fiona wasn't the stranger to Craddock that she'd pretended to be. She was in there with Laing, indignantly haranguing the man in the bed. And he, surely the injured party, appeared on the defensive, until the others drew breath and then he was on to them.

Interesting: and certainly quite a hell of a triangular relationship.

Eventually some kind of pact was reached, the talking slowed, faltered to a stop, but no one was smiling. As Morgan and Laing made movements to leave, Z rejoined them. 'Just one thing I meant to ask you,' she said, Columbo-fashion.

Craddock returned another weak smile.

'The house keys found on you after the accident,' she reminded him. 'What address were they for?'

His face went whiter than the gauze on his head. He looked round desperately at the other two. 'I – I don't know. Weren't they mine? If not, I guess I must have picked up someone else's.'

Through the window of his loaned office at the Castle, DS Beaumont noted the return of Z's car. He dismissed the kitchen porter who had proved a non-starter and pressed in Z's mobile number on the desk phone. He watched her get out of the car, move apart and listen for his message.

'Z, I'll see Warren Laing again now. Bring him in, will you?'

Waiting, he rose to stretch his legs and rotate his stiff shoulders. At home, before this recent outbreak of serious crime, he'd been involved in redecorating his bedroom. He'd been obliged to abandon half-papered walls and furniture piled in one corner.

He still refused to share a bed with his distanced, but regretfully returned, wife. Semi-detachment suited them both, because she still blamed him for provoking her walk-out. After months of mutual almost-tolerance, the situation hadn't healed enough to save him from spending his nights on the sitting-room sofa, which was anything but roomy. It left him hard to please.

'Mr Laing,' he said as the man was ushered in, 'let us take a little walk together. I have something to show you which I'm sure you'll be delighted to explain.'

Oh God, thought Sandy, they've found the body and it connects with me. That cow, Fiona: what has she let me in for now? I should have followed my instinct and informed the police when it happened.

But the DS was leading him upstairs, with the woman detective trailing behind. He looked back from the gallery and saw Fiona's white face upturned to watch. Keeping out of it! Well, it hadn't been her room Rosa had chosen to collapse in, so maybe he should try to keep the police off her as long as he could.

There was activity in the corridor leading to his room. Men in white paper coveralls were examining or photographing walls, carpet and doors.

Of course, Rosa would have bled all over the place in getting to his room. Because the Berber carpet was a deep mulberry shade he hadn't noticed it himself, and the corridor lighting was of the dim hotel kind. It had taken today's exceptional sunshine to betray him.

Beaumont stopped opposite his door, and automatically Sandy moved to drop his key card into the electronic slot, but the DS put out a hand. 'Crime scene,' he warned, with undisguised satisfaction. He nodded to one of the SOCO specialists who came forward and shone violet light on the panels of the door. In the cracks where panels and main frame met, lines of brightness suddenly appeared.

Then Sandy remembered, at some point in the muddled sequence of events Fiona had gone out with a wet towel and done something to the door. But not perfectly enough, it seemed.

'In case this proves to be of the same blood type as the missing woman's, Mr Laing,' Beaumont purred, 'can you explain why she should pick on your room to run to during the night?'

'She wouldn't have known it was mine,' he protested. 'I never discussed such things with her. I barely knew the woman.'

'Nevertheless that's what she did, injured in some way and bleeding. And if we continue our examination beyond the door, just what may we expect to find inside?'

More blood traces, and desperate attempts to scrub them away, Sandy thought. Also soiled bedclothes that had been dragged through the window to drop in the shrubbery, and then hastily smuggled back by Fiona, while he distracted the night porter.

They went in, Beaumont having confiscated the key card, and looked around. The lower window sash was raised a few inches. The DS went across and looked through. 'This had been sealed. You removed the screws.'

'I couldn't reduce the heating. I'm something of a fresh air fiend.' He heard his own excuses getting lamer and lamer. Soon he'd reach the point where only the truth would do. It would be a relief to confess, except that that must open a fresh can of worms. He wanted to come clean about who he was, but the real Laing was desperate he keep up the pretence a little longer. He still believed his life could be in danger.

He slumped on the bed and in an instant realised that under his hand the linen was crisply laundered. A maid had been in during the morning and changed duvet cover and pillowcases. But was that enough to save him?

'I'm a heavy sleeper,' he said. 'I doubt I'd be woken by anything short of an earthquake; especially after that.' He pointed to the empty bottle of single malt left on the dressing table. 'I always take a stiff nightcap.'

Beaumont turned away from the window as if satisfied. He hadn't leant out, so saw nothing unusual in the springy bushes below. 'Right, sir,' he said portentously. 'We'll wait to see what turns up under further examination, shall we? In the meantime this room will be taped off as part of the crime scene and you must be housed elsewhere. I will have your belongings collected and transferred.

'Oh, and sir, don't think of leaving the premises for any reason, until I have arranged for a senior officer to interview you.'

'Premises?' Sandy bleated,

'The Castle buildings, sir. And its grounds, of course. We mustn't deprive you of going outdoors, seeing you're such a fresh-air fiend, sir.'

CHAPTER EIGHTEEN

No classes were held at the Castle on Sunday mornings. A hired minibus had arrived at ten o'clock to take off the staff for a variety of churches in Slough. Seemingly a devout workforce, almost all except the excessively weary took advantage of this service, whether returning loaded with carrier bags from the 24/7 supermarket, pot plants from a garden centre or clutching well-thumbed missals.

From the window of their shared office Beaumont remarked on the fact to Z as the minibus discharged its returned passengers a little before midday.

'And what's more,' he added, 'your words have been heeded by La Morgana. She is just about to be driven out in a tan Vauxhall Vectra.'

Zyczynski briefly looked up from feeding notes into her laptop. 'We're not into zero tolerance on that anyway. She's a spirited girl. I hardly expected her to take notice. I wonder what she made of Laing's latest news. He must have told her about the blood smear.'

'Yup, I saw them conferring in the bar ten minutes back. So is she a rat abandoning ship? Or rowing out on some mission of mercy? The Vectra belongs to Gordon Beasley, the Art tutor.'

Z added a final line to her report, logged off and closed her laptop. 'Rats don't row. They just sneak down the mooring ropes or swim for it. Anyway, are you sure Laing wasn't lying on the car's floor under a rug, evading your grasp?'

'No sweat if he was. He could have been telling the truth about sleeping through Rosa's visit; especially if he locks his door at night. She didn't kick up enough racket to disturb anyone in the rooms on either side. I'm just surprised he didn't claim Ms Morgan was with him overnight as sleep-in alibi. They're close enough, in both senses of the word. The tutor, Gordon, is right off the mark claiming Laing was having an affair with the Burford woman.'

'Maybe he was just snuggling up to her jewellery. He had an unusual interest in it, for a man. Knowledgeable too: do we know what his profession is?'

At the door, she turned. 'Did I tell you that Laing's gran was a Bob Hope fan?'

'The things you pick up: I never cease to marvel.'

'That was his excuse when I caught him whistling "Thanks for the Memory" at, rather than to, Fiona. Specifically the bit that goes, "You may have been a headache, but you never were a bore".'

'Was that the worm turning, or bowing himself out?'

'Whichever, I leave it with you. I'm off home; so *ciao*!'

Beaumont sat stabbing his pen into his notepad, reversing it between his fingers at every jab. So Laing had a gran. Well, most people had at some time. It could hardly be significant.

He yawned, considered what he might fancy for lunch and

idly wondered whether the gran would be mother to the quoted Alicia, shared by Laing and his half-brother Craddock. Or maybe she was on Laing's father's side. Not that it mattered.

In hospital, Warren Laing lay seething over his personal possessions being kept out of reach. He could see the locker where they'd been transferred, but any demand for the return of his mobile phone would certainly be refused. He doubted the ban on its use inside the building covered a real risk to electronic equipment: just another officious way of keeping the patient in a state of subjection.

The most he could expect was to have the phone trolley wheeled in where someone could overhear what he needed to say, and anyway he'd forgotten the number Alicia had given him for her new state-of-the-art mobile. By now there would be a stack of texts waiting to be read inside the locker, and the old girl would be going loopy over his lack of response. Unless, of course, some interfering nurse had switched the bloody thing off; in which case Alicia would imagine him dead and buried. He should have got Sandy to rescue the thing for him while the visitors were here.

Sandy could have been a problem, turning up like that, but fortunately he'd tripped into some hole of his own, happily claiming to be Warren after he, Warren, was wrongly identified as Sandy.

Now the idiot wanted to come clean about both their identities. Warren wasn't altogether sure the promise he'd extracted from Sandy to keep schtum for the present was worth much weight. And the biker could get taken in by the name-swap and go after the hapless idiot, who would be scared into admitting who he actually was.

Taken all round, it was time to get clear of the hospital before more trouble caught up with him. Get clear of everything, in fact.

He lay stewing over his predicament until one ray of sunshine lit an edge of the cloud. That girl Sandy had brought along was quite something. He hadn't imagined his substandard half-brother capable of pulling someone of that calibre. Fiona, she had announced herself, in an expensive, cut-glass voice. The funny thing was, he thought he'd seen her somewhere before, but not to speak with. Maybe she'd appeared on TV: she had enough zing to be an actor. Later, when all this mess was cleared up, if it ever was and he didn't land in prison, he could maybe look up Sandy and get to know the girl really well.

Dazzled by winter sun, low even in early afternoon, Z tried to focus her mind on driving. A long sequence of dull days had caused her dark glasses to get buried at the back of the glove compartment. Riffling through as she was halted by a red light, she snagged a finger on something sharp. Blood began to ooze from the corner of her nail.

Red and amber were followed by green. She moved forward in a slow queue of Sunday drivers. A smear of blood marked the steering wheel. She sucked at her finger and found it was no great flow.

There'd been enough to leave a trace, though. Like Rosa's blood on the outer panel of Warren Laing's door. That didn't mean the woman was badly injured: just had blood on a hand.

Beaumont could be reading too much into it, assuming it meant that Rosa must be dead. And how could he be sure it was her blood, or even deposited there on the night she disappeared? True, it was of the same quite rare group that Burford had claimed was his wife's – AB, Rhesus Negative – but nothing would be sure until the DNA test results came back.

She turned off the main road into the lane leading to Ashbourne House and sight of home chased every thought of work from her mind. An ambulance was standing by the entrance, its rear doors open while a uniformed paramedic struggled with the end of a loaded stretcher.

Beattie, collapsed? Or some domestic accident?

Z braked, sending gravel flying. The paramedic was walking backwards, taking the stretcher's weight: *unloading* an injured patient.

She ran across and saw with horror, above the tight-wrapped red blanket, Max's wan face, with one half swollen under purple bruising.

DCI Angus Mott had been down in the basement, talking to Sergeant Collins, who must have been old enough to recall the Sidney Street siege and seemed suitably located there in charge of archives. When he felt his mobile vibrate he excused himself and listened to Beaumont reporting.

'There's always been the possibility, but maybe now we've enough to make this a full-blown murder case,' Mott told him. 'I'll refer it to the Boss. Where's Z?... Good, she's due time off, and from tomorrow there'll be more pressure all round.'

He waited to reach his car before ringing through to Yeadings. The call reached him in the Kidlington mess, where he was a guest for lunch. 'Go ahead,' the ACC (Crime) assured him.

Yeadings listened to Mott, grunted, and demanded, 'Is it safe to take the minder off Craddock? If the Burford investigation is extended, we'll need every available man.'

'I could get Z's slant on this. She visited Craddock this morning, with the man's brother and his girlfriend from the Castle. Sir, I don't like the way that pair's involved with both victims.'

'You think there's a connection between Rosa Burford's disappearance and the biker incident?'

Mott hesitated. 'Could be, but I don't see how. Then again, I'm beginning to question whether the biker business really was a deliberate attack.'

'Is Craddock nervous about his own safety? Better go and see him yourself, Angus. We haven't had much feedback from him as yet. Then decide.'

Yeadings closed the connection and turned to the assistant chief constable. 'Tomorrow I'll be informing the press that the Rosa Burford case is being treated as possible murder.'

The senior man nodded. 'Quite right then, to stand down personnel from fringe cases. We could run into considerable expense with overtime. And I suppose you'll be putting in for a profiler?' It sounded like an accusation.

'Yes, sir.' Yeadings sighed, thinking, *as though I'm demanding a personal valet!*

Warren Laing, examining DCI Mott's ID, felt some unease. Why now was he being treated to monkeys from farther up the tree?

The detective went carefully through known details of the incident, treading a well-worn path. 'Are you sure you can't think of anyone who might wish to harm you?'

'Not a soul,' Laing lied emphatically. 'Look, you know what I do for a living. And God knows I've not much of a life outside it. It's not even that I'm especially clumsy and upset my boss by damaging stuff for auction.'

Too much the wide-eyed innocent, Mott thought. But maybe it was the sceptic in himself digging in its toes. Tentatively he raised the question of withdrawing the constable on protective duty, and Craddock appeared amenable. It was still a risk the DCI would prefer not to take, but persistent pressure from above made trimming of costs inevitable.

Great, Laing thought, as Mott took himself off, together with the uniform officer: that's one obstacle removed. Now as soon as I'm fit to put feet to floor I can start planning my own tactical retreat.

On Z's insistence, Max had been transported in a wheelchair to the spare bedroom in her flat, protesting that he didn't want to burden her and could cope quite well on his own.

'It's more convenient here,' she said. 'Otherwise I'd be forever running across to see how you were. And I'm getting an agency nurse in to help out, at least until the Boss OKs me for compassionate leave.'

He gave up protesting, thanked the paramedics and watched them pass to her the doctor's note.

'It's simple aftermath of dislocation and bruising: nowhere as bad as it looks.'

'And hellish painful, I'm sure. What exactly happened? What were you doing in a light aircraft anyway? I thought there was a regular flight from Marrakech. And anyway your text said the air traffic control system was down.'

Max eased himself on to one shoulder, grinning lopsidedly. 'What safer time to fly? You've all the sky to yourself. I was offered an unofficial lift to Tangier by an ex-RAF guy with an old Piper Cherokee. There would be a better chance there of getting to Europe and picking up a London flight.

'Take-off was OK, then one of those sudden dust devils caught us and we tipped, losing height. The left wing caught the edge of a village minaret and we were flipped over like a pancake; hit sandy ground. No great speed fortunately and I've no broken bones.

'Alex wasn't so lucky, He's hospitalised out there with head, shoulder and chest injuries. I'll have to go back to give evidence later. From the fuss you'd think we intended revenge for the Twin Towers.'

'I'm not surprised. But how on earth did they let you go? In this state, Max?'

He blinked at her, pathetic-looking without his glasses. 'Oh there are ways. I promised the doc to do a bit on his hospital and fax it from a London paper. He arranged for an air ambulance.'

Fiona was uncovering his chest. Patches of yellow and green edged wide areas of purple where haemoglobin had had time to break down. 'Max, these aren't fresh bruises. When was the crash?'

He waved an arm, meaning to be casual, winced, then admitted, 'Wednesday, I think.'

She stared at him, unbelieving. 'So when you sent me that text...'

'I wasn't sure they'd let me go. But it was true about air traffic control being down. I wouldn't lie to you, Rosebud.'

'You just left the most vital information out. Max, it's not good enough.'

'Honey, you've enough to keep you on the boil with the Job. You don't need me worrying you any sooner than I have to.'

She saw the point and should be grateful; although she hadn't quite reached that point of forgiveness. She still resented his silence, but the underlying thing that got to her was the unnecessary dangers he so often ran.

She had to avoid appearing like a police wife scolding her man for taking on risks. That was the way real divisions opened up. Max was good at his job, choosing to travel to risky places. It was more than a professional requirement: a need for excitement was in his blood. Without it Max wouldn't be Max.

'It all makes for good copy,' he wheedled, as if he'd followed what was in her mind. 'I've pre-sold a column to the *Spectator* and another to the *Telegraph*.'

She rebuttoned his pyjama jacket, took his undamaged hand and sat beside him on the bed. 'Your pilot friend could be on serious charges. You too, for conspiracy, when you go back.'

Max grinned disarmingly. 'I'm hoping he'll wriggle out. It seems he knows the King from way back; used to give him clandestine lifts before he made it to the throne. Let's hope HM still appreciates some of the stunts they got up to together.'

She stared at him. One of the things she most loved about him was that on the surface he seemed so reassuringly ordinary; but not now, his face puffed and discoloured. And the longer she knew him the clearer it became what a complex personality she'd got herself involved with.

And could never bear to live without.

CHAPTER NINETEEN

The alternative model was posing from 2 p.m. This left Sandy more than disappointed. He made a half-hearted attempt to sketch her outline in pencil, and then abandoned the linear for sweeping strokes with the charcoal stick, flat side on. This gave satisfying depth of shadow, the illusion of a third dimension.

He found he was less distracted than when Fiona was facing him there in the nude. It was easier to regard this woman as some anonymous stone figure unearthed at a Mediterranean dig.

As the afternoon wore on he sketched with sufficient application to persuade himself he deserved some later reward when Fiona reappeared. He slipped out during the coffee break, took his polystyrene beaker round to the front of the main building and was relieved at seeing that the maroon Jaguar was still there. Fiona hadn't mentioned any intention of going out; but the thought of her driving the car after a police caution offended his normally law-abiding outlook.

He had missed her at lunch, and persuaded himself that she'd a right to time on her own, but as evening came on and she wasn't in her room dressing for dinner, he grew more anxious. A second check on the courtyard informed him that the Jaguar had now disappeared. Perhaps it would be wiser not to draw attention to her absence. And yet – the police presence was partly, after all, to make sure nothing worse should occur.

He fumed throughout the meal, keeping an eye on the doorway. Halfway through his dessert he was aware of DS Beaumont standing behind and leaning over.

'Your young lady not hungry tonight?'

Torn between excusing her with a fictional headache and confessing his worry, Sandy babbled, 'Looks like it.'

'Or gone off for a more fancy meal perhaps? Let's hope she doesn't get shut out. The main gates get locked now at eleven on the dot. There's a notice posted in the hall to that effect.'

'She should be back by then.'

'"Should be"? Not *will be*?'

The man was playing with him. It was infuriating when Sandy was already worried. 'What would happen if she didn't make it in time?'

'She would have to start explaining a lot of things in more detail than she's cared to offer so far.'

'And if she doesn't return?' he blurted.

'Then we'd have just you, to account for the movements of you both, wouldn't we? Enjoy the rest of your meal, Mr Laing.'

Darkness and a slicing wind had come on as early as five o'clock, but nothing deterred certain young of Maidenhead from deserting the family hearth as soon as the evening meal was disposed of and gathering in nighthawk groups at their recognised rallying points.

The riverbanks had several of these, where the darkness was deepest. Where it wasn't, volunteers were happy to shin up old-fashioned lamp standards and fix the bulbs. Along by Boulter's Lock two groups were accustomed to pursue their business with small packets of grass, bottles of glue and under-age girls.

Infrequent sweeps by a police patrol car barely disturbed them. Nothing improper was ever found by the time the officers lumbered out, set their caps back firmly on their heads and strode across. It was accepted that such small game was not worth the trouble of booking. Speedy action was only required when a state of war broke out between gangs and it became police duty to prevent the little scrotes from ripping each other to pieces.

There was no patrol car in sight at a little after 9.15 p.m. when a tantalising aroma of fried chips signalled the *Boulters* moving in on the *Springers'* patch. The alert given, the defenders squared up, a central bunch of five hulking thirteen-year-olds, with an outer fan of nimbler juniors ready arming themselves with anything suitably vicious as they prepared to perform a pincers movement.

In a burst of wild whooping the first volley of greasy chip papers flew in, wrapped around sizeable broken bricks, and then the real business began, the two gangs piling into each other, shouts and oaths punctuated by treble squeals as the girls were torn between joyfully joining in and waiting for romantic rescue.

There was the inevitable chucking in, accompanied by loud splashes and protests. At least three boys were struggling in the water, still gamely going all out against each other, whether unrecognised friend or foe. It was five or six weeks since such a satisfying outburst of testosterone to test their tribal loyalties.

By now, indignant residents from detached houses lining the river were starting to show at their gateways, protesting against the uproar. 999 calls had been made, and the distant *hooh-hah* of a police siren warned that the battle was soon to be broken up.

Some dispersed into the darkness. Others delayed to pull struggling swimmers up the slithery bank. Shedding water and breathless, a small rodent-faced nine-year-old was almost hysterical. 'He's gone down,' he managed to get out. 'Pug's gone down! I couldn't do nothin'. He musta hit his head.'

A rough count confirmed that Pug was certainly missing, and he'd been one of the first to be slung in.

The patrol car swung into view. There was further scattering, but the drenched boys hung on, one of them returning to the water and striking out towards midstream. By now adults had gathered to complain and, as two constables joined them, competed to give their versions of what happened.

The shorter PC tore off his uniform jacket and started to wade in, almost instantly up to his armpits in the river, then striking out in a crawl.

He stopped where the other swimmer was and bawled something back. The crowd's excited babble cut suddenly off. '*What?*' his partner shouted from the bank

'There's an obstruction.'

He duck-dived clumsily, a wild waving of dark trousers, and was gone for a few seconds before surfacing. They saw he had something in his arms. It was the limp form of a smallish boy. The policeman rolled over and began a slow sidestroke back.

Arms reached out to help them ashore. The body was laid out on the grass and a woman claiming to be a doctor knelt to try for a pulse. A space was cleared while she started on resuscitation.

'How long was he down?' the rescuer demanded. Not long, was the unhelpful general opinion.

With a great belch, water came suddenly gushing from the boy's mouth.

'He's going to be all right,' said the woman comfortably, ceasing to pump. 'It takes a lot to knock lads of his sort out. But it's an ugly gash on his temple here. Whatever's in the river needs to be cleared before any boats run into it.'

The police hero of the moment was back in the water. He swam out a short distance and then started to rise above the surface until his whole chest was clear. He bent forward, his legs came up, and he disappeared again.

Everyone waited while the shuddering, half-drowned boy was wrapped in a man's loaned coat. The taller PC was back in his car phoning through for an ambulance.

'And CID,' his partner ordered when he reached land again. 'It's a car down there, so we may need divers. The boy was lucky to remain on its roof. The water's thick with detritus, so I can't be sure, but I think the driver's still in it.'

Max was determined to show he was no invalid, but flight fatigue was taking its toll. He swallowed the painkillers prescribed and that was all he knew for the next five hours. Waking in the dark he reached for the bedside lamp, and its light, flooding the corridor, brought Z hurrying from the next room.

'Something to eat?' she enquired.

Instantly he knew he was ravenous. 'I can get it myself. Don't cut short your beauty sleep, Rosebud.' He threw back the duvet, rolled over to get out, winced and fell back on the pillow. 'But no hurry.'

'Stay put. I'll get you some smoked salmon while I deal with the steak. I've a nice Sancerre, but I guess it won't go with the medication. You'll have to suffer watching me enjoy it.'

'Steak,' he said ecstatically, 'with what?'

She reeled off the choices and he settled for tinned artichoke hearts, red peppers and stacks of onions. 'Invalid fare,' he suggested with a leer, 'but I'll come to the table; which I'll set, if you give me a couple of minutes. I have to get moving or the old body will seize up.'

She'd no intention of arguing. He had sense enough to know his limitations. Busy in the kitchen she heard him limp through, open the sideboard and begin to take out the cutlery. 'Lay a place for me too,' she called. 'I didn't feel like eating earlier.'

'That's why you've lost weight: pining for the absent loved one. Or so I hope.'

He came and leant in the doorway. He had unearthed his glasses and, with them restored, he appeared less vulnerable. She could look at him now without that piercing sense of pain.

'I'll open the wine and taste it for you. You'll surely allow me that.'

'It's open. You could carry through the starters.' She

watched him lift the prepared plates, carefully reverse direction and limp back to the dining room. He was gaining confidence with every movement. He would be all right now he was home. And she'd make sure he didn't overdo it starting back to work too soon.

They took their time over the meal. At its end he said, 'Join me in bed, love.'

He went back on unsteady feet. She stayed to load the dishwasher. When she followed, kicking off her slippers to slide in beside him and share his body warmth, he was asleep again and smiling.

There was little hope of the driver in the sunken car having survived. No witnesses had reported seeing it go in the water, and it must already have been there when the *Boulters* delinquents began to assemble after 8 p.m.

As soon as the ambulance had departed with the boy and two remaining ex-swimmers, his rescuer returned to the police car with the lady doctor and took hurried notes before roaring off into the night. At the Maidenhead station the idea of waiting for daylight was unanimously scotched. A retrieval squad was put together and a closed white van sent to the scene where it disgorged a number of uniformed constables with traffic cones, bollards, and reels of yellow/black crime-scene plastic tape. This they proceeded to set up, driving the crowd of spectators and a few leashed dogs back on to the pavement.

Firefighters brought auxiliary lighting and a generator from their station next to Area's own, and a heavy crane was driven close, ready to lift the car on to a flatbed lorry.

Despite the hour and the night chill, the crowd of gawpers

had grown. There was an air of excitement like before a firework display. For many this was outside real life. They were extras participating in a crowd scene, both actors and spectators: the more so when camcorders started whirring and even a tele-news van turned up to add a taste of celebrity.

Two divers in black wetsuits entered the river to attach a cable under the car's rear end, one riding the roof as the car started to lift free of the water, then dropping to get clear when it hung, swinging, over the river. Cascades began to pour from every crevice in the chassis. The volume burst open the bonnet's lid and the flow became a torrent.

The thing hung long minutes, barely swinging, then stilled. In the brilliant halogen glare a pallid shape began to show against a streaming front window.

The crowd murmured, thrilled and appalled. One or two started to move away. Others pressed closer to the yellow and black police tape for a better view.

A uniformed inspector, called in from his wife's fiftieth-birthday celebration and caught in a dinner jacket under his black overcoat, consulted with one of the divers, then resorted to his mobile phone. The call was routed through Area Control, since he hadn't direct access to Beaumont's number. But he had read all the latest messages coming in before he knocked off for the evening. This was certainly the licence plate his men had been advised of, on a locate-but-do-not-contact basis.

Yes, he confirmed: a Jaguar X, some darkish colour. It could be red or brown. There was somebody in the driving seat, presumed dead: further details to follow.

* * *

The call caught DS Beamont in his car, about to enter his own street. He let the mobile ring until he was opposite his driveway, which appeared blocked by a large white refrigerated van.

Cursing quietly, he pulled up to read the message.

Bloody hell, this was the ruddy limit. Hadn't he done enough for the day, with both Mott and Z knocking off early and leaving all the hard graft to him? And yet wasn't this also exactly what he'd been waiting for? – the case making a sudden lurch out of negative phase. Another body.

He slammed the car door and made for the house, ringing to bring his son to open up.

'Mum's in the kitchen. She's got that cooking woman...'

'Yes, I'm not blind.' He brushed past. Audrey was seated at one side of the melamine-topped table with her business partner opposite. The air was a-buzz with glorious scents of baking. Their handiwork was stacked between them and they were flush-faced with achievement over beakers of coffee.

'We've been trying out some new recipes,' his wife excused herself.

Well, obviously. Why did his family imagine all his five senses were kaput?

'I've just dropped in for a flask of soup or something. It's an all-night emergency.'

'We'll wrap you some fodder,' the partner offered. She was a tough cookie herself, pretty butch in his opinion, but she always attempted to be acceptable.

'No time,' he said brusquely. 'I just need to get by you to the cupboard.'

The large woman moved her chair a couple of inches so

that he was obliged to brush her arm in passing. He located the family-size tin of Heinz Tomato and took his litre Thermos from the lower drawer. Both women sat on and let him fend for himself, all three observing the recognised rules of barely verbal marital truce.

He warmed the flask, heated the soup in a saucepan and transferred it without spilling. Then he dumped the saucepan with their unwashed clutter above the dishwasher.

'Right then, I'm off,' he announced.

Nobody commented.

'Turn down that row,' he shouted at the closed sitting-room door as he passed. Nothing changed, and back in the car he could still hear the wail of some strangled string instrument above a deafening bass.

Kids and wives: he didn't know which was worse.

There was no reason why the DCI shouldn't have his evening wrecked as well. Before he set off, Beaumont pressed out Mott's number and noted the caution with which Angus answered. In the background something quiet and orchestral was being played. Not exactly smooch music, but something to soothe the savage breast. Or was it *beast*?

'The Morgan girl's had it,' he announced brutally. 'In her Jag, in the Thames, at Maidenhead. Thought you should know, but there's no call to bring you out.'

'I'm on my way,' Mott responded. 'I'll see you there.'

Well, of course. That's what DCIs got the extra moolah for. Paula would have to get used to it. How long before she started nagging about the Job interrupting her magic moments?

'Boulter's Lock, then,' and he shut off.

It took him twenty-four minutes to get there, only to find the Jaguar, plastic-wrapped, being transported to the police pound, to be left under cover. Normally its examination would wait until daylight, but in view of the body it was decided to call Professor Littlejohn at once. He was a stickler for viewing the corpse *in situ* and as soon after death as practicable. Until then the car was to remain wrapped.

As a uniformed constable Beaumont had worked out of Maidenhead for five months before being transferred to Bicester, so he knew better the summer version of it, with smart river launches gliding through topped by bikini-clad girls, and clumsier craft slowly progressing on half-day charity outings. On board elderly parties scoffed chicken salads from polystyrene boxes and fanned themselves in the heat. This was something else.

The pathologist was eventually located at his old college in Oxford. Even with a police escort speeding him on his way, this meant more delay. Beaumont put this to Mott when he arrived.

'Right then, I'll stay on here. You get back to the Castle. Say nothing until I ring you that she's officially dead and formally identified. Meanwhile, make sure Laing in particular doesn't slope off to bed. And find out who's spent time away from the place since Miss Morgan drove off. Just in case.'

CHAPTER TWENTY

Awaiting developments, Mott strolled off into the car park and made two phone calls. The first was to the Boss, and it caught Yeadings watching an Attenborough nature film on television. There were quiet sounds of spoons clinking on chinaware in the background and it all sounded too cosy for a man standing out in the cold and deprived of home comforts.

Yeadings's reaction to the update was a grunt, then, 'So what are we to make of that?'

'We'll not know before morning. The licence plate identifies the Jaguar as the one Fiona Morgan was driving. Examination of the car won't start until daylight, but the prof's already on his way for an initial look at the body. We may get a provisional opinion on it sometime tonight.'

'Accidental, intentional, or dirty work at the crossroads: it seems we get the full choice this time. So let's keep an open mind. Thanks for ringing, Angus.' He paused. 'It's good having you back.'

Next Mott put through a call to DI Salmon. The man was touchy about his place in the hierarchy, so he did more than pass on a résumé of the action. He asked him to relay it to DS Zyczynski, instructing her to visit Craddock again next day at

St Luke's. She was to get all she could on his half-brother Laing and the Morgan girl.

There were no discernible background sounds to this call. Perhaps the downtrodden but self-righteous Mrs Salmon was gagged during work calls. Or remained in thrall to some serious knitting.

When Professor Littlejohn put in an appearance a SOCO photographer was standing by. The pathologist moved in. Over his shoulder Mott took in the slumped figure in the driving seat.

'The body is that of a woman,' Littlejohn declared. 'And life is extinct. You may bag her.' He withdrew his head to face the police group. 'And that, gentlemen, is all you will be getting out of me tonight. I'll be staying at Frederick's, and I hope to see some of you tomorrow at the morgue. The hour will be notified in the morning.'

He then rammed his tweed hat firmly on his head and strode back to his car, his caped overcoat flapping in the wind.

'Who's Frederick?' demanded a reporter, scribbling in his notebook.

'The hotel!' came a contemptuous chorus.

'Oh.' The hack was disappointed. He'd scented a mild scandal.

At the Castle, Beaumont decided to knock off. He checked in the bar for late drinkers, noted Burford slumped in an armchair, and was informed that Laing went up to his room half an hour earlier: probably to spend a sleepless night, since he'd clearly been in a sweat about the girl having taken off. It was as well he didn't know about the incident at Boulter's

Lock. The DS intended to be there next morning when the truth hit him.

With luck, Beaumont considered as he drove home, there'd be some leftovers from the women's marathon bake-up to tuck into; unless the young prodigal had scoffed the lot.

On waking next morning, recall struck Sandy like a lead-loaded sock. He made for Fiona's room and scratched at the door. Receiving no answer, he knocked loudly, calling her name; finally went back for his electronic gizmo to fiddle the lock.

He might have saved his energy. The girl had not returned. Nor had the bed been slept in.

He knew she was the model booked to pose from nine-fifteen, so this was cutting it close. He admitted he'd no right to resent her leaving without explanation, but it hurt. If she'd decided on some rash action, he'd have tried to dissuade her. And that action could cover an unimaginable vista, because so much of her life was still secret from him.

He returned to shave and shower, having missed the news flashes from Three Counties Radio.

At breakfast small groups were in earnest conversation which suddenly broke off as he entered. The two male detectives were back. Sandy carried his loaded tray to a small corner table where he could watch the door, and tipped up a chair to reserve a place for Fiona. He was aware of a sudden hush. He gazed around and found people avoiding his eyes. A woman from his art class was sniffing into her handkerchief.

The senior detective, fair-haired and youngish, detached himself from a group and came across to his table. 'May I join you?'

All he had was a coffee, so maybe he wouldn't linger. 'I was saving a place for my friend,' Sandy warned, 'but since she's not up yet...'

Mott slid into the seat opposite him. 'Some of the—' he baulked at calling these mostly middle-aged and elderly people 'students' – '*guests* appear to have heard the early morning news. I wonder, did you?'

Something dire was coming. Sandy blanched. 'No. I don't watch morning TV. And I missed the radio news. What's happened?'

'Last night a car was retrieved from the river at Maidenhead, near Boulter's Lock, a dark red Jaguar, and—'

Sandy's jaw dropped. He clenched his fists. 'Oh God! Like her sister!'

Mott stopped, equally stunned. 'What do you mean?'

'It's Fiona, isn't it? Is she all right? Where is she? I have to go to her.'

The DCI was watching him closely. 'Sadly, the driver didn't survive. But I can assure you it wasn't Miss Morgan, Mr Laing. I was there when the car was opened.'

Sandy stared back, at a loss for words.

'It was an older woman. But what did you mean by "like her sister"?'

'She – you're sure it wasn't Fiona? Some other car, then? So why tell me?'

'It was the car she brought you here in, Mr Laing. But last night someone else was in the driving seat.'

'Well then, where is she?'

'That is what we are hoping you can tell us, Mr Laing.'

This constant reiteration of the name was getting to Sandy,

the more because it wasn't his own. It made him afraid the detective knew he was a phoney and was repeating it to goad him. But there was more that Mott seemed to be holding back, and Sandy dreaded further revelations.

'If it wasn't Fiona, who was it?'

'A post-mortem examination later today should bring that to light. And forensic specialists are already starting on the car for clues to what happened.'

'Thank God it's not her.' Sandy pushed his plate away, unable to face food. 'But something's happened to prevent her getting back. You have to find her. What are you doing about it?'

'Everything we can, sir. We need Miss Morgan as a vital witness. She may have lent the car to a friend. It was her key in the ignition. The ring attached to it had the silver initials FM set in black leather.'

Sandy nodded. That was hers. So perhaps Mott was right and she'd actually loaned out her precious car. Or had someone taken it from her by force?

'You mentioned a sister. Perhaps Miss Morgan has gone to stay with her. If you will give me her address I can find out.'

'I can't. She's dead. And anyway I never knew her.'

Mott regarded him evenly. Laing seemed little short of panic. His breath was coming fast and his face had flushed.

'What I meant was—' Sandy gabbled. 'When I thought it was Fiona in the car, well, that's how she was killed: the sister, Marty. She was Fiona's twin. Her car went off the quayside at Limassol. It happened last September.'

'But you said you never knew her.'

'Fiona told me about it. She was very upset.'

'And momentarily you thought grief could have driven Miss Morgan to kill herself in the same way?'

'No, she wouldn't! Kill herself, I mean. And anyway she didn't think her twin's death was suicide either.'

'Accidental, then?'

'I don't know. But somebody else had been driving. She was immobilised somehow, on the back seat. A witness saw her struggling before the car sank'

'So what happened to the driver?'

'There wasn't one by then. He'd gone off.'

'Who was it? Did the police get him?'

Sandy shook his head. He had mastered his breathing and now leant over his forearms on the table, head sunk between his shoulders. 'There was an inquest. They called it misadventure.'

He didn't dare say more, because the real Laing had attended it, hadn't he? It was at the inquest that Fiona said she'd seen him for the first time. Sandy had no reason to think she was lying about that.

If this detective went probing any further into the matter the anomaly could be exposed. Every day he was getting deeper into the mire. He should never have taken up this stupid pretence. As soon as Mott had finished with him he must get to see his half-brother and insist they straightened their identities out.

'So is "Marty" short for Martina?'

'Or Martine. I wouldn't know.'

'Martina or Martine Morgan, then.' Mott was writing in his notebook. 'And this happened at Limassol, Cyprus, last September?'

'Her surname wasn't Morgan. She'd been married. It was something longer, three syllables.'

Mott waited but Sandy couldn't remember; or preferred not to.

'Right,' said Mott. 'Let me know if the name comes back to you, but no sweat. There are other ways of finding out.' He put the notebook into an inside pocket of his leather jacket. 'Oh, by the way, we don't seem to have noted down your profession, Mr Laing.'

'Er, financial adviser and property manager,' Sandy offered miserably. That was how Alicia had always described Warren. He'd done well at a major building society, then set up on his own, dealing in property.

'Thank you, Mr Laing, you've been very helpful.'

The two detectives moved off together. Sandy was free to go. His fried breakfast had congealed on the plate and his coffee was cold. Although he felt quite hollow with hunger he knew he'd not keep any food down. He queued again for fresh coffee and moved to a different table. It was time he took stock of his situation and started planning ahead.

He dared not leave the Castle while Fiona was still missing in case she turned up and he missed her. There was a sinister slant to the business of the car, serious enough to ensure the police would follow up on it. Taken all round, he'd be happier now if they did keep up their interest in Fiona.

For himself, he needed to sort out his own identity. Perhaps he could trust the detectives to cover Fiona's disappearance, and by afternoon make a quick visit to put pressure on Laing to come clean.

*   *   *

Rosemary Zyczynski made noncommittal noises back to Salmon when he tasked her by telephone. She had intended contacting the Boss to ask for a few days' leave, but it sounded now as though the situation at the Castle was making demands on the team, which left only her to deal with the biker incident. Now the notion of its victim being connected, however loosely, with recent developments suggested she might end getting a part in the drowning investigation too. She couldn't miss the opportunity.

She had left Max soaking his bruises in the luxury Jacuzzi which had been a strong inducement for her to buy the apartment. He had hobbled to it, even stiffer today, and she had supported him into the water. The expanse of swelling and discolouration had grown. She couldn't imagine how painful the injuries must be. The nursing agency had promised to ring her back and she hoped something could be arranged before she had to go out.

Max had scorned the idea of a qualified nurse, but she had won him over by warning that, if he were left alone in his present state, Beattie would insist on coming up for invalid-sitting, doubtless bringing quantities of herbal remedies and old wives' versions of miracle cures.

'Kindly meant, I know,' he granted. 'And I'm as fond of the old warhorse as you are, but at that I have to rebel. A professional to care for my intimate bits would be preferable.'

And when the nurse turned up at a little before ten-thirty, it was a tough-looking young man with a sunny smile and a no-nonsense attitude.

Z kissed Max on an unblemished patch of his forehead and left him settled at the window with a choice of music CDs and the day's *Telegraph*.

Leaning on two aluminium sticks, Warren Laing had limped once around his private room without falling, but was relieved to get back to the chair beside his bed. He had been almost wordless during Z's visit, and he'd still not been given the key to his locker. When he was woken from an after-lunch doze by his half-brother's arrival, his immediate request was for that. 'Can you bust the lock?' he demanded.

'No problem,' Sandy assured him. He was the one normally called upon at Hennigan's when one of the lots on offer turned up as a locked-box mystery. It was a skill Charlie had taught him and he'd found he had a knack with it. The cheap NHS lock provided no surprises.

He pushed aside the clothes, strangely similar to his own working outfit, and unearthed the mobile phone. 'You can't use that thing in here.'

'I'm not ringing out. Just want to pick up the messages.'

'But that could still…' Oh, why bother? Laing was the sort to trample over anyone and anything once he had an aim in view. Sandy knew he'd have enough trouble getting his own demand across without having crossed him over using the phone.

'Keys,' Laing ordered next. 'They're in my trousers pocket.'

They were in his jacket, where Z had returned them: a set of five house keys and a separate electronic one for a BMW.

'Take them. I'll give you a list of things I want from the flat, and then you're to go to Worldwide Travel in the High Street and get my outward tickets changed for tonight's flight. Get an upgrade if necessary. I'm going to leg it from here. Or, better, you're going to get me out in a wheelchair and drive me to Heathrow. Once that's done, the car's yours, understand? You'll have to fork out for any extra costs incurred because my money's all tied up, and I left my current cheque book at home, but the BMW will more than cover that and pay for your services.'

Sandy trudged across to fetch himself a chair and brought it back to face his half-brother. 'What makes you think I'll do any of that?'

'Because once I'm gone you can go back to being yourself, plus you'll have a valuable car.'

'Do you realise I'm part of an ongoing police inquiry, under your name?'

'Tell them you swapped under duress. I forced you into it.'

Sandy thrust out his lower jaw. 'They're not going to believe that, because I shan't say that.'

'So wise me up, how else will you be getting out of this?'

Sandy didn't answer because he saw no way of ever getting sorted. Not without going down for impersonation, fraudulent use of another's cheque book at the Castle, and wasting police time. Then there was always concealment of a dead body.

'Fiona was right,' he growled. 'You are a stinking ferret.'

'Fiona? Ah yes. I've remembered why she looked familiar. Marty had this photo in her bedroom: three women, two of them young and the other older: the twins with their mother, taken when the girls were fifteen. But I don't know what I've done to make Fiona call me that. We never met until you brought her here.'

'She must have picked it up from her sister. They were close.'

Anger flared in Laing's eyes. 'Marty thought the sun shone out of my arse. At least she did up to a few days before she was drowned.'

'Were you with her on Cyprus?'

'No, but I should have been. I gave her the money to book our holiday at the Park Beach Hotel, but I was held up by a project that went sour just then. She did a sulk and flounced off without me. I heard what happened on the news, saw the hire car dragged out of the water. They showed a photo of her, one I'd taken a month before, down at Winchelsea.

'I flew out to identify her body, tried to find some sense in what had happened. She only played at being the dumb blonde. She had all her wits about her, and a damn sight more than most. No matter what she'd had to drink, she wouldn't have played the fool parking near the edge.'

'So, if not you, who was the tall, dark Englishman who was taking her around?'

Laing stared. 'There wasn't one.' His voice had gone quiet. 'I checked at the hotel, in case she was taking me for a mug: just the one room, originally booked for us. Hers was the only English name in the register.'

'So he was booked in elsewhere.'

'Anyway, that's water under the bridge. Do what I'm asking now, and afterwards you can let on who you really are. The woman detective dropped in this morning asking about you and your girlfriend. I made sure she didn't leave here any wiser.'

CHAPTER TWENTY-ONE

Gordon was having a bad morning. Fiona had failed to put in an appearance and the other model, who lived in the village, had her phone turned off. His offer rejected by several of the Castle's domestics, he'd been obliged to abandon tutoring, strip off and ascend to the model's throne himself.

This was demeaning, and the shift from authority left him bitterly resentful. He was also conscious that he wasn't the young Adonis he'd once been; frankly, he thought, observing himself in the mirror of the cupboard appointed as model's dressing room, a leery, shaggy-shanked satyr.

At their first coffee break he abruptly departed with the excuse of making some in-house arrangements. He flung on sweater, trousers and sandals, and fled for a stronger brand of caffeine in his bedroom. On the way there he ran into Beaumont.

'No classes today?' the DS enquired breezily.

Gordon disliked the man. He suspected that behind the wooden face an impish, if not malicious, sense of humour lurked. As in the case of a Mafia Godfather, respect was something the tutor needed in order to maintain his persona.

Loftily he explained the situation in Studio 1. 'I doubt you would care to replace my missing model?' he asked sarcastically.

Beaumont simply looked at him, inner thoughts concealed. Eventually, as Gordon began to edge past, he offered, 'We're really more interested in Miss Morgan herself. How long have you known her?'

'Barely at all; this is the first occasion on which I have used her. And certainly the last.'

Barely, Beaumont thought. How appropriate in the circumstances. 'So how did you choose her? Is there a register for artists' models?'

'She was recommended by my previous model. Her sister.'

'Would that be Marty, by any chance?'

Beasley pretended not to hear. The man was wasting his time, and now he blocked his passage as he tried to get by.

'Martine wasn't a professional, but she used to pose for this course and for one on portraits which I hold here twice a year. She didn't really need the money; she did it more as a favour. Now, look, I must get along. My class will be waiting.'

Beaumont let him go. He had been heading for the bedroom corridor but now he turned back the way he'd come. Gordon had thought better of arriving in class with alcohol on his breath. He would snatch a coffee from that execrable vending machine and the students could just wait.

Beaumont made for the principal's office. 'More questions?' his secretary asked, guarding the inner sanctum.

'One which I should have asked before, and it's something I'm sure you can help me with.'

'Anything, as long as you don't disturb Himself.' She smiled saucily, fancying him.

'Aren't I the lucky one? It's about Mr Beasley's models: where they come from and so on.'

'That's simple. He's only ever had two: Mrs Gillespie for three or four years, and now Fiona Morgan, who's new. Then there's a girl from the village, Monica Trotter, who sort of stands in.'

'And before that?'

'Goodness knows. Before that he wasn't a tutor here.'

'So why did he give up on this Mrs Gillespie?'

'Oh, that was awful. She died in an accident last autumn, abroad somewhere. She was so nice, really pretty; blonde with big blue eyes and a gorgeous slim figure.' She was clearly envious.

'I prefer a girl with generous curves myself.'

'Really?' She adjusted her spectacles and waited to be asked out.

'Like my wife,' Beaumont lied. 'So you got to know this Mrs Gillespie quite well?'

'Only to talk to in here, making arrangements. She was a bit – well, not snooty exactly, but posh. You know.'

'And is Fiona Morgan the same?'

'Not a bit of it. She's someone you can let your hair down with. You know: girly talk. It doesn't matter who you are, she just fits in.'

Maybe Marty kept her charm for the menfolk, Beaumont considered. Blondes could be like that, he'd found; while Fiona seemed to go for *people*. He thanked the girl and returned to his borrowed office, there to consult with Mott.

There were a number of questions his last two conversations had raised. It would appear that the regulars in Gordon's class could have known Fiona's sister over some years. And if such as Mrs Rosa Burford did, then certainly her husband George did every bit as well, being a man. Not that that helped the present conundrum, because Martine was out of the equation. But maybe George had earlier got to know Fiona through her. The model and his wife: one still missing and one recovered dead from the Thames. George was certainly his favourite suspect.

It was time to have him in and question him in more detail about his movements over the past few days. He'd spent some time absent from his taxidermy class, but he couldn't have spent all those hours in the bar. A second search of his room and car wouldn't come amiss.

Then again, Beaumont decided, he hadn't entirely finished with Gordon Beasley. One mystery that now struck him was how Martine could have recommended her sister to him when she was already several months dead. Unless, of course, she'd done so last year, knowing that she would be withdrawing her own services in future: perhaps a rift in relations between tutor and prize model?

'The prof's secretary rang,' Mott interrupted him at this point. 'Post-mortem's at 2.30.'

'So I guess it's a light lunch for one of us.'

'Both of us,' Mott said shortly, 'and I could do with Littlejohn putting more of a spurt on. We need to know if there's anything iffy about this death. Laing has just told me Fiona Morgan's twin sister suffered much the same abroad: death from drowning in a submerged car.' He filled him in on the Cyprus death as they walked to their borrowed office.

'That could look bad for Laing. Was he anywhere near at the time?'

'He says not; but apparently flew out for the inquest. It's something we can check, but in any case there's no close parallel, because our dead woman is not Fiona Morgan.'

'But her car? So who the hell is she?'

'I got a look last night, and I'd guess it was the other one who's missing. If so, I'd like to know just how well she knew the Morgan girl.'

'Rosa Burford? Swipe me! I had her down as a walk-out.'

'Maybe she was, at the start. Then somehow the two joined forces, Burford took the car and Fiona took over the disappearing act.'

'If Laing flew out to Cyprus for the inquest he knew the other sister pretty well. Twins, so maybe they were a threesome.'

'Is that relevant?'

'Maybe not, but it's a point we might get him rattled about.'

'If we're not too busy with George Burford, once it's certain that the drowned woman is his wife.'

Mott was right about the victim's identity, but by early afternoon his other assumption was proved well off the mark. Rosa Burford had not drowned. Placing her in the driving seat before sending the car into the river now looked like a sardonic kind of joke, because the killer had not troubled to remove the knife driven up under her left scapula. There was no way she could have been stabbed there while she was strapped in.

The knife was slightly curved, fine-bladed, with a black wood handle and a sharp point. Professor Littlejohn, who appreciated dark humour, welcomed such twists breaking the routine of autopsy. He spent some time carefully removing the knife, measuring it, waiting for photography and then replacing it for further shots, removing it a second time and having the wound photographed again with a fine steel ruler inserted and another alongside. When, as customary, his manly bass broke out it was into a chorus from the *Pirates of Penzance,* and more than a little triumphal.

He scrutinised his assistant taking a swab of the knife blade. As she was about to bag it the professor called her back.

'Take several more samples; at different points. Be particular where it joins the handle.'

'Something unusual, sir?' Mott asked.

'Fascinating. I could have missed it. Many would.' He was almost purring with pride. With gloved fingers he pulled open the wound to show them.

'The weapon was used to kill the lady all right, but after a period it was removed and then replaced. The flesh had time to dry out between. She was stabbed a second time while very much dead.

'There's something else too, but I suspect we'll get a better view of it when I take a section of the buttock or thigh. Madam was well fleshed, as you'll appreciate by now.'

The examination continued, with the pathologist in increasingly good humour. All last night's irritation at being wrested from entertainment at his old college had gone. Mott guessed that this subject at present under the prof's knife would feature in some future lecture to his postgraduate students. The promised section of buttock or thigh should be worth waiting for.

*   *   *

Once it seemed certain that the woman taken out of the Thames was indeed Rosa Burford, Mott had moved to a corner of the lab to ring through to Zyczynski. 'What are you doing at the moment, Z?'

'I'm on my way to have another word with Barry's mother. He was one of the lads who found Mr Bell's body. He's only ten and I suspect he's a latchkey kid. His mother's a working single who usually doesn't get home until seven. There's no one else there and Barry has to get his own evening meal. Today's her free half-day.'

'Don't invent work for yourself, Z. Refer it to social services.'

'It's positive policing, Angus. He's a good lad, a bit wild, but they did right to report what they found, despite it getting them in hot water. I don't want to make it any more difficult for the mother. She's a cleaner and she's quite a bright lady. I've spoken to the head of her boy's school. There may be a place for her as a class assistant for Year Three. It would mean her getting the same hours and holidays as Barry. It's just a question of wising her up for the interview.'

Mott groaned. 'Charitable intentions, Z! I've been there, done that, and the T-shirt is worn out. Believe me it's not worthwhile. In the end they'll both let you down.

'Anyway, I've a job for you. Of the worst kind: informing George Burford that it could have been his wife in the Jaguar pulled out of the river. He'll need to identify her at the morgue here, but there's no hurry, so go ahead now with Barry's mother. The body will need tidying first, once Littlejohn has finished.'

'Did she carry ID?'

'No. That's why I'm saying "could be". But the flimsy evening dress is as described, and no top clothes despite the temperature hitting zero. Also, significantly, all the jewellery she was supposed to have been wearing is missing. The prof says necklace and rings forcibly removed, and both lobes are badly torn where the earrings were ripped off before death. There would have been considerable blood loss.'

'And the Jag was the one Fiona Morgan claimed as her own?'

'That's so; which ties the murder to the Castle, as does the manner in which the dead woman was dressed. Anyway, I must go. The prof's just going in for the organs.'

Sandy was certain he didn't want further involvement in his half-brother's plans. On the other hand, any chance of hastening confession of his own deception would be welcome.

But then, he couldn't come clean while it risked dropping Warren in the shit.

Maybe, as intended, the chancer would succeed in getting abroad until the fuss died down. There was the possibility that he himself could get in trouble for colluding in Warren's escape, but he could truthfully plead ignorance of any reason why his brother should be detained. Although he suspected him of something dodgy, probably connected with money, he'd no hard evidence to support this. Innocent until proved guilty, wasn't that it?

Seated on a cold stone bench in the pretentious little garden at the rear of St Luke's, he considered the keyring. Following instructions he must catch two buses to reach Belvoir Court and get past the man on duty in the foyer; he could do that.

Warren had described the door that led to the underground garage. The BMW was there, waiting.

All he had to do then was drive to the travel agent, get the flight date changed to tonight, collect the receipt and a package from the printer's, and take them to Warren.

But that wasn't the end of it. Finally he had somehow to smuggle him out of the hospital and drive him, a disabled patient, to Heathrow Airport. It would require him to borrow a porter's or doctor's uniform and a wheelchair. With all that extra deception thrown in, wouldn't it look like deliberate abduction?

A fine sleet began falling, which provoked him into moving on. He pulled up his collar about his ears and made for the nearby bus stop. His watch showed it was almost 4 p.m. A lot was expected of him before closing time in town and still he didn't feel up to making a choice. Whichever bus came next would decide whether he followed his half-brother's instructions or sloped back to the Castle.

The bus rattled straight on into the town centre. For the Castle it should have turned off at Welder's Lane. So he was committed. He sat wondering why he was such a patsy even to consider what Warren had asked of him. Perhaps it was because he'd discovered that, in a way, they were so much alike; at least in their sense of sardonic humour, if not of what was proper. If it hadn't been for poor old Gran instilling in him all those negative rules, who could say whether he wouldn't have turned out an equal rogue.

There was always a chance that at some later stage the plan would be frustrated, but at least he'd show willing by making the preliminary moves.

He was greeted by name at the travel agent's: that is, by his half-brother's name, to which he was now quite accustomed.

'I was a bit worried to tell you the truth, Mr Laing. I tried phoning and texting you, but no answer,' the manager told him.

'Something came up,' Sandy explained obliquely. 'I've missed the flight, of course, but I'd like you to fix me an alternative. I believe there's a late one going out tonight?'

'Let's just see what comes up on the screen then.' The man swung it so that the customer could share the information, and began pecking a way through his keyboard.

'There is indeed, with seats available, and it's a little cheaper. That's because it means changing at Madrid. Not the best place to get marooned, I find; but there's an hour and twenty minutes' gap: time enough to get between the two terminals. And it's still a single, Mr Laing?'

'We'll leave the return open.' He handed over the credit card and stabbed in the PIN number Warren had confided.

'Good, it's booked then. Just collect your tickets at Heathrow, from Iberia Air. And enjoy a pleasant holiday, sir.'

So far, no problem. Next stop was the printer's, a couple of streets away.

The package was waiting. The girl who handed it over seemed not to know Laing and was too busy nursing a defective photocopier to take stock of him.

He'd left picking up the car till last, because he hadn't been sure he would ever get this far. Now it began to look as though Laing had a chance of departing as planned. Sandy grimaced at his watch and decided on a taxi from the station to save time.

At Belvoir Court he again braved the man on duty in the foyer, who barely looked up from his evening paper, but mouthed, 'Evenin', Mr Laing,' as he went past.

The lock on the front door to Warren's flat showed no evidence of earlier tampering. Legitimately this time, he used the key. He made straight for the mini-office inside the wardrobe and collected the car's documents together with the computer discs which he'd left scattered about; then a selection of clothes. They all went into a supermarket bag found in a kitchen cupboard, and after that he was ready for the basement garage, to pick up his reward.

Professor Littlejohn's self-satisfaction promised something a little out of the ordinary. Choosing the left thigh for his section he went in enthusiastically with an electric saw.

'There,' he said with some pride, 'isn't that beautiful?' He was displaying a crimson joint, in colour not far off good beef topside, and thickly surrounded by a wall of yellowish fat.

Mott failed to admire it. After considering the case-load, he'd sent Beaumont off to look further into the doubtful background of the hanged man. Now he wished he'd gone himself and left his DS to play up to the pathologists's twisted aesthetic sense.

'What exactly are we looking for?'

'Here. See how the flesh is flabby and appears layered. There are diminutive spaces which show how it's been stretched by the formation of fine ice crystals. The lady has been refrigerated, Mr Mott: shut in a freezer for at least thirty-six hours, at my estimate. When did she disappear?'

'During the night of Friday–Saturday,' Mott told him. 'Would that meet your estimate?'

'Indeed it does. And given her acceptable body temperature when taken from the water-filled car, we shall be able to calculate how rapidly the river's flow could bring about a total thaw. From which, in turn, experiment will show, to within a few hours, just when the car came to enter the water.'

All of this could lead somewhere, Mott realised. And surely the Castle must be involved. Ample freezer space would be available there in its catering department.

'Take heart,' Littlejohn mocked. 'It's all quite straightforward mathematics and you have it handed on a plate. See how I do your work for you!'

CHAPTER TWENTY-TWO

Z was feeling down. Mott's phone call left her considering his new cynicism over helping the public. He'd been different before his Bosnian experience.

Dealing with Maisie Bell had been gruelling enough. Before facing any further angst she had to phone Max at home and make sure he was all right.

The landline went unanswered. His mobile number was engaged although she tried three times. She gave up on it and decided that her appointment with Barry's mother was the nearest she'd get to believing there was hope yet for the planet. She drove out there in driving sleet and found her waiting, with a kettle ready boiled and some freshly baked scones.

At St Luke's seven or eight wheelchairs were ranged along one wall beside Reception. Not too difficult to whip the farthest one off and disappear up the corridor to the lifts, but it would take more panache than Sandy felt at present. Some kind of uniform was essential to give him the necessary cover.

He sidled up outside the porters' room, seemingly absorbed by a poster cautioning the public to search for little lumps. He flicked a sideways glance through the open door and noted no fewer than three men in there, resting between calls; and nothing in the way of spare uniform jackets to be seen. So he must venture elsewhere.

It seemed immaterial which corridor to take, but he turned left and passed several doors bearing the names of doctors or ancillary staff. He reached the end and found himself outside a ward. Inside, nurses were moving among the beds and he shrank from their scrutiny. Halfway back towards Reception he took refuge behind a door marked Staff Only. It contained twin rows of numbered, grey-painted steel cabinets.

A locker room: now that was more encouraging. And he didn't need to bust any locks because a crumpled white cotton coat hung from a knob at the far end. It was suitably stained with small spatters of blood, which could account for its being abandoned. Sandy slid into it and found he was labelled Dr Magda Clunes.

Impersonating a half-brother had been quite enough; cross-dressing went beyond the limit. He removed the card from its plastic envelope, spat on the inked name, smudged it with a thumb and replaced it. A stethoscope in one of the large, square pockets would have been welcome, but he must be grateful for what fate had already provided. Grinning affably he bounded back to the reception hall, liberated the end wheelchair and trundled it towards the lifts.

Such of Warren's clothes as had survived his accident and the emergency treatment would have been ruined, so he must escape wrapped in a blanket, and then change in the back of the car on the way to the airport. Sandy had chosen an outfit to look unremarkable: casual tweed jacket, jeans and pull-on shoes, grey sweater, grey check shirt. They would save Warren having to open the suitcases he'd left ready-packed in the car's boot.

In the approach passage to the surgical ward an immense trolley was being stacked with used crockery from the patients' last meal. Sandy negotiated the obstacle, unquestioned by catering staff who drew back for him to reach Sandy's side room. Nurses were nowhere to be seen.

'God, not a moment too soon!' Warren greeted him. 'Quick, get me into it. They threatened to move me into the open ward tonight. Have you got…?'

'Everything. But before we go, there's this.' Sandy produced the car registration form from an inner pocket. 'Just sign the transfer page. I'll fill in the rest.'

Warren raised a quizzical eyebrow. 'Is it me you don't trust or your ability as a forger?'

'Whichever, get on with it.' Sandy shoved a pen into his hand, and pulled the blanket from the bed, wrapping it round Warren's shoulders. 'Clothes are in the car. It's parked close, in a disabled drivers' slot.'

'Everything indeed. Did you remember to feed the cat? No? – OK, *joke*!'

'What about your medication?'

'Just strong painkillers and antibiotics. Where I'm going you can get them without a prescription. And there should be aspirin or something on the plane.'

'Maybe they'll question your travelling. There's something in the small print about being acceptably fit. And how will you manage in Madrid, changing planes?'

'I'll deal with that when it comes. You have to make your own way in life, Sandy; not wait for it to slap you in the face.'

That's where we differ, Sandy reflected. Maybe that outlook was what got Laing into the present situation: not a recommendation for the lifestyle.

'Whatever you say,' he told him, wheeling the chair out through the doorway and setting off back to the lifts. Nobody interrupted their progress on the way out, although a small lady in a slightly cleaner white coat who got on at Floor 2 screwed up her eyes trying to read the name card on his chest. Sandy nodded authoritatively to her and she seemed satisfied. Outside, the wind tugged at Warren's blanket and they had to stop while he was tucked in again.

As they approached the car a dark-uniformed man stepped out of a white van and walked purposefully towards them. Sandy's white coat was no trump card out here. To have been sussed at such a late stage in the Great Escape was bitterly cruel.

The man smiled at Warren and opened the car door wide, allowing Sandy to lift him and decant him on to the back seat. He even offered to return the wheelchair to Reception.

Not a police officer, but a Red Cross worker. Fate, it seemed, was still smiling on them.

Mott returned to the Castle to find that Zyczynski had already broken the bad news to George Burford and was in their office writing up her notes.

'How did he take it?'

'Wretchedly. He said that by now he was more than half prepared for something bad; not that he understood why Rosa should take someone else's car when she had her own keys to theirs. And nothing's going to persuade him she'd ever attempt suicide: she was too full of life and had all sorts of plans ahead for them both

'He could believe she might fancy a night or two away with some man she'd picked up here, but he couldn't suggest a name. It had all happened before. That's why, at first, he wasn't unduly alarmed, just a bit depressed, so that it had put him off the work he'd come here to do.'

'Suppose I have a word with him now? Some new aspects have come out of the PM which I'd like him to consider. Do you think he's discreet enough to keep them to himself?'

'He's gone even more morose, drinking in the bar while he makes up his mind what to do. He seems quite at a loss. As for passing on sensitive material, there's nobody he seems to talk with except Warren Laing, and he's not been in for most of today.'

'Any idea what he would be up to? Was there any message for him from Fiona Morgan?'

'Not to my knowledge. He was mooning about in the grounds this morning, and then went off in a taxi after lunch. So maybe she did phone him. He hasn't handed his key in and he didn't take any luggage.'

'Anything new from the boy's mother you went to see?'

'No. She's keen to try for the teaching-assistant job. I don't see why she shouldn't get it. No special qualifications are needed, except to be an experienced mum and patient with children.'

Mott grunted. 'Right; I'm off to the bar for a sandwich, then. Are you coming?'

'I'd rather finish this report and go home. Max is there and he's not too well.'

'I'm sorry to hear that. Nothing infectious, I hope?'

'Not unless rash judgement is catching.'

'Oh.' Mott shrugged. 'I hope not. There's enough of that in my home at present.'

It sounded, Z thought, staring after him, as though the honeymoon period was well and truly over. Maybe Paula's pregnancy had gone to her head.

Mott returned to the Area station, went through to the Incident Room and sat, still in his coat, to contemplate the whiteboard. It needed sorting. There were too many detached names floating on the edges, and at present what buzzed in his mind was their connection. He went across, cleared a space and wrote *Rosa Burford* in the centre with a line extended to her husband, another to Fiona Morgan and a third radiating to Warren Laing. Next he linked Laing and Fiona, George and Laing. He considered where the dead Marty connected on the periphery; certainly with her sister and Laing, but Beaumont had rung to give him the gist of his conversation with the tutor, so it seemed Gordon Beasley was involved with her too, as were all of his class who had attended his earlier life classes.

Was it stretching coincidence to consider Marty at all? Bringing her into the pattern created a network of lines in all directions, a sort of Union Jack off-centre from Rosa. But Rosa must surely be central as she was the one killed here.

Two deaths involving cars sunk in water: he needed to know more about the incident in Cyprus, and doubted he'd find what he wanted in any news column. Maybe Yeadings could help; some years back he had spent several months out there chasing a fraudster who'd left a trail of suspicious deaths behind in the UK. He was a great believer in keeping up with acquaintances in the Job, and would certainly know a high-ranking Cypriot policeman.

Mott rang through and caught the Boss after dinner. He listened while his DCI sketched the story, and grunted approval. 'Yes, it's worth following up. I was mainly working in Nicosia, but I know someone in Limassol who would be glad to help. Given the time difference, I'll need to ring him early morning. You can leave it with me, Angus.'

As Mott closed the call the internal phone buzzed. Sergeant Bailey in Control had a message to pass on from the forensics lab. 'I thought it might be urgent,' he said. 'They sounded quite keen at the other end.'

And the message?' Mott demanded, impatient with the man's chattiness.

'I'll read it out. "Blood found on the knife was from two sources, one from the woman's body under examination. The other was not human. Precise nature of the second specimen is under further analysis." Have you got yourself a case with visiting aliens, Inspector?'

'Thank you, Sergeant. Is that everything?' He rang off.

Not human meant animal. And hadn't Burford signed on for a course here in taxidermy? If the subjects used were freshly killed they would need skinning and gutting. It was time he visited the lab in question and took stock of George Burford's tools. He remembered Beaumont mentioning rodents Burford was meant to be working on.

He rang back to forensics, but their switchboard had closed for the night. He left a message on the answerphone. 'Query if the second sample of blood is from polecats.'

It took him twenty minutes to drive back to the Castle. Once arrived, it took thirty to chase up the right key to let himself into the lab and then to identify the bench where the polecat skins were under tension. Near the base of the clamp lay a black tool-roll. Mott unfastened it and ran his eye over the selection of implements. There were two knives slotted in. The dark handles were of the same kind as the one left in Rosa Burford's body, and one of the three securing loops was empty.

Could Burford have been so stupid as to leave evidence leading directly back to him? Mott considered the dejected man Z had left slumped in the bar. Perhaps he just didn't care any more and, finally outraged by his wife's behaviour, his reason had blown. He'd gone for a skinning knife and attacked her with it. Snatching her necklace and tearing out her earrings could have been a tardy attempt to throw suspicion elsewhere. But it had never seemed to hold water; there was no other suggestion of a jewel thief in the neighbourhood.

At last there was a clear direction for the investigation to take. Mott left, locked the lab, returned the key. He looked in at the bar and Burford was still there, barely conscious. He sat down beside him, saying nothing but feeling some pity stir at his wretchedness.

Eventually, 'Earlier, did my sergeant take you to view the body?'

Burford raised his head. 'Yes. My wife,' he said, like a sigh. 'It was Rosa.' He was silent a while, then, 'I can't imagine life without her.'

'Have you got very far with your polecats?'

Burford stared as if Mott had suddenly broken into a foreign language. 'What? Not really.'

Clearly not interested, Mott registered. He would leave the man to his misery and question him properly tomorrow.

'Where were you when I phoned?' Z demanded, releasing herself from Max's welcoming embrace.

'Next door. I went across to my flat because a whole pack of hacks arrived and I didn't want them messing up your place.'

'Thoughtful,' she appreciated. Do you want me to go over and clear up?'

'No. I did it myself: beer cans, full ashtrays; the lot. I'll go later and shut the windows. It got like El Vino's in the old Fleet Street days.'

'I hope you're not overdoing things.'

'M'm, I shall need an early night' He leered at her. 'especially since I've made a risotto that'll charm your taste buds. I swear, it's aphrodisiac.'

Because Laing had insisted he couldn't leave without picking up supplies of his particular brand of tea, they were making a slight detour through Windsor. If he was quick about the transaction they should be OK for time, but Sandy fretted, being someone who liked to be at an airport three hours before departure, rather than two.

On the way Warren made up for lost time in St Luke's by phoning through to his mother. It was ironic that this time it was she who had switched off. He breezily left a message by voicemail, adding, 'You'll never guess who I'm with at the moment: Sandy Craddock. Or Alexander, as you'd call him. He's a great guy. We must all get together someday soon, do some partying. Be talking later. Bye.'

The small shop Laing directed him to was in the narrow Eton High Street, between a high-class stationer's and a philatelist's heaven. Parking was restricted and Sandy was obliged to pull up on the opposite side. He offered to do the required shopping but Laing was insistent he must hobble there himself. Besides, they might have shut, but they'd open up for him.

Sandy helped him on to the pavement, bent to retrieve the hospital blanket that had fallen out wrapped about his legs, and thought he heard Laing give a loud gasp. He had hobbled a little way into the road and now staggered forward, one arm clutching at empty air ahead.

On the far pavement a group of senior boys from Eton College broke up as a man darted through and hared down the street towards the bridge.

Laing cried out hoarsely, lunging in the man's direction, swayed and fought to stay upright in mid-road. Beyond him, Sandy saw with horror a furniture van bearing down at speed. There was a brief instant when he thought Warren had made it, then the scream, a screech of tyres, and the van skidding, its bonnet ploughing into glass and bricks.

In the frozen moment after the crash, silence was total. Then Sandy was running, converging with the boys at the van's side. A lower leg protruded from under the wreck of the front wheel. As he watched, it quivered, jerked once and stayed unmoving. A slow flood of crimson began to spread outwards.

'Poor sod,' muttered one of the boys, white-faced. 'He's bought it.'

The driver, his face streaming blood, managed to climb from the less damaged side of the van and stood hanging on the door. 'Oh my God!' he cried, 'why did he do that to me?'

Behind him, as he perched at the open door of the passenger seat, waiting for the police to get round to questioning him, Sandy heard Warren's mobile ringing: Alicia, expecting to catch up with him at last.

He wasn't going to pick it up. She could leave a message, to join all her other unanswered texts. He hoped she hadn't already wiped Warren's voice off her recording. That was the last time she was going to hear it.

A uniformed constable had finished with the Eton boys and was now coming across for his statement. So who the hell am I going to say I am? Sandy demanded of himself.

CHAPTER TWENTY-THREE

'Is this your car, sir?'

Of course, that had to be the first question; and not a hard one because he had all the necessary paperwork in his pocket. He handed it over, which left no room for evasion.

'And you are, sir?'

'Alexander Craddock,' he confessed. 'The injured man is my brother. He was crossing the road to buy some tea.'

The constable looked at him, clearly thinking *this is a weird one*. 'I'm afraid he was more than injured.'

'It – it was so sudden. I can't believe...'

Nevertheless the PC needed his driving licence, which he didn't have on him, and continued with questions, heavily pursuing the rules according to the book. Sandy felt a weariness coming over him and leant back, eyes closed.

'Are you all right, sir?'

'No I'm bloody well not! I'm confused, devastated.'

'You can take your driving licence into your local police station within the next seven days. Can you give me your address, sir?'

Under pressure, Sandy complied, adding, 'But at present I'm doing an Art course at a place called the Castle. I think it's somewhere near Medmenham.'

'And your brother's full name and address?'

Behind him Sandy was aware of firemen crowded at the front of the shattered furniture van with hoisting gear. Operations were held up while one of them lay down and began to squirm his way under the wheels. Sandy had a split second to push the policeman away as he was violently sick.

'Can't you leave the poor devil alone?' growled a bystander.

Sandy looked up to see a second crowd of gawpers had gathered, with himself as the centre of fascination.

The constable was embarrassed. There was more than enough to keep him busy here until reinforcements turned up. 'Just his name and address, sir, for identification.'

'Warren Laing. We have different surnames because we had different fathers.' He added the Belvoir Court address for good measure.

'Right, sir. Do you feel up to driving yourself? If so we can leave things until tomorrow. We will be in touch.'

From somewhere in the crowd a bottle of mineral water was produced. Sandy swallowed gratefully, pouring out the remains to clean the pavement by his feet. He staggered out of the car and walked unsteadily round to the driving side. Once seated there, he felt his head clearing.

Driving back to the Castle would be the easy part. There'd be a lot to sort out when he got there. And then Warren: what the hell was he to do about him? It seemed impossible. He'd been so vitally alive and full of plans one minute and then – nothing.

Sandy hadn't thought much about death since Gran's departure, but now it was all around him, getting ever closer.

But at least this one had been provably accidental.

* * *

He lost himself once on the way there, stopped and put his head in his hands. Then he opened the window to a blast of chill air, reversed in a cul-de-sac and started to apply his mind to the route. When he finally parked in the Castle's courtyard he had decided not to stay on. He was himself again, and it would take too much explanation either to resume here as Warren Laing or make the change back.

He would collect his luggage – that is, Warren's borrowed stuff – ask if he owed anything, and then get home. He doubted there'd be any great hue and cry for the Alexander Craddock who'd absconded from St Luke's; at least for a day or two. Then, perhaps, the post would bring a formal admonishment from the NHS, enclosing an outpatient appointment card.

At the Castle, what he didn't expect, as he leant on the counter at Reception waiting his turn, was the rapid tapping of high heels on the tiles and a pair of warm arms flung round him from behind. He turned and hugged her back. 'Fiona, where the hell have you been? I was worried sick something had happened.'

'Silly old goat,' she said fondly. 'I had something to do which wouldn't wait. Didn't Gordon give you my message? Look, leave whatever you were waiting for and let's go upstairs. I've something to tell you.'

So had he, but it seemed it must wait. There was a more urgent matter, and this was not the time to pass on bad news.

Even then they were interrupted by an insistent rapping on Fiona's door. 'Detective Sergeant Beaumont,' a voice announced. 'My chief inspector has arrived and needs to see you, Miss Morgan.'

Fiona swore softly, cradled against Sandy's wildly beating heart.

'I'm just changing,' she shouted back 'Hang on, will you, and I'll follow you down.' She scrabbled for her clothes. 'Sandy, I wanted to tell you first, but come with me and I'll explain it all.'

In their office, Beaumont and Mott were ranged like an interview board on one side of the table. Facing them a single chair was offered to Fiona. 'Mr Laing?' Beaumont queried.

Sandy swung another chair alongside Fiona's. 'Actually, no. That's – that *was* – my brother's name. I was just using it here.'

The chief inspector looked up from his papers with interest. 'And why would that be, Mr...?'

'Because he'd already taken mine. I'm Alexander Craddock.' That sounded perfectly logical to Sandy. Apparently it satisfied DCI Mott, for the moment. He turned to Fiona. 'Miss Morgan, a few questions.'

'Where I've been for the last few days.'

'And why, since you were specifically asked to stay in touch. I must remind you this is a murder investigation and you appear to have some connection with the dead woman.'

'Rosa Burford,' she said. 'Not really. I mean, there's no connection I'm aware of.'

'Except, perhaps, through your car?

'That, yes. That's the first thing they told me when I got back. I've no idea how she came to end up in the Jag. Is it a write-off?'

'You didn't lend it to her?'

'Lord, no! I'm particular who drives it. I'd left the keys to it in my bathrobe pocket in the studio cupboard. Rosa must have taken them from there and just driven off.'

Mott considered this before going further. 'So perhaps you would explain why you left here without informing a member of the inquiry team.'

She turned to Sandy. 'This is what I wanted to tell you, love, once I got my breath back. I had a letter, you see, from a girl my sister Marty got to know in Limassol. It was one of those sudden attachments that happen in the girly world. Anyway, she wrote that Marty had left some stuff with her. We hadn't met because she was working in Larnaca and couldn't get free to attend the inquest.

'I suddenly thought I might find a clue out there, among whatever Marty had left behind. I'd little enough to go on, before. Like me, Katya couldn't believe Marty would have killed herself or been such a dumb fool as to drive off the quay accidentally.'

'So did you find anything?' Mott sounded less stiff, almost intrigued.

'A little box of letters, some pen and ink sketches, and a few paperback books that Marty had been going to throw away. But Katya hung on to them. She knew my name, and she knew of the Castle, where Marty used to model. It was pure luck that she put the two together and found me here. But there was nothing important. As she'd said, it was just stuff.'

Stuff, Sandy thought. And there's all Warren's stuff I'll have to go through. I mustn't leave it unprotected in his car: well, my car, once I've sent the new registration slip in. Maybe, if I look, there's something there that links him with Marty.

Mott repeated his instruction to keep the police informed of their movements, then dismissed them both. It wasn't clear whether he was satisfied or intended to take Fiona's story further.

'Get your coat and come with me,' Sandy insisted when they were released. He thought she would demur, but she gave him a straight look and went off without a word. He waited by the main entrance. She came back in the short fur jacket she'd arrived in.

'Where to?'

'You'll see.'

He led her towards the BMW, flicked its lights with his key and grinned at her raised eyebrows.

'You've come into money.'

His face fell. 'I've inherited it. Get in; I've a lot to tell you and most of it's awful.'

She sat silent while he reeled it all out: the farcical attempt to get his brother out of St Luke's and smuggled to Heathrow.

'I don't know why he had to get away, but I had this – this sort of fellow-feeling. I think if we'd had more time together we'd have got on fine. So I did what he wanted; and in the end it was all – useless.'

'Were the police waiting for him?'

'No. It was pathetic. He got out of the car and was run over.' He heard her gasp.

'It was in Eton High Street. He was wobbly on his legs, but he tried to dash across. Then a furniture van hit him. I can't believe it. This time it really was an accident.

'What the hell am I going to tell Alicia? He was phoning her from the car while I drove. He left a message he was with me and we should all meet up sometime. Fiona, I killed him, whipping him out of hospital when he wasn't fit to stand on his feet!'

'Sandy, it wasn't your fault. If I know you at all, you were just going with the flow. He insisted, didn't he?'

'You could say I was bribed.' His voice was bitter. 'The car was my price for doing what he wanted. Not that I needed it. I thought you might like it, if the Jag was a write-off. That is, if you ever intended coming back.'

'You are unbelievable. What a hell of a time you've been having while I was away. As for your brother, Sandy, I'm sorry. It's sad for you.'

He stared out of the misted windscreen. 'He's left his luggage in the boot. Tomorrow I'd better take it to my room for safe keeping. Then I'll have to go through it. Fiona, are you quite satisfied he had nothing to do with your sister's death?'

'Utterly sure: I did find out something from what she'd left with Katya, but I wouldn't let the police know that until I've had a better chance to think about it. For the present we've a lot to catch up on.'

Next morning a message from the forensics team confirmed that the animal blood on the murder knife was indeed a polecat's. The blade had been wiped off, but a minute quantity had dried into the join with the handle. This sample predated the human blood that came from Rosa Burford's body.

'So we go for the husband,' declared Beaumont with relish.

'It looks that way,' Mott conceded.

They enquired and learnt he had returned to the lab to pack up his things, having no heart for going further with his project. 'I'll pick him up before he can get rid of the evidence.' Beaumont offered.

He brought Burford in, together with two plastic bags. One contained the man's tools, and the other the pelts of three dead polecats. He also introduced a strong whiff of disinfectant into the office.

Burford gestured to one of the bags and complained, 'It's not complete. Someone's nicked one of my knives.'

'Mr Burford,' Mott warned him, 'I must ask you to accompany us to the local police station, to be questioned regarding the suspicious death of your wife. The interview will be recorded and a sealed tape of it given to you at the conclusion of the interview.'

Burford appeared unsurprised. 'Am I being arrested?'

'Not at this point. Your presence will be voluntary. You may be accompanied by your solicitor, if you so wish.'

'That sounds grim enough. I didn't do it, you know. And I haven't a clue to who did. Still, I want to get to the bottom of it, and I just wish the bastard, whoever it is, could still be hanged.'

Students and staff were beginning to drift through the hall and the corridor that led to the bar, for pre-lunch drinks. The departing policemen escorting George Burford excited some interest, but less than did the see-through parcels Beaumont was carrying. There would be no shortage of speculation during their meal.

In the courtyard a slicing wind hit them, but Burford made no demand to go back for a coat. As they got into Mott's unmarked car, Sandy, unloading the BMW's boot, glanced across. The departing car's headlights caught him and Fiona dragging wheeled luggage towards the main entrance.

'Better check with Traffic on the Eton incident,' Mott warned Beaumont under his breath. 'Just in case that body turns out to be ours as well.'

'In which case Burford could have competition for prime suspect. And what are we doing about this Craddock using an alias at the Castle on some fantastic notion that his own name's in use elsewhere?'

'We bide our time, that's what. And in the meanwhile find out how he paid for his course at the Castle. We can always pull him in if he's billed it on his brother's account.'

'Half-brother,' Beaumont corrected him. 'If you can believe that much.'

They had stacked Warren Laing's bags in Sandy's room, then retired to Fiona's where she sat on the bed dealing out her finds from Cyprus like a twosome game of cards.

'The letters first,' she suggested as he joined her. 'Read through that lot and tell me where that gets us.'

CHAPTER TWENTY-FOUR

'Quite a war zone,' Mott commented dryly next morning, laying the diary in front of the Boss. 'Thames Valley's breaking out over my return.'

Yeadings grunted, surveying the list of post-mortems and inquests. 'There's another death too, that we shouldn't overlook: that of Martine Gillespie at Limassol last summer. I've been in touch with the area commander there, so perhaps I'd better cover that corner.'

Mott faced the team. 'Today DS Zyczynski and DI Salmon will be attending the post-mortems of Gillian and Roger Bell at Wycombe. That's scheduled for twelve noon, which doesn't leave them much time to either side. So we're thin on the ground. I don't foresee any problems over there, and it's possible the whole thing will be sewn up in one go.

'The inquest on Rosa Burford will be on Friday: purely formal identification, time and place of finding. I shall request an adjournment pending further inquiries. DS Beaumont and I will be giving evidence, along with Professor Littlejohn.

'Professor Littlejohn will be dealing with the post-mortem of Warren Laing, briefly aka Alexander Craddock, tomorrow at Wexham Park Hospital. Medical staff from St Luke's will give evidence at the later inquest, covering his state of health and hidden identity. Windsor Area police will also give evidence, and I'm sending Z to both on a watching brief.'

He looked around at them. 'Any questions? No? Right then, further tasking. In depth questioning of George Burford falls to DS Beaumont and myself.'

'Good cop, bad cop,' came as a low murmur from Beaumont's direction, which Mott chose not to hear, while Yeadings glowered at the ceiling.

'This morning, until required at the Wycombe post-mortems, DS Zyczynski will be questioning students and staff at the Castle, with special attention to the taxidermy class, the bar regulars, and the life class. DC Silver will accompany her and continue after she leaves. We meet up here at 6.30 p.m. for debriefing. Written reports in before you knock off. Any problems there?'

A few questions were aired about transport and meals, which he dealt with rapidly, noting at the same time that Yeadings had wandered across to Z and appeared to be giving her extra instructions. He guessed they would be connected with the Limassol death, which he'd referred to as a corner he could take on.

Cornering it, Mott reflected. And, however straight-faced, Yeadings had spoken like Little Jack Horner on the point of pulling out a plum. So was there something in that aspect that he, Mott, had missed out on?

'Z, a word with you,' he called as she was leaving. 'Get Fiona Morgan talking about her sister. Anything at all that might have a slant on our present case.'

She nodded. 'I was hoping to do that, Angus. I'll have to

catch her when she takes a break. While she's modelling they'll not let anyone in, and she'll clam up if I start insisting.'

'Good, as long as you're aware that there is that angle. I rely on you to play it by ear.'

'There's something else we should look into,' DI Salmon claimed. 'SOCO are examining the Castle's walk-in freezer, but how about a refrigerated van? If the Burford woman was killed outside the building, why carry her back in? Keeping her somewhere mobile simplifies transferring her into the Morgan Jaguar later.'

'Good point. I'll need a list of all caterers owning or using those vans. Get a DC from the augmented team to follow that up. Anything to add? If not, go to it.'

Beaumont consulted his mobile which had vibrated in a pocket during the briefing. It showed his home number, with the message, 'Ring me asap.'

The boy would be – should be – in school, so that meant the wife. With a sinking stomach he thought he guessed what Audrey could be in a flap about.

He rang through and was proved right. In a voice an octave higher than usual, she dived in, complaining that her precious catering company had been broken into over the weekend.

'And your van stolen,' he assumed.

'Yes, the big refrigerated one. Angela's frantic. But how did you know? Has it been found? Is it badly damaged?'

'Not found yet, as far as I know, but we have been informed of its use in the past few days. How come it's only today you noticed it was missing?'

'Because we hadn't an outside contract on the books until

midweek, and normally nobody goes into the garage between loadings.'

'Right. Don't panic; we'll put out a call. One of our cars will pick up on it. No need to assume it's been ditched.'

Poor cow, he thought. In the months since her disillusioned return after abandoning home and family to 'find herself', this working partnership with Angela had become the centre of her existence. He had been accepted as incidental furnishing in the home; young Stuart as only a little better. With common assent Audrey had exiled herself to the spare bedroom. To his eternal regret, congress had twice been achieved, almost by accident, on the living-room sofa since then. In a moderately discreet way he'd found alternative fish in the sea, and those with no bad fishwife repercussions.

Now he must accost his appropriately fish-named DI, to admit that the wife of a Thames Valley detective was the latest victim of the deplorable goings-on at the Castle. He doubted the man would see any humour in it.

Zyczynski reached the Castle twenty minutes before classes were scheduled to start. Fiona and Alexander Craddock were still in the otherwise deserted dining-room, elbows among the debris of breakfast, with their heads together, plotting.

'Hello there,' she greeted them. 'Do you mind if I join you? There's such a lot to get sorted in what's happened lately.'

'That's what we find,' Sandy agreed. 'The management here haven't taken kindly to my change of name. You would think I had leprosy.'

'I'd better go and get ready. I'm modelling this morning,' the girl said abruptly.

'But I was hoping you would tell me more about your sister. Was she a professional model, and that's why you're standing in for her?'

'She was a nurse. I'm a qualified chef. I filled in so as not to let Gordon down. I'd not modelled before.'

'Can they spare you from your – what is it – hotel or restaurant?'

'I took a six-month sabbatical. It will be up at the end of next week.'

'I see.' She didn't, in fact; but at least Fiona was permitting her questions. 'Do you ever drive one of those refrigerated vans?'

'I haven't done. I could, I suppose. You don't need a Heavy Goods licence, as far as I know.' She sounded lightly amused. No guilt in it, apparently. But then she could be a good actor.

'Look, Sandy will take care of you. I have to go and eat humble pie with Gordon. I really did let him down, going off like that. See you both later.'

'Don't forget to swear at him for not passing on your message,' Craddock said grimly.

'What was that about?' Z asked.

Sandy explained. 'I was half out of my mind worrying what had happened. He said he forgot to tell me, but I think he's plain malicious, because he fancies Fiona and wants me out of the way.'

'Maybe he feels protective of his models.'

'It's something other than that.'

'Maybe there was something between him and Fiona's sister?' she wondered aloud.

Sandy shrugged. 'She certainly was involved with my brother,' he said.

Now it was *brother*, Z noticed. Earlier it was always 'half-brother', so perhaps any coolness between them had thawed out. Otherwise, why would Craddock have been driving Laing to the airport and conniving in that cloak and dagger escape from St Luke's?

'It was terrible for you, seeing him run down like that.'

'Lightning striking twice,' he said bitterly. 'But this time it truly was an accident. I would swear to that. It was just that for a moment...' He fell silent, uncertain.

'For a moment?' Z prompted.

'It was nothing: my fancy.' He stared round the room. 'Everyone's cleared out. I'm going to have another bash at drawing Fiona. Can we talk another time?'

'Of course.' She watched him leave, and then made her way out to the lab block, to pursue the taxidermists. At some point she would need to contact the police at Windsor and find out if any other witness had misgivings about the accident in Eton High Street.

Sandy caught up with Fiona before she struck her pose. He was still annoyed by Gordon's failure to pass on her message. 'How come you picked on him to tell me you were going off?' he demanded.

'Because he was there. He offered me a lift in to Slough. Then I got a taxi to the airport.'

'Why didn't he take you all the way?' Sandy was ready to pick on any shortcomings of the irritating man.

'He had business of some sort near Slough, and going

farther would have made him late. Anyway, he didn't know I was aiming for the airport.' She was trying to be patient with him, but his next words set her aback.

'I'm going to come clean about Rosa and what we did to her.'

'You are not! Sandy, have some sense. You can't involve us. Just wait. We'll talk about it.'

'You won't change my mind. I don't have to mention you.'

'Good morning. Settle down, everybody,' shouted Gordon. 'We're almost at the end of the course and there are things I want to comment on. A little feedback for you, after all that hard, if sometimes misdirected, work…'

'Wait!' Fiona hissed again. Sandy shrugged. They both took up their positions.

Two post-mortems to attend in two days. Three, if you were counting bodies, Z complained silently. The Bells had the worst implications: a family tragedy which left Maisie burdened with the double guilt of surviving both her child and her husband, and surely for some complicity in letting matters reach such an end.

Examination of the man brought nothing spectacular to light. He was sturdy, healthy, apart from some early atherosclerosis. 'A smoker,' the young pathologist declared with virtuous disapproval, removing the lungs. He had detailed the injuries to his neck: fractured hyoid bone, dislocated cervical vertebrae and lacerated flesh, a bloody patterning of rope abrasions.

The little girl was thin, and in the single large wound to her left temple minute flakes of paint showed where she had been swung against some solid structure. There were also several small areas of older bruising on her upper arms and wrists which suggested hard gripping by adult fingers. Z recalled that a query had been raised regarding physical abuse to an older child, who had died of pneumonia before the family's move to Thames Valley.

And yet the father had given Jilly an expensive scooter for Christmas. She could almost picture him, small, mercurial, cursed with a short fuse. Was that letting imagination run ahead of proof? Maisie was the only one of them she had met, and nothing about her implied she could have stood up against a domestic bully.

DI Salmon stood throughout the examinations without producing any comment or questions. Z couldn't judge whether this indicated repugnance or lack of interest. Darkness had fallen when they parted at the exit to the morgue. A detour via Windsor would mean her being late home, and she wanted to be there to cook something special for Max tonight, but her curiosity was stung and she needed to know more about the incident in Eton High Street.

The constable who had been first on the scene had gone home by the time she arrived, but there were two male DCs working on in the CID office. She declared her interest and they pulled the computer files relating to the accident.

'The dead man's half-brother is still stunned by what happened,' she told them, 'so I'm particularly interested in the witness statements.'

'Boys from the College,' one of them told her. 'We had practically to fight our way past their housemaster to get access. Not that their version disagrees with what Craddock gave us. Except for the bit about the man who ran away.'

'What man?'

'You didn't know? It seems that Laing was just being helped out of the car when he spotted someone on the opposite side of the road and tried to get across unaided. The man started to run, and turned down Meadow Lane, heading towards Eton Wick. He could have parked somewhere down there. One of the boys walked to the corner, but the man had disappeared.'

'And they thought Laing was trying to chase him?'

'All of them told the same story. The man was a stranger to them; medium height, bareheaded, dark hair, and his coat collar pulled up to his chin.'

Z considered this, and then scrolled through the statements for herself. 'There's one here quite specific. He says the man was walking past them when the one in the road called out. That made the pedestrian look across, and that was when he started to run.'

'I remember that boy: tall guy, must have been six-four, six-five, wore glasses, very precise. Probably become a lawyer one day and a flipping future prime minister.'

'It's interesting,' Z said, 'because up till then Laing appeared to have been lying low, hiding his identity. Suddenly he's the one doing the chasing. I'd give a lot to know why.'

'Ask the guy with him. His brother, wasn't he? Unless he got struck blind, he shouldn't have missed something of what was going on. We haven't yet got the full story from him ourselves.'

*   *   *

Z was ten minutes late for the after-hours debriefing. The nuclear team had assembled in the Boss's office and Yeadings was dispensing coffee.

'I understand Max is home and needs nursing,' Mott told her in an aside. 'So, if there's nothing urgent to report, you can write it up now and leave it on my desk.'

'Nothing spectacular: everything much as expected. Thanks, Angus.' She ran down to CID office and booted up to get her notes on file.

DI Salmon looked sourly after her. If women had to take fully paid jobs and expect promotion in the police force they should be prepared to do equal unpaid overtime and not get let off with domestic excuses. Now he was left to give the verbal account of the two bodies autopsied at Wycombe. And that meant he'd be late back for his supper. It would probably have shrivelled up.

Zyczynski printed up her notes and, looking through them, realised she would not get free of the Job that night until she had checked the Eton boys' statements with Craddock. So, having left her report on Mott's desk, she drove again to the Castle to confront him.

He appeared to have steadied in the interval, but there was still a missing part in his version of what happened in the High Street. He insisted he'd not properly seen much across the road: just a group of people and an indeterminate figure running. It was later he realised who the boys were, by their tail coats and white ties.

Laing had ventured forward on his own while Craddock bent to pick up the fallen blanket from the gutter. When he looked up, all his attention was on his brother staggering into the path of the traffic. He'd seen little of the person running away, but Warren had been focused on something ahead. He had reached forward and called out, although by then he must already have been falling.

The furniture van had been coming fast and could never have stopped in time. The driver took evasive action too late and went into the building opposite. He thought maybe it was part of the College library.

'Thank you,' Z told him and closed her notebook for the day. She'd wasted time, and now she'd need to ring for an Indian delivery. But, arriving home, she found Max had borrowed an aubergine from Beattie and conjured up a moussaka, to be followed by ripe nectarines with a ginger sauce. Comfort food, she thought. And comfort man.

CHAPTER TWENTY-FIVE

Next morning's team briefing began with disagreement over the accidental death of Warren Laing.

'He recognised someone,' Z repeated: 'someone so important to him that he would have chased after him, sick as he was and living incognito.'

'You say "chased", as if he had something against the man,' Yeadings cautioned. 'Couldn't it have been a friend he urgently needed to contact?'

'One of the witnesses was specific: Laing looked furious. That could account for his lack of caution. He'd seemed quite unaware of the danger he was in.'

'Aren't we getting sidetracked here by Zyczynski's interest in the man Laing? He has no direct link with the case in hand, the murder of Rosa Burford,' DI Salmon objected.

'Perhaps we should all find him interesting,' Yeadings suggested. 'Not Laing as Craddock, but Laing as himself, as he was when he had flown out to Limassol for the inquest on the girl he loved. I don't think he was a stupid man, or one who would take a tragedy lying down. Suppose, like Fiona Morgan, he convinced himself that the coroner's findings were wrong, and Martine Gillespie had been murdered. He would feel as any of us would: that he must get to the bottom of what happened and why. I believe it is possible that across the High Street he recognised someone who could have been there at the time of her death, or was in some way involved with the girl.

'You may consider that's as far-fetched as bird's nests from China, but don't close your minds to the possibility. There are circumstances and people common to both crimes. We don't have to settle for the Rosa Burford murder being an open and shut case against the husband. I am sure it's a whole lot more complicated than that.'

Salmon leant forward and stabbed a finger at the others. 'But we have the weapon, which Burford has admitted is his own skinning knife. It has traces of the polecats' blood underlying that of his wife,' he insisted. 'All we need now is a confession, before we put it to the CPS.'

'We also have a stolen refrigerated van probably used to store the body,' Beaumont put in forlornly, 'and the only person who has even the remotest connection with that is a detective sergeant of Thames Valley at present at this table.'

'I appreciate the irony,' said Yeadings, 'but if SOCO find anything significant in the van, which has been retrieved overnight from a wooded lane near Cliveden, it may lead to someone known to the victim.'

'To someone connected with the Castle?' Z suggested. 'Or am I sidetracking again?'

'Let's leave it there for the present,' Mott said. 'We'll be appealing on TV for information about the van's movements, with a film simulation, on next *Crimewatch* programme. In the meantime I'm seeing Craddock and Fiona Morgan here at nine-thirty. They rang in early requesting an interview. It may well be relevant, since Miss Morgan chooses to cut into modelling time to talk to us. DS Zyczynski, I'd like you with me as you've had quite a bit to do with them. DI Salmon has the timetable for you others.'

'I'm down for the post-mortem of Warren Laing later this morning,' Z reminded him. He'd clearly forgotten, and hesitated.

'I don't mind sitting in on Craddock and the girl,' Yeadings said blandly. 'It might be good to have an outsider's view afterwards.'

The Boss an outsider? Mott grinned. Trust him to get involved in the nitty-gritty. 'I'd appreciate that, sir.'

Mott kept the couple waiting, and then sent a constable to escort them to a vacant interview room. He nodded to them on entering and introduced Detective Superintendent Yeadings. They appeared duly impressed.

'We shall be recording this interview,' Mott told them, 'and a copy of it will be given you at the end.'

'We're giving a voluntary statement,' Fiona said sharply.

'And you will be free to leave at any point. Now, how can you help us?'

'I'll start,' Sandy offered, plunging in with being woken in the early hours by a scratching at his bedroom door; expecting it to be Fiona, but having Rosa Burford collapse on to him in the act of expiring.

The superintendent's bushy black eyebrows rose towards his hairline. Mott stayed unmoved. 'And you have waited all these days before coming to inform the police?'

'I know. I can't believe that, myself. It was a shock. And

then things started to happen so quickly.'

The girl had taken over, Mott guessed. He turned to her. 'Is that the point when you came in?'

Between them they gave him the whole story, which sounded feebler and less credible by the minute. By now Yeadings was looking thunderous. 'Do you realise how you have hampered the investigation?' he demanded. 'Your actions amount to an indictable offence. At very least you could be charged as accessories after the fact.'

'It's too late to undo it,' Sandy confessed miserably. 'At the time we wanted to avoid explaining a body found in my bedroom. After all, she was nothing to do with us. We thought that with daylight someone would find her where we left her and ring 999. When nothing happened and the body had disappeared we couldn't understand. I thought at first that Fiona had gone down again and driven her away. But, of course, she couldn't have lifted the body on her own. Rosa would be twice her weight.'

'You intended to make an inside job look like a mugging by some unknown prowler in the courtyard? That is deliberate misdirection of any likely police investigation.'

'I hope neither of you is needed elsewhere,' Yeadings said firmly, 'because we shall need a considerable amount of detail from you on what you observed. It could take the greater part of the day. If you wish to depart before we are finished with you, we have enough to prefer charges and detain you. Is that understood?'

The two stared at each other. 'I said it would turn out like this,' complained the girl.

They all took a break at eleven, when Sandy and Fiona

were escorted by a WPC to the canteen. They queued for coffee and found a table together where they watched the policewoman tuck into an oversized blueberry muffin.

'At least it's done now,' Sandy consoled himself.

Fiona frowned in concentration. 'I suppose they'll go after George Burford with more relish now they know it happened inside the residential block. Were their rooms on our corridor? She couldn't have staggered far in the state she was.'

'I don't know so much. I read once that a murder victim walked for half a mile with a dagger in his back. The blade sort of kept it sealed. The blood on my carpet and door all came from her ears. I can't see Burford ripping her earlobes like that to get a few diamonds off. He could have helped himself at any time from her jewel box.'

'Even if it happened in her bedroom,' Fiona wondered, 'it didn't have to be George in there with her. It could have been one of her pick-ups.'

In Yeadings's office he and Mott were following much the same trail of musings. 'For what it's worth, the Burfords had separate rooms,' Mott reminded the Boss.

'What I wonder,' Yeadings countered, 'is whether she was taken to the knife or the knife to her. Was it an opportunist act or premeditated? But I doubt the stabbing occurred in the lab used by the taxidermy class, because that block is a good fifty yards away from the residential one. Also, Craddock's bedroom and the Burfords' rooms are on the upper floor. It beggars belief she could have staggered that far without encountering someone, even in the early hours. Where was the night porter in all this?'

* * *

When questioning resumed, the girl was less obstructive. Craddock appeared to have convinced her finally that they had done the right thing.

'Describe the conditions you left the body in. Was it covered? Exposed to the weather?' Mott pursued.

'She was wearing the dress and shoes she'd had on in the bar earlier,' Fiona offered. 'But no jewellery.'

'The sleet had stopped by then, but the ground was puddled. There was a vicious wind. It was blowing half a gale that night,' Sandy followed up.

Yeadings was nodding. He had hopes of traces left in the refrigerated van. Access to that form of transport was the killer's weak spot. Who would have known of its existence, and where it was kept? Beaumont's wife and her catering colleague would be the next in line for questioning.

'I should like to show you something,' Yeadings said mildly. He took a postcard-sized envelope from his pocket and dealt three photographs on the table between them. 'Is there anyone here either of you recognise?'

Fiona drew a surprised breath. 'That's my sister.'

'And the other two?'

'Yes, they are of Martine as well; but I'm not sure about the girl with her in that one. Her face is turned away.'

'I think you do know her. Her name is Katya Adrianou. You have recently flown out there to meet her.'

'These were taken in Limassol?'

'Yes. Mr Craddock, do you know anyone in these photographs?' He spread all three in front of the man. 'Look carefully.'

He shook his head 'I've never been to Cyprus. Never met Fiona's sister.'

'All the same, take a very good look.'

Sandy picked up the one which showed the two girls on a café terrace. The curly blonde he recognised as Martine. The other was small and dark, but her hair hid her features. They appeared to have finished a meal and were lingering over coffee. Perhaps they had asked another diner, or the waiter, to photograph them together, and then Katya had turned her head. A group of people was moving away in the background. Behind them an apparently short-sighted woman was reading the menu close to her face. Something about the sculpted top of her hairdo and the fleshy arms made him take a second look.

'Fiona, that woman at the back, under the awning; do you think it could be...'

She took it from him and stared for a moment. 'Oh my God,' she exclaimed, 'I believe you're right. It's Rosa Burford.'

There was a short silence.

'I'd like to know,' Yeadings said slowly, 'who was behind the camera. His shadow falls on the next table. From the sun hat, I would say it was a man. Could that be husband George?'

At Wexham Park Hospital Z had parked in the corner by the mortuary, her Yaris dwarfed by Professor Littlejohn's new Lexus. She was on time, but the prof was a stickler for punctuality at the slab. She found him inside, already in his plastic apron and clipping on his miniature mike.

'Z, m'dear, how are you?' he boomed at her.

'I could do with fewer of these occasions,' she told him.

'Yes, I heard you had a couple yesterday. Ever think of

taking it up seriously? Women make fine pathologists, you know: all that finicky detail.'

She assured him she was happy enough as a cop.

'You know the Coroner's Officer, Sergeant Cowley, and PC Whitaker from Windsor station? Splendid! So let's get on with it.'

The body was hideously mutilated. Patiently Littlejohn separated and identified the two occasions on which Warren Laing had been run down. The head, shoulder, left arm and chest injuries dated back mainly to the first collision with the biker. Crushed pelvis and partially severed lower limbs came from the more thorough destruction wrought by the furniture van.

'I understand that the driver suffered a heart attack. He's here in Cardiothoracic and has twice been resuscitated. We may yet get the unfortunate man on the slab later.' Littlejohn ogled Z over his half-lenses.

Bloody ghoul, she told herself. But maybe that's the only way he can face all this mangled human flesh.

Fiona had struggled with her conscience during a further short break when Mott and the superintendent retired, leaving a uniformed officer on guard beside the door. So far no attempt had been made to separate them.

When the two detectives returned she had made up her mind. 'I've already explained to you, Chief Inspector, why I flew out to Cyprus for a couple of days. It was to meet Katya Adrianou in Larnaca where she's working as a legal secretary, and to pick up some things Martine had left behind when she was killed. Katya had written to tell me about them.'

Mott waited.

'And I said there was nothing important among her stuff.'

'But?'

'There were letters. Several were from Warren Laing, regretting he still couldn't get to her for a few more days, but to keep a warm place in her bed for him. "Only, not with that loser Whizzo."

'I don't know who he meant by that, but there was also a note from someone signing himself "W". It gave his time of arrival at Larnaca airport and declared his undying worship: really sloppy stuff. I can't imagine Marty going for anyone who could write like that. Still, it appears she hadn't prevented him flying out to make use of Laing's absence.'

'What did you make of her relationship with Mr Craddock's brother?' Yeadings asked.

'I knew they'd shared some business project,' she allowed. 'I got the feeling that...'

Everyone waited.

'...that it was a bit iffy.'

'Your sister was a nurse? And her most recent post was at a nursing home in Hastings?'

Mott looked sideways at Yeadings. The Boss seemed to have been doing some homework on the case.

'Yes. You're right.'

'And one of her patients was a Major Trevor Barnes, who was in the final stages of Alzheimer's disease?'

'She mentioned him, yes.'

'This would be the same Major Trevor Barnes who owned a substantial house in Winchelsea, modestly called Jasmine Cottage?'

'She didn't go into any detail about him. Just that she felt sorry for him and he once apologised for being so awful to her.'

'He also owned a car, a classic Jaguar, which she claimed he gifted to her?'

Fiona fell silent, covering her face with her hands. 'Oh God, this is awful. I'm sure she didn't mean to cheat him out of it. He'd said that in front of another nurse, so she had a witness to the handover. Then I accepted it as part of her estate, which was to come to me anyway in her will.'

'But, as DS Zyczynski pointed out to you, ownership was in question because Major Barnes had failed to notify Vehicle Registration of the change.'

'Well, how could he? He could barely talk, let alone sign anything.'

Yeadings was relentless. 'The major had been a war hero, a helpless old man waiting to die, who would say one thing one minute and its opposite the next. Were you happy with that?'

'Anyway, the car's a write-off now, isn't it? So none of this really matters,' Sandy protested in mitigation.

'Will anyone be making a claim on the insurance?' Yeadings asked innocently. 'It will be interesting to find out.'

There was no answer. 'I think,' Mott said, 'we can leave it now. You are both free to go, but we shall certainly be asking you to return for further questioning. Thank you, Miss Morgan, Mr Craddock.'

CHAPTER TWENTY-SIX

DI Salmon, as near glowing with virtue as he ever allowed himself to be, was following up his theory on the refrigerated van. Beaumont's admission of his wife's frantic call about the break-in and robbery had led him straight to Angela Farr's house in Aylesbury, where he set his borrowed DC to questioning staff while he awaited impatiently the arrival of forensics experts.

Audrey Beaumont was helping produce details of addresses where the van had been used, and of clients who would be aware of where it was normally kept. Twice in the considerable list was a booking for the Castle covering full banquet service. The first occasion was in late March of the previous year; for 135 covers, and again in mid-June for 150. On each occasion Angela's serving team of five had supplied back-up to the Castle's two chefs and regular catering staff.

'This proves their familiarity with the layout of the buildings,' Salmon told the DC with satisfaction. 'And the Castle's regular employees would certainly learn where the freezer van came from.'

A fantastic scenario was starting to form in his mind: of Rosa coming across some serious mismanagement while exploring the kitchen quarters by night and being summarily dispatched with a chef's knife to prevent her reporting it to higher authority.

That would fit in well with Mott's new thesis that she had been killed inside the main building. It also accounted for the snatching of the van to keep the body preserved, while allowing time for setting up an alibi and finding a permanent means of disposal. And the latter had been the Jaguar left in the courtyard while the Morgan girl went chasing off to Cyprus. After a couple of days the body had been transferred and the Jaguar was run into the Thames at Maidenhead.

The planning was little short of genius, and his disentanglement of its intricacies would astound Yeadings when he came to reveal it. It remained now only to discover the whereabouts of the van while the body was lodged in it, and to name the person at the Castle who could have pulled it off.

And to account, he realised despondently, for Burford's skinning knife being substituted for the preferred kitchen knife. Then, of course, there were also the blood traces on Craddock-Laing's bedroom door to be explained.

He was unsure whether to present this imperfect solution for the team to pour cold water on.

'So what next?' Mott demanded of the Boss.

'For me, back to the desk where I belong,' he said primly.

His DCI wasn't sure that cleared him out of the firing line. To mix metaphors thoroughly, Yeadings, left alone with a telephone, could yet shoot the ball straight into the back of the net. He had a mischievous temptation at times to creep up on his team and go one step ahead.

It had been like that with the information from Cyprus. The letters left behind by Martine Gillespie could have been read by the local police investigating her death before they were passed back to her friend for safe keeping. The sort of friends Yeadings had in police forces abroad would have taken care to be thorough. He'd certainly been advised of the letters' contents before Fiona Morgan divulged them. Nothing in them had surprised him. So, working on his famed intuition, did he intend to act on further information yet unshared?

DS Zyczynski found a text message on her mobile when she left the mortuary at Wexham Park Hospital. The number was of Yeadings's outside line, and it said simply, *A word in your ear, Z, asap.*'

'Just a minor loose end you could tie up for me,' he said when she arrived. 'It means driving down to Winchelsea in Sussex, and sweet-talking some house agents. You could show interest in purchasing a sizeable property, cash down. And be sure they tell you everything about Jasmine Cottage and its recent history.'

'How far do I commit myself?' she asked warily.

'Show interest but don't make any promises,' he warned. 'Real estate merchants are sharks. You give them your address, and you never get free again of their circulars.'

It had been DS Beaumont's turn again to cover the Castle. Craddock and his girlfriend were notably absent. At Reception they were thought to have gone out early, intending to visit Area police. He wondered if this accounted for Burford not having been picked up for further questioning.

At lunch the DS positioned himself with a good view of the man without himself being easily observed. Today he looked less the grieving widower and was making some effort to mix with others. A tall, rather sharp-angled woman had taken her tray across to him, and Beaumont learnt from the boy clearing tables that she was the taxidermy tutor. Burford was eating little, but continued with the whisky.

On his other side sat a stocky woman seen queuing outside the life class studio before Gordon Beasley came to unlock it. It seemed that Burford would not have far to look for womanly consolation.

As on other days the food was good, with a choice of hot dishes, salads and a vegetarian preference. Beaumont, a solid trencherman, had gone for asparagus soup, the steak and kidney pudding with oysters, followed by a double banana split. He took coffee in the lounge, a whole cafetière which failed to help his eyelids fight gravity. He fell asleep thinking how well this level of living became him.

Gordon Beasley padded round the dining room looking for the missing pair. This morning Fiona hadn't given warning of her disappearing act. He'd had time to regret overlooking her earlier disappearance for two whole days, let alone unknowingly giving her a lift part-way to the airport.

What was that motto he'd seen on a fridge magnet? – *Give a woman an inch and she thinks she's a ruler.* Well, Fiona was one of those; nothing like her malleable little sister. He couldn't imagine why he'd let her persuade him to give her this modelling slot in the first place. And Craddock, who had passed himself off as his own half-brother: he was a dangerous man. Only three days more, thank God, and he could be rid of them both.

Meanwhile he had to find a model to fill the space. He'd sat in again that morning for rapid charcoal sketches, but unless he found a substitute fast his class would be out of patience with him. As an artist he barely made a living, so it was essential to keep on this Adult Education post.

He passed into the lounge, to confront the sleeping detective. It was a pity the man couldn't be transported, stripped off and left nude on the model's throne. His face on waking would be well worth portraying.

Through a mist Beaumont was aware of being stared at and opened one eye to follow the tutor's retreat. Sunk deep in a neighbouring armchair, Burford gave a snort. His voice came out slurred. 'She – was – besotted with him.'

Had he meant Gordon Beasley? But his eyes were shut. He'd spoken of whoever was present in his drunken dreams: lost in a memory of his promiscuous wife.

Besotted? So was Rosa killed by a desperate ex-lover with no other way to get rid of her? Usually crimes of passion were for the reverse reason: the cast-off lover killing from jealousy and anger. *If I can't have her, then no one shall.*

Somehow that didn't fit with the impression of Rosa Burford they'd built up from general opinion. She was too easy. So what exactly was it that brought her back here year after year? Was a love of Art sufficient lure for a warm-blooded would-be vamp like Rosa Burford, trailing a bored and compliant husband? Or was she overwhelmed by a foolish middle-aged woman's late-blooming passion? And had that husband at last grown so exasperated at her besotted state over someone here that he'd taken one of his knives from the tool-roll and followed her to her bathroom to finish her off?

Burford's suggestion, of a nose bleed causing the minute traces of her blood remaining on the tile grouting there, had been totally unconvincing. That had to be the crime scene.

After their final uncomfortable interview with Mott and Yeadings the absent couple slipped back into the Castle at a little after twelve-thirty. There had been a lunch-hour staff meeting for the tutors and Fiona was expected to take her meal with them at High Table. It left Sandy to pick up a sandwich from the bar and settle at last to going through Warren's luggage.

Keys to the cases had been returned to him together with his brother's wallet and travel tickets. There were two Samsonite cases similar to the one he'd borrowed and a briefcase which he left until last.

The clothes were of two kinds, suited to European or Argentine climate, which seemed to prove that Warren had planned the trip some time ahead and probably intended an eventual return. Suits, underwear and shoes were of high quality, as was the casual wear: all well beyond anything Sandy had ever envisaged owning. There'd be a serious tug-of-war in his mind between ingrained penny-pinching and an instinctive distaste for borrowed plumes. But, having once used Warren's name, how could he baulk at taking over his wardrobe?

The briefcase's contents were, as he'd expected, of more interest. There was a small package of handwritten letters secured by an elastic band. He opened it and found them headed *Park Beach Hotel* and signed M with a flourish. They were all fondly erotic. One had an enclosure which he stared at in amazement. He turned it over and read the message across its back: *So even poor Whizzo has his uses!*

It was incredible, and yet...

He couldn't wait for Fiona to get free of the tutors. The detective, Sergeant Beaumont, had been asleep in the lounge; he would have to do. Sandy threw everything back into the briefcase, slid off his bed, retrieved his shoes and stormed off to voice his suspicions.

Superintendent Yeadings returned the telephone to its cradle and sat pondering the latest revelation from Windsor police station. The sketches which Craddock had drawn from memory had come up trumps. A jeweller in Eton Village who had received a copy being circulated throughout Thames Valley had got in touch with them.

Several of these pieces had been offered to him only two days back, but he had turned them down, because none of them was genuine: good fakes, but fakes, and he didn't deal in such things. And he had described the man who brought them in.

Yeadings scrolled through his screen to find the Eton boys' description of the one who ran away in the High Street. Both versions could be of the same man, except for the height. The jeweller had called him tall. Katya Adrianou had also described as tall the dark Englishman seen in Martine's company in Limassol. But Katya, from her photograph, was petite. Her idea of tall might not be the same as that of a 6 foot 4 inch eighteen-year-old. And maybe the jeweller, bending over to examine the fake jewellery through his loupe had been sitting low behind his counter. So the differing opinions on height could be immaterial.

Yeadings reached for his internal phone and dialled Mott's office. 'Coffee?' he invited.

DCI Angus Mott knew the Boss well enough to guess the reason for this summons. He was required as a sounding board. Yeadings had come up with something worth taking a long look at.

The phone was ringing as he tapped at Yeadings's open door. He was nodded in. The Boss pressed the button for open speech and Sandy Craddock's voice came over clearly. Mott slid on to a chair to listen while Yeadings thanked the man and insisted he keep his findings strictly to himself. His DCI would see him shortly.

'That's particularly interesting,' Yeadings said, 'since the circular regarding Rosa Burton's missing jewellery has brought a response.' He explained what he had learnt of the visit to the jeweller in Eton village.

'This could be the man seen running away when Warren Laing recognised him across the street.'

Mott was on to it in a flash. 'A new suspect! Do we have a photograph?'

'Phone Beaumont to get one. Then what, Angus?'

'Get it ID'ed by the Eton boys and the jeweller. Then pull him in.' Mott was already on his feet.

'Not wait for a line-up?'

'No. We've waited long enough for this. The press has got us written up as a load of woodentops.'

Yeadings leant back and hid a smile behind his hand. 'So go for it, lad.'

Fiona and Gordon Beasley came back together. The afternoon class was ready and waiting. Sandy stood by his easel, almost bursting to tell her of his discovery, but he'd sworn to say nothing, and anyway there wasn't time. He clipped up a fresh sheet of A2 heavy cartridge paper and dashed straight in with charcoal.

On an adrenalin rush, careless of measurements, even he could see that the result was brilliant. He'd no need to regard the model as coffee pot or Grecian statue any longer: it was pure, one hundred per cent gorgeous woman.

Beaumont had taken several photographs as the tutors filed out from their meeting. The flashes startled them, but the attention was generally accepted as flattering.

He printed out one full figure and faxed the result to Area station, where Mott dispatched a patrol car with copies to Eton village and the College.

By 4 p.m. the paperwork was completed, an interview room booked, and Mott rang through to advise Beaumont he could bring the man in.

'And if he refuses?'

'Arrest him on suspicion of double murder.'

CHAPTER TWENTY-SEVEN

The interruption had occurred during afternoon tea break. Beasley had refused to answer Beaumont's knocking at the studio door until Fiona was robed and queuing at the drinks machine. Then, recognising him, he had opted to hold their discussion in the corridor. Beaumont's polite request was met with a show of testy protest, but finally there had been no need to make a formal arrest.

'I cannot imagine why your chief inspector couldn't speak to me here. I trust this interview will be as short as possible. The class cannot be left unsupervised. Do you realise how very inconvenient this is?'

'One of your class has suffered worse,' Beaumont reminded him. 'This is a murder case, Mr Beasley.'

At that point the man had telephoned the principal's office for a member of staff to take over, and with a bad grace permitted himself to be driven off in Beaumont's unmarked car.

'My students will probably imagine I'm being arrested.' He managed a weak laugh as he folded himself in.

The DS made no comment, flicking an imaginary speck off the windscreen.

* * *

Superintendent Yeadings contrived to be near Reception when the suspect was brought in. Apparently involved in checking the notice board, he viewed him over the top of his half-lenses.

An unremarkable figure, the man had one of those indeterminate faces where a small goatee beard is meant to compensate for a weak chin. As with many such additions it was greyer than his thinning hair, of which the lustreless black suggested touching up with dye.

The man's features were small, his movements jerky; his overlying air of self-satisfaction unconvincing. A bit of a bluffer, Yeadings decided: perhaps even a bully when in a situation of his own choosing.

Beaumont showed the visitor into the farther interview room and closed the door on him. He encountered Yeadings on the staircase. 'DCI Mott sent me for Gordon Beasley. I thought we had Burford in the frame.' He sounded affronted.

'That's right. Did he show any reluctance to come in?' Yeadings asked.

'He blustered a bit; got pompous: his class unable to continue without him. But eventually he'd no objection to helping the police with their inquiries.'

'Good. Send a constable in on standby, and report to Angus in his office. He'll put you in the picture. And tell him not to hurry down. It's good to leave the pot to simmer.'

Angus Mott glanced up as Beaumont appeared in his doorway. 'There's been a development,' he announced. 'Beasley has been identified as the man seen running away when Laing was run over in Eton village. It seems he was there to sell some jewellery resembling the sketches provided by

Craddock, and it turns out the stuff's all fake. Since Burford maintains it was the real thing, it seems Rosa could have had copies made and hocked or sold the originals.'

'But Beasley, a killer? What about means, motive and opportunity: all that old crap?'

'As staff, Beasley would have access to the lab keys which are kept in the secretary's key cupboard. He could have taken Burford's skinning knife at any time when the lab was empty. To kill Rosa Burford he'd as much opportunity as anyone familiar with the main building. She cultivated male companions and could have invited him back to her bedroom while Burford was propping up the bar.'

'She was besotted with him,' Beaumont remembered. 'That's something Burford muttered when he was half asleep; and he could have meant Beasley, who was around at the time. But I wouldn't put good money on him for motive. Maybe the man is a pompous git with a short fuse, but it's expecting a lot to claim he did her in because she was a persistent, embarrassing bore.'

Mott stretched his long legs under the desk. He was already experiencing promotion's price in stiffening muscles.

'I hope there's more to it than that. Blackmail perhaps? Was she ready to reveal some sordid secret that could cost him his job? That's something we have to get out of him ourselves.'

'So – softly, softly catchee monkey.'

Mott nodded. 'And it all links up somehow with the Cyprus death of Martine Gillespie. Beasley must have known her better than anyone at the Castle except her sister. For several years she was his model for the annual life class, although full-time she was an agency nurse and a sometime live-in girlfriend of Warren Laing. There's a whole network of relationships.'

'But the Burfords knew her well too, because they were regulars at the Castle. They weren't by any chance at Limassol when the Gillespie girl drowned?'

'According to the Boss, George wasn't, because he was attending a conference of Master Builders at Llandudno that weekend. But Rosa appears in a crowd scene behind Martine and her friend Katya on a hotel terrace. The photograph has been enlarged and enhanced. There's no doubt about it: Rosa's there, lurking in the background.

'Further investigations are now under way in Limassol where lax security was reported at the gates to the container park on the quay, and a watchman has recalled a second car with a tourist licence plate parked for a short period near the entrance before he raised the alarm. And finally, since the Boss's intervention, the girl's body is to be exhumed for a second post-mortem. They hope to find some indication of why she was unable to get out while the car was partly above water. Any kind of restraint was ruled out earlier, but the body was never tested for drugs.'

'But again, where's the motive? You suggested double murder. Was Beasley even out there at the time?'

'The local police are checking hotel and B&B registers. We've faxed a photograph. If his name comes up, we should know soon. Martine's letters written to Laing at that time contain slighting references to "Whizzo", and one enclosed a clever pen and ink sketch of her. I'm curious to hear what Beasley has to say about that. I'm inclined to agree with Craddock that, like the other sketches, it comes from the pen

of an accomplished artist. Did Beasley consider himself
"whizzo" at getting a likeness?

'But for the present let's keep to the Rosa Burford case and
see where it leads. If you're ready, I suggest we go down and
start gently grilling.'

Beasley declined the offer of a duty solicitor, but grew slightly
alarmed when shown tapes and recording equipment.

'We find it helps later to clarify any doubts about what
was actually said,' Mott explained comfortably. 'You will be
asked to sign both copies and you may retain one for your
own use.'

It does seem unnecessarily formal,' Beasley complained. 'I
am happy to tell you anything I can about the dead woman
and her husband.'

'Thank you. We've one or two points to get cleared up.'

Beasley relaxed and sat back. 'Fire ahead then.'

They began with questions about the classes in general, the
mixing of students and tutors in free time, and
accommodation at the Castle. Gradually Mott led up to the
number of years Beasley had covered courses and threw in the
name of his earlier model, Martine Gillespie.

About her, Beasley fell silent. Then, 'Her sister is less
reliable,' he complained. 'A bad timekeeper; she goes absent
without warning; and appears to be having an affair with one
of my new students. None of which is satisfactory if serious
work is to be achieved.'

'Yes, it was unfortunate about the other girl. I understand
she was tragically drowned on holiday abroad.'

'In Cyprus, last autumn; tragic, as you say.' A flicker of

some emotion passed over his face, and the small red mouth tightened among the greying bristles.

'A lovely island, Cyprus,' Beaumont murmured dreamily. 'Do you know it at all?'

'I have been there, yes.'

'I really fancy a villa at Paphos, but I've only ever stayed in Limassol.'

Beasley was disinclined to continue the conversation.

'Let's not reminisce,' Mott said severely. 'Mr Beasley is rather pressed for time.' He turned back to him. 'I believe you gave Miss Morgan a lift on her way to the airport recently, Mr Beasley.'

The tutor bridled. 'I had no idea she was going abroad. I overheard her ringing for a taxi at Reception and offered her a lift. It suited us both to drop her off in Slough. She must have taken a taxi from there, and she was away for almost two days without notice or permission.'

'She went on to Heathrow? Where were you bound at the time, Mr Beasley?'

He spluttered. 'I – I had business in Slough: there was art equipment to purchase and so on.'

'Not in Eton village?'

'No; why should you think that?'

'Because that's where you went on the following day, perhaps having been unsuccessful in finding what you required in Slough.'

Beasley teetered on the brink of denial, but chickened out, unsure what Mott's assumption was based on. 'Yes, there are some delightful little shops there which stock specialised items.'

'Shopkeepers who deal in genuine articles. Such as a jeweller who rejects fake gems?'

Beasley collapsed against the chair back. He appeared to have difficulty breathing.

'Constable, fetch Mr Beasley some water,' Mott called over his shoulder, and the PC slid out.

'Would you like to reconsider our offer of the duty solicitor?' Beaumont tempted.

'No. No, I'll ring my own man. I'm allowed one call, aren't I?' His whole body was shaking, his face suffused with blotched colour.

'That foul woman! She deserved far, far worse than what happened. She killed her, mercilessly, left her to drown. I never knew until later who Marty had gone out with for a meal; but that last night, at the Castle, Rosa was drunk; she taunted me. She *boasted* about what she'd done!

'She knew I would have given my own life to save that wonderful girl. It was magic even knowing her. And we were getting so close, so intimate. How could I have cared for that blowsy old tart, when there was lovely young Marty?

'But Rosa wouldn't leave me alone; she'd followed me out to Limassol, and must have been watching our every move. Hell indeed knows no fury like a woman scorned. But how could I know what devilry she'd get up to. Oh, my darling girl!'

'And the knife?' Mott gently probed.

Beasley looked up and a twisted smile opened in the facial hair. At that moment he looked more evil than demented. 'Burford was a fat fool. He should have kept her under control. It was only just he should take the blame.'

* * *

Huddled together by the lounge window, Sandy and Fiona waited for Beasley's return.

'Surely it can't take so long,' she wondered. 'How much could he have known about what happened to Marty? They weren't that close. She made fun of him. He was only someone to go around with on holiday, while Warren was held up over the Jasmine Cottage deal.

'What was that about? You said they had a scam going on. There was more to it than the Jaguar business, wasn't there?'

'Oh, you know about the car already. She was nursing this old chap with Alzheimer's who was quite sweet really. Well, sweet to her. And Warren Laing was renting his house down in Winchelsea as a summer booking. That's how they came to meet, when Warren drove to Hastings to see the major in the nursing home. He invited her across to Winchelsea for her free weekend, and they simply fell in love. It went on from there.

'She told me about it at the time: how major Barnes had no family and either he hadn't made a will or he'd managed to lose it. So Jasmine Cottage was there for the taking. I don't know if they got him to sign it over to Warren, or if it was a forgery, but when Warren had sold it they were to take a month's holiday in Cyprus together.

'But something went wrong. I believe Warren took deposits from more than one buyer and it caught up with him. I didn't get the full story of that because Marty and I had broken off contact by then. Well, it was such a scabby thing to do.

'In the end he only managed to get there for the inquest, which is where I saw him for the first time.'

'And you let me think you were his mistress, although you despised him. I couldn't understand you.'

'I lied about everything. I didn't know who you were at first. I had to account for breaking into his flat. I was desperate, and deeply suspicious of Laing. I meant to try and find some proof that he'd been responsible for Marty's death.

'Earlier the janitor had told me he was away, and then there you were, in his bed, asleep and sozzled out of your mind. I seized the opportunity, but one moment I was convincing Laing I was a pick-up from some bar the evening before, and next I discovered I was fancying you. It was weird.

'Then the newspaper story about an accident to that other Sandy Craddock gave me a glimmer of light about you. That and your ruddy chest hair.'

Sandy felt he was getting bogged down in unrelated complexities. 'So what was Warren running away from when the biker hit him?'

'The aftermath of that Winchelsea scam, I guess; or of some other. He was a rogue, you know, even if an attractive one. But then con men usually are.'

'So where did the Castle come in?'

'I was curious to know what Marty had been up to there. She was so giggly about it. So I thought I'd come and see for myself. I'd signed up to model in her place before I knew it would be in the nude. Then I thought, if she could face it, so could I. Then I sort of acquired you, and you wanted to disappear too, so I brought you along.'

Sandy nodded slowly. 'And then all the wheels started dropping off, and we got involved in a murder. I saw in the local paper that a man's just received six months' community service for perverting the course of justice. That could happen to us, or even worse because of concealing the

312   CLARE CURZON

body. Not that I've got a job to go back to in any case. How about you?'

'I'll be all right. My lot can't do without me.'

'Some restaurant, if you can take time off for half a year.'

'It's a really great one. But then I think that because I happen to own it.'

'Oh,' Sandy said flatly. 'I don't suppose you can offer employment to a half-trained antiquary?'

'Funny you should say that, because I've had an idea, but I'll need to consult with an old friend about it. I'll tell you later.'

Sandy looked unconvinced. 'You know, I don't think Beasley's worth waiting up for. We can see him in the morning.'

'You're right. Better things to do. Bed, then.'

Arrived in his room, Fiona retired to clean her teeth, accompanied by her mobile phone. Through the bathroom door he heard her laughing, explaining, waiting for an answer. She came back smiling. 'You have a new job, if you want it.'

'Waiter or bottlewasher? Thanks, Fiona, but—'

'Hear me out. My dear old friend Jacob is seventy-five years old and has been longing to take life more quietly, retire. He has an upmarket antique shop just round the corner from my *Da Giulia*. His offer is as manager on a six months' trial. You'd get a free run, no interference. If you're a success there's an option to buy. Why not?'

'I'd have to think about it, but—'

'We'd be neighbours; could become more. Sandy, I've only just found you. Please don't walk out on me now.'

But, he thought. And that 'but' covered serious misgivings. He'd discovered in himself a doglike need to be cared for, while she was like the cat that walked on its own. He wasn't sure that sort of partnership could endure.

She was lying back on his bed, eyes closed and a dreamy smile on her lips.

'What are you thinking about?' he bent over to ask.

She propped herself on her elbows and faced him. 'Our being together. It started with deceit on both sides, but I find I've never trusted anyone in my life as I do you.'

A warm feeling was spreading through him, dispelling the doubt. He recalled one of the last things Warren had said to him: 'You have to make your own way in life, not wait for it to slap you in the face.' So why not at last make a move, for once overtake the impetuous Fiona?

'I'm old-fashioned,' he warned her. 'I think we should marry. I want you, and I want your children; and all the antique shops and auction houses in the world can go hang if I don't get you.'

She stared long and hard at him.

Oh God, he thought with shame, I've really botched up this time.

Then she smiled. 'I might even consider that, sometime. I'd really miss you; your crinkly smile; your growly voice; the awful gaffes you make; all those unfinished sentences.'

Mott and Yeadings sat late over the case. They had Beasley's written confession for the murder of Rosa Burford. When it came to court there was every chance he would plead guilty under extreme provocation. Martine Gillespie's death remained under Cyprus jurisdiction, but at least with exhumation there was to be a fuller investigation. And if Beasley's story could be believed, then her killer had passed beyond human justice and the case could be quietly closed.

It was hard to believe that Rosa Burford had been so desperate not to lose Beasley that she would risk all in killing the girl he was besotted by in his turn.

Yeadings fingered the copy made from the photograph of her sister which Fiona had given him. In it Beasley was shown laughing, clean-shaven and without glasses, a younger-looking, more handsome man than the one they were accustomed to. It was surprising that, across the narrow Eton street, Laing should have recognised the man he'd glimpsed in Limassol five months ago. But then, according to the schoolboy giant's statement, the man's coat collar had hidden the lower part of his face, so the goatee beard was hidden. It could have been something about the way the man moved, that nervy jerkiness that he himself had picked up on. Wasn't visual acuity as much part of the make-up of a skilled con man as of a good detective?

'How about Craddock and Morgan?' Mott asked. 'Do we refer them to CPS for perverting the course of justice and concealing a suspicious death?'

'Young idiots,' Yeadings sighed. 'I suppose they did help us in the end. Perhaps a formal warning this time, and trust they don't make a habit of disposing of bodies. I think in any case they've already found a better alternative to expend their energies on.'

He rose, stretched and went to drain off the bronze and cream chrysanthemums standing to soak in his hand basin.

He'd chosen them for Nan that morning. She would enjoy arranging them in the new copper jug from Hennigan's which graced her prized seventeenth-century oak table in the hall. Once his wife got into bidding at auction, it seemed there was no halting the habit.

He smiled. These chrysanths should last until he could bring in his first white tulips from the garden.